A Promising Kiss

Captivating Kisses
Book 8

Alexa Aston

Text by Alexa Aston
Cover by Dar Albert

Dragonblade Publishing, Inc. is an imprint of Kathryn Le Veque Novels, Inc.
P.O. Box 23
Moreno Valley, CA 92556
ceo@dragonbladepublishing.com

Produced in the United States of America

First Edition June 2026
Trade Paperback Edition

ARE YOU SIGNED UP FOR DRAGONBLADE'S BLOG?

You'll get the latest news and information on exclusive giveaways, exclusive excerpts, coming releases, sales, free books, cover reveals and more.

Check out our complete list of authors, too!

No spam, no junk. That's a promise!

Sign Up Here

www.dragonbladepublishing.com

Dearest Reader;

Thank you for your support of a small press. At Dragonblade Publishing, we strive to bring you the highest quality Historical Romance from some of the best authors in the business. Without your support, there is no 'us', so we sincerely hope you adore these stories and find some new favorite authors along the way.

Happy Reading!

CEO, Dragonblade Publishing

Additional Dragonblade books by Author Alexa Aston

Captivating Kisses Series

An Unexpected Kiss (Book 1)
An Impulsive Kiss (Book 2)
An Innocent Kiss (Book 3)
An Unforeseen Kiss (Book 4)
An Enchanting Kiss (Book 5)
An Urgent Kiss (Book 6)
An Unforgettable Kiss (Book 7)
A Promising Kiss (Book 8)

The Strongs of Shadowcrest Series

The Duke's Unexpected Love (Book 1)
The Perks of Loving a Viscount (Book 2)
Falling for the Marquess (Book 3)
The Captain and the Duchess (Book 4)
Courtship at Shadowcrest (Book 5)
The Marquess' Quest for Love (Book 6)
The Duke's Guide to Winning a Lady (Book 7)

Suddenly a Duke Series

Portrait of the Duke (Book 1)
Music for the Duke (Book 2)
Polishing the Duke (Book 3)
Designs on the Duke (Book 4)
Fashioning the Duke (Book 5)
Love Blooms with the Duke (Book 6)
Training the Duke (Book 7)
Investigating the Duke (Book 8)

Second Sons of London Series

Educated By The Earl (Book 1)

Debating With The Duke (Book 2)
Empowered By The Earl (Book 3)
Made for the Marquess (Book 4)
Dubious about the Duke (Book 5)
Valued by the Viscount (Book 6)
Meant for the Marquess (Book 7)

Dukes Done Wrong Series
Discouraging the Duke (Book 1)
Deflecting the Duke (Book 2)
Disrupting the Duke (Book 3)
Delighting the Duke (Book 4)
Destiny with a Duke (Book 5)

Dukes of Distinction Series
Duke of Renown (Book 1)
Duke of Charm (Book 2)
Duke of Disrepute (Book 3)
Duke of Arrogance (Book 4)
Duke of Honor (Book 5)
The Duke That I Want (Book 6)

The St. Clairs Series
Devoted to the Duke (Book 1)
Midnight with the Marquess (Book 2)
Embracing the Earl (Book 3)
Defending the Duke (Book 4)
Suddenly a St. Clair (Book 5)
Starlight Night (Novella)
The Twelve Days of Love (Novella)

Soldiers & Soulmates Series
To Heal an Earl (Book 1)
To Tame a Rogue (Book 2)
To Trust a Duke (Book 3)
To Save a Love (Book 4)
To Win a Widow (Book 5)
Yuletide at Gillingham (Novella)

King's Cousins Series
The Pawn (Book 1)
The Heir (Book 2)
The Bastard (Book 3)

Medieval Runaway Wives
Song of the Heart (Book 1)
A Promise of Tomorrow (Book 2)
Destined for Love (Book 3)

Knights of Honor Series
Word of Honor (Book 1)
Marked by Honor (Book 2)
Code of Honor (Book 3)
Journey to Honor (Book 4)
Heart of Honor (Book 5)
Bold in Honor (Book 6)
Love and Honor (Book 7)
Gift of Honor (Book 8)
Path to Honor (Book 9)
Return to Honor (Book 10)

The Lyon's Den Series
The Lyon's Lady Love

Pirates of Britannia Series
God of the Seas

De Wolfe Pack: The Series
Rise of de Wolfe

The de Wolfes of Esterley Castle
Diana
Derek
Thea

Also from Alexa Aston
The Bridge to Love (Novella)
One Magic Night

PROLOGUE

Harrow School—June 1795

NO ONE WAS coming for him . . .

Matthew sat by the window, which looked out on the front of Harrow School. He had not left this spot all day, hoping that someone would show up for him. Some boys had fathers who arrived to bring them home for the summer. They emerged from the school with their arms wrapped around their sons' shoulders or patting their sons affectionately on the head. A few boys had both parents come, while a handful had a servant show up to claim them.

This was the third time he had been forgotten about.

It was also the last time he would be leaving Harrow School. Next year, he was slated to attend Eton, where his own father had gone. Though he dreaded what came next, he supposed he would need to go and speak to the headmaster now and find a way home.

He glanced about the room a final time, neither happy nor unhappy that he would never see it again. Matthew was a quiet boy, more like his mother than father in nature. The Duke of Reddington was loud and boisterous, always smelling of spirits no matter what time of day. His father neglected his ducal responsibilities, continuing to run with a fast crowd, despite having a wife and child.

Matthew exited the room, closing the door behind him. He made his way downstairs to Mr. Morgan's office. Pausing outside the door a moment, he collected his thoughts and then raised his fist, rapping on the door with a confidence he did not feel but would nevertheless project.

"Come."

Entering the headmaster's office, he waited while Mr. Morgan finished writing something. Then the older man glanced up.

"Mr. Keaton. You are still with us, I see."

No courtesy titles were used at Harrow School. Only one boy, who was an earl, was called by the title he held.

"I will need to find transportation home to Redfield, Mr. Morgan."

The older man frowned. "This is the third time this has happened. Is that correct, Mr. Keaton?"

He hated the tone the man took with him. It was not his fault that no one had thought to come for him. But it was easier to blame a twelve-year-old boy than it was to place blame at the feet of a duke of the realm.

Matthew simply looked blandly at Mr. Morgan, waiting to see what the headmaster would say. He tried to project modesty, a trait the school valued in all its students. Harrow School tried not only to teach boys academic subjects, but its tutors also tried to mold their character. Above all, humility was expected.

And it was beaten into you if you didn't properly show it.

Finally, the headmaster said, "I suppose we can find a way to get you home. This will be the last time we speak, Mr. Keaton. I hope you have enjoyed your time with us."

For a moment, the older man looked at Matthew with sympathetic eyes. He swallowed, not wanting to break in front of him.

"Yes, sir. I am set to attend Eton next year. I know I will be prepared because of my time spent here." He paused. "I have the funds needed to purchase a ticket on the next mail coach."

"That is good to hear, Mr. Keaton. You have excelled in your studies. Wait here."

The headmaster left the room, not offering for Matthew to take a seat. Because of that, he remained standing.

He wondered where his father was and what he might be doing. The London Season was in full swing now, and Matthew assumed the duke was in town, which is why he had been forgotten about. If it were left to his mother, Matthew never would have been stranded at school, but the duchess had no power in her own household. For ten years, he had seen her move through the house as a ghost. Then two years ago, once he returned home from school, Mama had simply disappeared. When he questioned the servants, they looked at him with pity and said they did not know where the duchess might be. When he confronted his father, Matthew was told that his mother had gone away for a rest.

For all he knew, she was dead.

He had seen the bruises on her. Heard the one-sided fights, his father berating his wife for her imaginary sins. There had been times Mama had been beaten so badly that she could not leave her bed for weeks. A doctor was never called, however. Mama's lady's maid always nursed her back to health until the next incident occurred.

The duke had broken his duchess. Matthew determined the same would never happen to him. For the most part, the duke ignored Matthew when he was at home. Oftentimes, Reddington was in town during Matthew's school holidays. Even when he was in residence at Redfield, son rarely saw the father. Matthew took all his meals alone in the schoolroom and roamed the estate, growing to know and love every inch of Redfield. He saw how neglectful his father was regarding the property. Fortunately, they had a decent steward in Mr. Crandall, and so the land and tenants were cared for to a certain extent.

Mr. Morgan returned. "There is a mail coach coming through the village in an hour. I have instructed Barrow to place you on it. He is collecting your trunk now. You may meet him outside."

"Thank you, sir," he said, leaving the headmaster's office, wondering how many more times in his life he would have to hide his embarrassment.

The foyer to the school was devoid of all the trunks which had been brought down early this morning. Matthew stepped through the doors a final time, seeing Barrow outside. The servant sat in a wagon which held Matthew's trunk.

He climbed up beside the servant. "I appreciate you taking time to help me, Barrow."

"Happy to do so, my lord. I'll wait with you until the mail coach arrives."

His throat grew thick with unshed tears. "Thank you," he managed to get out.

They rode in silence the entire way to the nearby village. Matthew liked Barrow, who had taught him and several of the other lads how to play chess. It was one of many things Matthew excelled at.

The wagon came to a halt, and he withdrew all the money he had, giving it over to the servant in order to purchase his ticket.

Barrow said, "Be right back, my lord," climbing from the vehicle. He disappeared inside the inn and returned a few minutes later, bearing a ticket.

"Here you go, my lord. Don't lose that. It will get you to where you are headed." The servant also handed him a few coins, the leftover change from the purchase.

Actually, it wouldn't. The mail coach would only drop him at Redgrove, which was three miles from Redfield. Somehow, he would have to find his way home. With the coins left over, hopefully a local from the village would take him and his trunk to Redfield. If not, Matthew could always leave his trunk at the inn and walk home, sending a servant to fetch it later.

"It shouldn't be long now."

"You do not have to stay, Barrow. I know you always have work to do."

Stubbornness filled the man's eyes. "I'll do as I please, thank you very much."

He knew Barrow had a soft spot for him, perhaps because Matthew had picked up the game of chess so quickly, regularly beating all his opponents, including Barrow himself.

"Are you happy at Harrow School?" he asked.

Barrow shrugged. "Happy as I suppose any servant can be with his lot in life."

"When I am the Duke of Reddington, I want you to come and work for me."

The man's jaw dropped a moment before he quickly closed it. "That's all well and good, my lord, but you may not be a duke for many years to come."

"Nevertheless, I shall come for you, Barrow. If you are not at Harrow School, leave word where you will be. I will find you."

Barrow's smile was genuine. "That's right kind of you, my lord. It's a great honor, working in a duke's household. I could do anything you'd like me to do. Work in the stables. Be a footman."

"Thank you," he said solemnly.

"For what, my lord?"

"For treating me decently. For teaching me how to play chess. For listening to me when I needed a friendly ear to bend."

Barrow's eyes misted with tears. "You're welcome."

When the mail coach pulled up in front of the inn, Barrow took Matthew's trunk and loaded it atop the vehicle. Matthew presented his ticket to the driver.

"We're all full inside. You'll have to ride with me or wait for the next mail coach."

He climbed up next to the driver and gave a wave to Barrow. Then the carriage set out once more. It stopped in five different villages along the way before it reached Redgrove. The coachman was kind enough to remove Matthew's trunk and place it on the ground, something he could not have done for himself. He thanked the man and gave him a coin, which the driver quickly pocketed.

Glancing around, he saw little activity on the streets and judged the time to be between seven and eight o'clock. He entered the inn, finding a few patrons in its dining room. He moved to the desk, where the innkeeper stood.

"My lord, what are you doing here?"

"The mail coach just dropped me off, Mr. Davies. Is there someone available who might take me and my trunk to Redfield?" He removed the last two coins from his pocket and placed them on the counter.

"I will take you myself," the innkeeper declared, slipping the coins into his pocket. "Wait here. I'll need to saddle my horse to the wagon."

"I will be outside with my trunk," he told the older man.

Within a few minutes, they were headed to Redfield. The innkeeper was a jovial sort and told him all that had been happening in the neighborhood since he had last been home from school. Matthew had a good memory for names and faces, and he recalled many of the people Mr. Davies gossiped about.

They arrived at Redfield, and a footman rushed out to greet them.

"I'll take your trunk to your room, my lord," the footman said.

"Thank you for bringing me home, Mr. Davies. I will not forget your kindness to me."

Matthew entered the house, where he was greeted by Ridley.

"We were not expecting you, my lord," the butler apologized.

"My school term has ended," he said flatly. "Is His Grace at Redfield or in town?"

"Here, my lord," the butler told him. With a pained expression, Ridley added, "His Grace . . . has guests."

He knew exactly what that meant. Raucous parties which lasted late into the night. Heavy drinking. Scantily dressed women dashing through the halls, hopping from one bedchamber to the next.

"I see," he said. "I will stay out of their way. Thank you for the warning. Might Mrs. Ridley bring me something to eat in my bedchamber?"

"I will see to it myself, my lord."

Matthew went up the stairs, finding two maids hastily making up his bed. As they left, he opened his trunk, which had been placed in the corner of the room. He unpacked while he waited for his food to arrive.

Mrs. Ridley brought the tray to him. "A few sandwiches, along with some fruit and cheese, my lord. Do you require anything else?"

"No, Mrs. Ridley. Please thank Cook for putting this together for me."

He sat in the room's only chair and ate every bite on the tray, not having had anything to eat since breakfast at the beginning of the day. He hated hearing that his father had guests. He should have asked Ridley how long they had been here. Usually, they stayed a week or so and then bored of the country, returned to town.

Once he finished his meal, Matthew found himself restless. He decided to take a walk. This time of year, the sun was just now setting, although he didn't need sunlight to find his way about Redfield.

He cut through the kitchens, which were quiet now, and went out the back door. Hearing voices, he paused, thinking they might be coming from the terrace. As he looked up, he saw a few people standing there, his father amongst them. They were laughing, snifters of brandy in their hands. His father held not only a snifter but also a bottle of brandy as he twirled about, laughing rowdily.

Then he heard someone say, "I dare you, Reddington. Walk it. The parapet."

From the shadows, Matthew watched his father climb onto the narrow stone parapet of the terrace. Slowly, the duke began walking along it, swaying as he went, his arms moving wildly as he tried to balance himself. All the while, his guests laughed with him—or at him.

A half-dressed woman climbed up on the far end of the ledge, beckoning to the duke, wriggling her derriere at him.

"Come this way, Reddington. Claim me," she teased.

His father said, "Wait until see what I plan to do to you," his words slurring as he unsteadily headed toward the woman, who now lay down upon the ledge, one bare leg hanging off, swinging enticingly.

Just before the duke reached her, he raised his arms in victory, causing him to stumble. Matthew cried out as his father began falling through the air. His body hit the ground below, causing Matthew to wince. The duke was sure to have a few broken bones from the fall.

In the meantime, a few of the women shrieked. Those on the terrace seemed to immediately sober, and not one of them came to render aid to their host. Instead, the entire group quickly vanished, scurrying inside like mice confronted by a menacing cat.

He raced to his father's side to tell him that he would summon help. When he reached the duke, Matthew saw his father's neck at an awkward angle. He rolled his father to his back, only to see vacant eyes staring up at him. Stunned, he shook the duke.

"Wake up!" he cried. "Wake up!"

But the Duke of Reddington was lifeless.

A sick feeling washed over him, and he hurried away, spewing everything he had just eaten into the nearby bushes. He removed his handkerchief, wiped his mouth, and entered the kitchen again. Going to the small office which Ridley used, he found it empty. Numbly, he moved down the hallway and knocked on the door to the Ridleys' sitting room.

The butler opened it. "What is it, my lord?"

Dully, Matthew said, "Send for the constable, Ridley. My father has had an accident. He is dead."

The butler swore softly under his breath. "Forgive me, my lord." Then his gaze met Matthew's. "I mean, forgive me, Your Grace."

The address took him by surprise. Yes, he had always known he was the heir apparent to the dukedom—but now that dukedom was his. Suddenly, he felt very small and helpless. Yet people would look to him. Depend upon him. Now was the time to rise to the occasion.

"There is nothing to forgive, Ridley. Please send for the constable at once. I am expecting a mass exodus of the current guests. They will be packing their bags now and leaving shortly."

The butler frowned deeply. "Should I rouse the servants? Have them prevent this from happening, Your Grace? The constable will need to speak with them."

Decisively, he said, "No, we are better off without them. I witnessed the accident. Let us get rid of them now so they do not loll about and expect to continue to be waited upon."

Even as they were speaking, Matthew heard bells ringing, signaling that various guests were sending for their maids and valets. He hoped Redfield would be rid of the lot of toadies by the time the constable made his appearance.

The next hour was a blur as guests left at a rapid pace. By the time the constable arrived, the last of them passed by him on the lane. Matthew stood in front of the house, watching them go. Not a single one stopped to offer him a word of comfort. The entire group had been worthless users. As the Duke of Reddington, he knew he would find himself surrounded by sycophants, and he determined to keep most everyone who approached him at bay.

He greeted the constable and said, "May we talk and walk? I would prefer for our conversation to remain private."

"Yes, Your Grace," the man said deferentially. Even at a such a tender age, Matthew would instantly receive respect, all because of his ducal title.

He led them to the rear of the house, where his father's body now lay covered with a quilt Mrs. Ridley had brought. Matthew had closed the duke's eyes before he covered the body.

"I am certain it is no secret to you that my father drank to excess."

Looking uncomfortable, the older man nodded. "I am aware

of that fact."

"His Grace had a group of guests staying at Redfield. They were out on the terrace, all of them deep in their cups. Including my father."

"You saw this?"

He nodded. "I arrived home from school earlier this evening. You can confirm that with Mr. Davies at the inn. He brought me home in his wagon."

Pity filled the constable's eyes. "That is not necessary, Your Grace."

"I decided to take a walk before retiring. That is when I heard voices on the terrace. It was apparent everyone had overindulged, and they continued to drink. One gentleman—I do not know which—dared my father to walk along the parapet of the terrace."

The constable winced. "And His Grace took up the challenge?"

"He did. Those present egged him on. He lost his balance and fell to the ground."

"So, no one pushed him."

"No," Matthew confirmed. "He got up on the parapet freely. He walked it unsteadily. And he fell to his death."

He paused, swallowing, the picture of his father in mid-air embedded in his memory.

"I shouted out. Rushed to him. The fall was not from so great a height. I assumed he might have broken a bone or two." He took a deep breath. "When I reached him, I noticed his neck at an odd angle. I turned him over. He was gone."

The constable walked to the covered body and raised the quilt, studying the form beneath it for a moment, nodding to himself. He dropped the quilt and returned to Matthew.

"Looks as if he landed wrong. Broke his neck." He placed a hand on Matthew's shoulder. "I know this is hard to hear, Your Grace, but perhaps this was for the best. I have heard of others breaking their necks in a fall and surviving, only to be paralyzed for the rest of their lives."

"He would have hated that. He was not a man who ever could be still. He was always in motion. Always impatient."

"I assume the other guests have fled Redfield."

"Yes. I did not think you would need them since I witnessed the incident. Yes, they were all drinking heavily. Yes, they encouraged the duke to climb up. But no one was near him when he fell. He merely lost his balance."

Nodding sagely, the constable said, "I see no need to learn the names of these guests from your butler and track them down, especially since we have your eyewitness account, Your Grace. I will write up my report and present it at the inquest. I can tell you now that the ruling will be death by misadventure."

"Exactly what does that mean?" he asked.

"It is a death which is attributed to an accident that occurred, due to a risk taken voluntarily by the deceased. In a simple accident, the manner of death involves no unreasonable, willful risk."

"Yes, death by misadventure would be the correct ruling," he agreed. "Will I be called to testify at the inquest?"

"It is a possibility. Of course, we could present a written deposition and see if that is acceptable, especially due to your age. And rank."

"I will do whatever is required of me," he said resolutely. "The sooner this matter is brought to a close, the better."

"I sent for the doctor. He should soon be here to make his official ruling so that the death certificate might be signed."

"We will look for him," Matthew said. "Thank you for coming so late."

The constable looked at him, sadness on his face. "I am sorry you are going through this at such a young age, Your Grace. You seem to have a good head on your shoulders, having intelligence—and the good sense to use it. Best of luck to you."

"Thank you."

The doctor arrived shortly afterward. Again, Matthew shared what he had seen, and the doctor confirmed that the duke had died due to the broken neck he had suffered. The physician gave his sympathies, and Mattthew allowed a few footmen to carry his father's body inside, where his valet would wash and then dress him.

Now past midnight, Matthew found Ridley and Mrs. Ridley having a cup of tea in the kitchens.

"Would you like a cup, Your Grace?" the housekeeper asked.

"No, thank you, but I do have an important question."

"Is it about the vicar?" Ridley asked. "I thought that I would send word to him first thing tomorrow morning. This morning, I suppose. I know you will need to meet with him."

"No, this question has to do with something entirely different." Looking intently at Ridley, Matthew asked, "Where is my mother?"

Mrs. Ridley touched her husband's hand. "He needs to be told now. After all, he is the duke."

"You're right," the butler said. Turning his attention back to his employer, Ridley said, "Her Grace was taken to an asylum two years ago."

"What?"

Ridley's agitation was obvious as he said, "Three men showed up at Redfield and carted Her Grace off. His Grace told the staff that Her Grace had been upset about things. That her nerves were acting up, causing her to behave irrationally."

"That wasn't the case, was it?" he said, a cold deeper than winter piercing his soul.

"No, Your Grace," the butler replied, shaking his head back and forth. "We—the staff—wanted to do something."

"You were powerless to help. No one can stand up to a duke, Ridley."

He thought of the horror stories he had heard regarding asylums. How not only were the mad committed to them, living in the worst of conditions, but also that men who tired of their wives also placed them in these asylums, hoping they would quickly expire, leaving them free to wed again.

"Do you know where Her Grace was taken?"

Ridley nodded. "I asked one of the men as they left. Throckmorton. It is not far from here. About ten miles north of Brandon."

"Have my carriage readied at first light. I am going to bring my mother home."

At a quarter to five, Matthew boarded his carriage. Ridley offered to accompany him, and he accepted the butler's offer. He also asked Mrs. Ridley to come, as well, thinking having a woman present might be comforting to Mama.

The coachman drove them to the town where Mama was kept, stopping the carriage at the gates of the building.

Matthew got out, saying, "Exchange the team for fresh horses and return here as soon as possible. I want to be back at Redfield as quickly as we can. The coachman can always return the rented team tomorrow and claim mine again."

"Yes, Your Grace."

The vehicle drove off, and the Ridleys accompanied Matthew to the gates. A guard was posted there, looking surprised to see them. He had the feeling not many visitors came calling at Throckmorton.

"State your business," the guard said brusquely.

"I am the Duke of Reddington, and I wish to see who is in charge immediately."

Quickly, the man's attitude changed at once. "Yes, Your Grace. Please come with me."

The gates were opened, and they were taken inside a large structure. Matthew thought it had, at one time, been a home, most likely sold off as unentailed. He heard a bone-chilling scream, causing his body to tense.

"Wait here," the guard said, going to another man. They had a whispered conversation, and the other man hurried away.

"Dr. Cheney will be right with you, Your Grace," the guard said, quickly exiting the building to return to his post.

As they waited, they heard two more screams and a low moan.

"It's a bad place," Ridley said grimly.

He couldn't have agreed more.

A thin, bespectacled man came down the staircase. He frowned. "You are not His Grace."

"I am now," Matthew said firmly. "And I am here to take the Duchess of Reddington home with me."

"This is most unorthodox," Dr. Cheney protested. "His Grace said—"

"His Grace is dead. *I* am the duke, and you shall answer to me. Now, are you going to allow me to leave with Her Grace in my care, or will I need to call in the authorities?" He glared at the doctor, who wilted before his eyes.

"Of course, Your Grace. But you will need to pay—"

"I will not give you a farthing more. Whatever His Grace gave you, that is all your greedy hands will receive, Dr. Cheney. Take me to my mother now, or I will do everything in my power to see this facility permanently closed. I may be young, but I wield the power of a duke. You do not want to cross me. Ever."

The doctor took a few seconds to think, then said, "I will have Her Grace brought to you."

Something in this man's eyes told Matthew he could not be trusted. "No. Bring us to her now. Without delay."

Dr. Cheney winced. "Very well. Follow me."

The next few minutes were a nightmare. They passed small, cramped rooms without doors, so privacy was nonexistent. Inmates inside these cells were chained to their beds. Other inmates were restrained in some kind of jackets, their arms inside these. They rocked. Moaned. Cried out. Screamed. Rats were everywhere, and the floors were covered in filth and feces, both animal and human. Bile rose in his throat, and he forced it down.

"Wait here," the doctor said, quickly entering a room and closing the door behind him.

The fact that this room had a door made him certain ominous things occurred behind it. Matthew wasn't about to wait and threw open the door.

To a vision of horror.

Mama sat tied to a chair, wearing a gunnysack so filthy the color could not be distinguished. Her long, beautiful hair had been shorn close to her scalp. Her cornflower blue eyes, the same as her son's, stared out dully. The entire chamber was freezing, and Mama was soaked to the skin, water dripping from her.

"I have no opinion," she said in a monotone. "I am never to speak. I have no opinion. I am never to speak."

He rushed toward her, glaring at the woman standing beside her. "What have you *done* to her?" he demanded, shoving the woman aside. She fell to the floor with a thud, a sound of bones cracking as she shrieked.

His mother kept repeating the same phrase as Matthew untied the restraints. Dr. Cheney started to help him, and he looked at the man, growling, "Get away."

Matthew finished loosening the knots and pulled the cords away, seeing Mama's wrists bloody and scarred.

"What *is* this place?" he demanded of Cheney, disgust filling him. "How can you treat women this way? Like animals."

The physician shrugged. "It is what their families ask. They wish to be rid of these women for various reasons. We do our best. It takes a great deal to keep them in line. My staff sometimes has to resort to . . . extreme measures."

"You are a monster," he said, his voice low, the anger obvious. "Leave."

"As you wish."

Tenderly, Matthew cupped Mama's face. "It is me, Mama. Matthew. I have come to bring you home."

Something flickered in her eyes. Recognition. She began weeping, fat tears streaming down her cheeks.

"You came," she whispered. "I knew you would come."

Her voice was raspy. If the words she had said over and over were true, she was punished for speaking and so did it rarely.

"Can you stand?" he asked, helping her from the chair, his arm going around her waist.

Ridley stepped closer. "It is Ridley, Your Grace. Might I help you to the carriage?"

"Ridley," she repeated. "I know you."

"And me," Mrs. Ridley said, tears swimming in her eyes. "I am here, too, Your Grace. We will take you home to Redfield."

Her sobs became louder now. "No. He will only bring me back here. Leave me on the road instead. Let me die there. Just not in this place."

Her body began trembling, and she shook her head violently. For a moment, he thought being placed inside a madhouse had driven her mad. Even if it had, he knew there was a vestige of his beloved mother still left within her. He would take her home and help nurse her back, physically and mentally.

Matthew captured her face in his hands, focusing his gaze on hers, forcing her to meet it. "Reddington is dead. Do you hear me, Mama? Your husband is dead. Gone. He cannot hurt you any longer. *I* am Reddington now. And I promise that I will always keep you safe."

His words seemed to get through to her. She calmed, allowing Ridley to get on the other side of her. Together, the two of them led her from the room and down the stairs. Matthew ignored all the screams and cries as they passed so many other helpless women.

They reached the front door, and Mrs. Ridley opened it, running ahead of them to make certain the gate was opened and the stairs placed by the carriage door. As they brought Mama along the walkway, his driver leapt to the ground and rushed toward them.

"Let me take you, Your Grace," he said gently, sweeping her from her feet and carrying her the rest of the way to the carriage.

Once they were all inside, Matthew said, "Sleep now, Mama."

"But the nightmares," she protested weakly.

"There will be no more of those," he promised, knowing those words might ring hollow to her. "Because you are going home. You are safe. I will never let another soul harm you ever again."

He saw her love for him in her eyes, which were beginning to lose their dull sheen.

"You saved me, Matthew. Thank you." She captured his hand and pressed a kiss to it.

"Sleep, Mama," he urged, nudging her so that she placed her head in his lap. Almost instantly, he caught the rhythm of her even breaths.

He would never forget the terrors within Throckmorton and knew it might be years—if not a lifetime—before his mother ever got over her experiences while there.

If his father were not already dead, Matthew would have killed him on sight.

Chapter One

October 1808—Norfolk

Lady Verina Fulton looked out the window of their carriage. She was eager to visit with Cousin Tia, who had wed Lord Merriman this past summer. Verina and her sister Justina had grown close to Tia and her twin sister Lia when the twins' father had passed suddenly before their come-out Season. Mama, who was a favorite in their extended family, had wanted to comfort the twins' mother, her aunt Alice, who was Mama's closest friend. So Mama had brought Verina and Justina with her to Millvale. They had stayed a few months at the ducal estate, and then Mama had invited them back to Traywick Manor in Cumberland. All those months had created a firm foundation of friendship between the four cousins, and she could not wait to meet Tia's new husband.

She glanced over at Justina, who sat with her eyes closed. Her sister was only a year younger than Verina, but they could not be more different. Where Verina looked forward to making her come-out into Polite Society next spring, Justina had no interest in attending balls and parties, much less finding a husband. Mama still hoped that Justina would change her mind about things, which might be possible as she watched Verina go through her come-out Season next spring.

For now, they would spend time in a part of England new to them. Merrifield was located in Norfolk, just west of Thetford, and was right on the border with Suffolk, the opposite side of England from where Traywick Manor stood. She looked forward to not only being with her cousin but meeting new people as she had when they had gone to Millvale two springs ago. Willowshire had also been a new part of England for her to see, and though she loathed long journeys by carriage, she had enjoyed the passing scenery over the last several days.

Her brother, who sat opposite Justina and her, stretched his long legs, their gazes meeting.

"We should be at Merrifield very soon, according to Lord Merriman's directions," he said.

The earl had enclosed his own letter of welcome along with Tia's, inviting them for an extended visit to Merrifield.

"I wish you could stay longer, Tray," she told her brother.

"I can stay for a couple of days, then I must return and visit with my business adviser and solicitor in town."

Verina thought about how her brother had been forced to grow up rather quickly. Their father and brother Lucius had perished in a horrific carriage accident when Tray, the oldest of the four siblings, was only ten years of age. While a guardian had been appointed for him before he reached his majority, overnight, Tray had become the man in the family, assuming many responsibilities. He had taken an active role at Traywick Manor, his country estate, and he was beloved by their tenants. Tray had recently finished his studies, and though Verina had not asked, she supposed her brother would be looking for a wife. Though he was young, Tray was mature beyond his years, and he would be aware, more than most, of how he must provide an heir.

"Tray, have you thought of taking a wife?" she asked.

He laughed easily, causing Justina to open her eyes and add, "I think you should do so."

"Since when have the two of you planned my life? No, little sisters, my goal is to see the two of you securely wed before I take care of myself. After all, I am young. It is more important for me, as the head of our family, to make certain of your futures before I see to my own."

"What if you fall in love?" asked Justina. "It seems that runs in the family."

Her sister spoke of the love matches six of their cousins had made. Their extended family was made up of three different ones—the Worthingtons, Alingtons, and Fultons. All four Worthington cousins, along with two of their Alington cousins, had made love matches over the past few years.

Verina did not think love was for her. Though she was eager to wed and start a family of her own, she did not believe lightning would strike again in her case. Of course, her own parents had been a love match, something quite unique for their time, and Mama had never remarried after Papa's untimely death. Mama mourned her husband to this day, but she still went on about her own life cheerfully, being a wonderful example of how to live a good life, being kind to all.

"I know love exists because I saw it between Papa and Mama," Tray said thoughtfully. "However, I want you to know that, despite what has happened for our cousins, love matches prove to be quite rare within the *ton*. When I do seek a bride on the Marriage Mart, I will look for someone who will make for a good countess. Love will play no part in my decision."

"I wonder if Tia and Lord Merriman are like Val and Eden," mused Justina. "They seem to kiss all the time."

"Lord Merriman must be very special for Tia to have wed him," Verina commented. "You know Tia had always spoken of having a Season of fun before she settled into marriage after a subsequent Season or two."

"Well, we will soon meet Lord Merriman for ourselves," Tray said. "By my estimate, we should reach Merrifield in the next half-hour or so."

Tray proved to be correct. Twenty minutes later, they turned off the main road, and the carriage drove up a lane lined with large trees. No matter where they visited, England seemed to be extremely green, and Norfolk was no exception.

Their coachman turned into the circular drive in front of the house, and Verina saw Tia dash out the door. The sunlight struck her cousin's strawberry blond hair, and she recalled how all their Worthington cousins had varying shades of red in their hair. Following Tia was a very tall man with jet-black hair. He looked lean but strong, and he joined Tia, slipping an arm about her waist as the carriage came to a halt.

Tia waved madly at them. Her cousin rushed to the carriage as the footman opened the door and Tray emerged.

"Tray!" called Tia. "How good to see you again. We were not expecting you. Just Aunt Agnes and the girls."

The cousins embraced, and he turned to hand down his sisters. More hugs were exchanged, and then Tia turned and went to her husband, looping her arm through his, bringing him closer.

"Cousins, this is my husband, the most wonderful man in the world. Hugo, this is Tray, the Earl of Traywick, and Verina and Justina, whom you've heard so much about."

Greetings were exchanged, and Verina thought how handsome Lord Merriman was, his black hair and brows an interesting contrast with his gray eyes. Her cousin was a very fortunate woman because Verina could see how he looked at her with love.

"You must call me Hugo," the earl said. "I have been told by others in the family . . . that you ten cousins are quite informal when in one another's company in private. That goes for the spouses, as well."

"We are happy to do so, Hugo," Tray said for the three of them.

"But wait!" Tia cried. "Where is Aunt Agnes?"

"Mama is caring for Mrs. Walters, a distant cousin," Verina explained. "She received a letter just before we left Cumberland. Mrs. Walters had taken a fall. She is a recent widow and had no one else to come and assist her. Mama rode as far as town with us, and we left her in the Fulton townhouse to care for her cousin. Tray went and fetched Mrs. Walters, so they will have the London staff to take care of them."

"Oh, I hope it is not serious," Tia said.

"Mrs. Walters broke her arm," Justina informed them. "It is

more of an inconvenience, Mama said. She knew her cousin was lonely, however."

"And Aunt Agnes felt obligated to help her cousin," Tia concluded. "It sounds just like her, putting someone else's needs above her own." She looked to Tray. "What are your plans? I know we had asked for Aunt Agnes and my cousins to stay through Christmas. Can you spare some time to visit with us?"

"Mama was to have escorted Verina and Justina here. Although I took her place, I can only stay a short while, and then I have appointments in town. I will return to Traywick Manor after that, and then close to Christmas, I will return to town, fetch Mama, and bring her here to celebrate with you. I hope that is not too long for my sisters to stay, Tia. For you, too, Lord Merriman."

"Hugo," the earl prompted. "I adore the family I have already met. I know the three of you . . . will be the same. Aunt Agnes, as well. Please, come in and have tea with us now."

"I am certain you would like to freshen up before tea arrives," Tia said. "Let me show you to your rooms. Do you wish to share?" she asked Verina and Justina. "We have plenty of bedchambers if you do not wish to do so."

Justina spoke up immediately. "Verina and I have always shared. I think it would be fun to have a bedchamber of my own for a few weeks."

"Then come with me," Tia said.

They followed their cousin up the staircase, footmen bringing in their trunks. Tia had told them not to worry about bringing a maid or any other servants because she had plenty at Merrifield to share with them. That would be a good thing because Mama had yet to allow them a lady's maid. Their mother had also decided not to replace their governess after Eden left them, thanks to Justina convincing Mama they could continue academic pursuits on their own. They had done so, continuing to read and write in their journals, as well as study things which interested them. Once in town next spring, Mama had said she would hire a dance master for them to both take lessons from.

The rest of what they needed to know in order to make their come-outs into Polite Society would come from Mama herself. She had already begun giving them lessons in the many aspects of running a household. They knew the role servants played in various positions and could speak knowledgeably about when to change linens and how often new ones needed to be purchased. Mama had created lists for them to study regarding activities which took place within a household, from beating the dust from rugs to canning fruits and vegetables in different seasons. Mama had even shared with them questions to ask when interviewing future employees, and things to look for in their answers when hiring for various positions.

Once in her own bedchamber, hot water appeared for her to wash with, and a maid unpacked for her. Verina was happy they had made this long journey to Merrifield. It would also be interesting having a bedchamber of her own. She and Justina relied upon one another a great deal, but if she were to wed in the next year or so, they should become used to being apart. Her Alington cousins Lucy and Dru had been fortunate enough to fall in love with titled lords who lived in close proximity to one another, as well as near to Ariadne and her husband Julian. Verina envied the three of them being so close to one another. Con, who lived on the western side of England in Somerset and had recently taken up his title, must be a bit sad for his sisters to live so far from him.

Verina collected Justina, and they joined the others in the drawing room. Tia poured out beautifully, and Verina saw a new maturity about her cousin which had not been present before.

"Marriage seems to suit you," she told Tia as she accepted a saucer and cup of tea.

"Speaking of marriage," Tia began. "We have news. I decided not to write to you because you would have missed my letter as you traveled here. Our cousin Con is no longer a bachelor."

It was common knowledge within the family that Val and

Con had determined to remain unwed until they came into their titles. Con's mother, their Aunt Charlotte, held tightly to the purse strings, and Con had to live a very frugal life in town. With his father's recent death, though, Con had come into his title, along with great wealth.

"Tell us about his countess, if you know anything of her," urged Verina.

"I am to thank, in part, for helping get Con and Rowena Stanhope together," her cousin revealed.

Hugo laughed and took his wife's hand, threading his fingers through hers. He lifted her hand to his lips for a tender kiss, affirming that they were very much in love.

"My wife, the matchmaker," he said. "You should let an objective party tell the story."

"I will tell this story, Husband," Tia said saucily. "I will not go into the particulars, but for a while during my come-out Season, I was at odds with Polite Society. Not that I was ever given the cut direct, but I was . . . pushed aside . . . for defending Hugo."

Justina gasped. "What on earth did you do, Tia? And you, too, Hugo, to alienate the *ton* and cause Tia to need to defend you?"

Tia waved the questions away. "We can discuss all that another time," she said dismissively, and Verina suspected the topic might never come up again. "The point is, a ball came—and no one would sign my dance programme. I was relegated to sit amongst the wallflowers."

"And that is where you found Rowena?" Tray asked, curious.

"It was indeed. Rowena Stanhope was known as a bluestocking, and Polite Society does not look upon women who use their minds with great favor. I found Miss Stanhope delightful, however. She was so interesting. And pretty, behind the gold spectacles she wore."

Tia took a sip of tea before continuing. "To make a long story short, I was forgiven for my imaginary sins, which led to my betrothal to Hugo. Knowing how charming Con can be and that if he danced with Miss Stanhope, it might draw some attention to her, I asked our cousin to do me a favor and dance one set with her. He agreed—and so began their most interesting love story."

Tia shared what she had learned from letters she had received from Con's sisters and Ariadne, who had been present at the very recent wedding in London held at Ariadne and Julian's townhouse.

"Apparently, Con was taken with Rowena and thought to call upon her the day after they danced at the ball together, something he had never done with any other woman," Tia shared. "Unfortunately, Uncle Arthur died after the ball, and Con and Aunt Charlotte returned to Marleyfield to bury him. Con, being a man, had not thought to send word to Miss Stanhope of the reason he was absent from her drawing room, after promising he would call.

"When he returned to town, he learned she was gone to the country. In Dorset. He also learned that she would be attending an upcoming house party at her neighbors' country estate."

"So, Con went to this house party to seek out Miss Stanhope?" Justina asked eagerly, obviously taken by the story. "But how could he show up without an invitation?"

"Ah, that is where the story becomes more interesting," Tia said, smiling. "Con managed to bribe Lord Clay, who had been invited to Pebblestone for the house party. He is known as a notorious gambler, and Con actually gave Lord Clay money to gamble with if he would remain in town and allow Con to take his place at the house party."

"That sounds quite romantic," Verina said, knowing how handsome and dashing Con was, thinking he had swept the wallflower off her feet. "Did Miss Stanhope agree to wed him the minute he arrived?"

"Not according to Lucy," Tia said. "It was a hard fought—yet heartfelt—week. Couples around them became betrothed, left and right. They wound up being the only couple present *not* engaged by party's end, but our Con came through, declaring his love to Rowena."

"I cannot wait to meet her," Justina proclaimed. "I may even be a bluestocking myself, now that I think about it."

The others laughed, causing Justina to blush profusely, and she asked, "What is wrong with being a bluestocking? You obviously do not have to hide how intelligent you are, and I like that."

"As I mentioned earlier, bluestockings are out of favor with the *ton*," Tia cautioned her younger cousin. "You do not wish to ruin your chances of finding a husband by declaring yourself one. I am not saying you must hide your intelligence, Cousin, but flies are attracted more to honey than vinegar."

Justina frowned. "What do flies have to do with bluestockings? Oh, well, it does not matter. I have no intention of wedding as it is."

"You are but six and ten, Justina," Tray said gently. "You may change your mind by your come-out Season."

"What if I do not wish for a come-out Season?" Justina said stubbornly.

"You would break Mama's heart if you do not do so," Tray cautioned, his tone brooking no nonsense.

"At least make your debut," Tia urged. "You can watch Verina make hers next year and learn a great deal. You do not have to take a husband that first Season." She chuckled. "Of course, I said the same thing, and look who I wound up with before Season's end." Tia looked lovingly to Hugo.

They talked another half-hour, and then Tia suggested they might wish to rest a while before dinner.

"Do not forget that Matthew and the duchess are coming for dinner this evening," reminded Hugo.

"Oh, that is right," Tia said. Looking to her cousins, she added, "Matthew is the Duke of Reddington. He and Hugo are close friends, along with Hugo's cousin. Anthony Drake is our local vicar. You will meet Anthony soon, as well. He is a frequent visitor to Merrifield."

They left to go to their bedchambers, and Verina lay upon her bed, telling the maid to awaken her in three-quarters of an hour so that she might dress for dinner. She had never dined with a duke before, other than her cousin Val, and that did not count. She wondered what this duke was like. Was he old and stuffy, or young and handsome, as Hugo was?

And what of his duchess? Eden, her former governess, was Val's duchess, but even Verina understood that was a highly unusual situation. Was the Duchess of Reddington friends with Tia? Hopefully, the woman would approve of Tia's cousins. With Verina making her come-out next spring, it might be nice to know this duke and duchess going into the Season.

No matter what, she hoped this couple would be the first of many whom she would meet during her time at Merrifield.

CHAPTER TWO

HE COULDN'T SAVE *them all.*

But Matthew did the best he could.

His carriage approached Dove Hall, the large manor house he had bought when he had reached his legal majority four years ago. The estate consisted of five acres, the house, a small stable, and seven cottages. More cottages needed to be built, and he would need to talk to Crandall, his steward, about purchasing the supplies to do so. Crandall would send a small team of tenants to the property once the supplies had been delivered. This crew had built the other cottages and knew to stay strictly within the area where the construction occurred.

Because other than Matthew, no men came to Dove Hall.

He still could see the terrible place Mama had been sent to by her husband. Years later, she still had nightmares about the asylum. Despite Parliament passing the Madhouses Bills a little over a quarter of a century ago, limiting the number of people committed to a place and calling for a yearly inspection and central registry of those confined to the premises, private madhouses still abounded.

Since his own mother had been victimized, Matthew had studied the laws carefully, going back to the Hawley case, which occurred almost fifty years previously. The House of Commons had created a select committee to probe the unlawful detention of patients in private madhouses, finding a Mrs. Hawley had been committed simply on the word of her husband, and he had paid a couple of guineas each month for her keep. Mrs. Hawley could not leave the house, nor was she allowed to communicate with anyone outside of it.

The committee found this had become commonplace, with no doctor's orders required to detain a person, and it recommended legislation be passed to intervene. Unfortunately, a bill was never brought forth. While the Madhouses Bills finally passed did regulate asylums now, all too often, private houses were still operating, such as the one Mama had been placed in.

Two days ago, Matthew, through a third party, had extracted Lady Treatley and Miss Stannis from one of these private houses and brought the pair to Dove Hall. Mama had been the one to name the place of refuge, and only the two of them referred to the women as damaged doves. After he had brought Mama home, she had a dream about doves, and together, they had researched all they could about the birds, finding doves were considered symbols of peace, hope, and transformation.

That was why they had chosen the name Dove Hall, wanting the place to be one of compassion and kindness for the women going through a difficult transition.

Matthew worked with a Bow Street runner, Mr. Larkin, in rescuing these women. The runner discreetly looked into the disappearance of women who were members of Polite Society and tried his best to locate them. Once Larkin established a lady was being held in one of these private asylums, he looked into the why of her being placed there. Most men who put away wives, daughters, or sisters did so for control. A majority of them never saw their relative again, merely paying a monthly fee to the owner of the asylum for maintaining the supposed lunatic.

None of the women Matthew helped went back to their abuser. Only two had been lovingly accepted back into the families they had belonged to before marriage and remained hidden away on those families' country estates. The others had no contact with their former lives. Some had settled into the cottages built upon the estate. They made items to sell, usually embroidered goods or quilts. One had become a seamstress, and she made new gowns for the doves who arrived. Two more doves had become companions to elderly women who never came to town. Three others now served as governesses, finding their positions through his mother. All who left Dove Hall assumed a new name, knowing they could never go back to their old life and position of prestige within the *ton*. Still, these women were grateful to be alive—and away from the prison they had been unjustly committed to for life, thanks to Matthew paying healthy sums to free them.

"Thank you for bringing me to visit our newest arrival, Matthew," Mama said.

Gazing at her, he saw her ethereal beauty. She had recovered physically from the two years of abuse she had suffered at the hands of the staff at Dr. Cheney's establishment years ago. She had also grown in confidence. No longer was she the young wife beaten senseless by her husband. The Duchess of Reddington possessed a calm, capable air about her, and she took great pride in the work her son did to aid women in hopeless situations.

"I believe Lady Treatley will adjust, given time," he said. Frowning, he added, "I am still worried about Miss Stannis, though."

Lady Treatley had been able to talk coherently from the moment they had gotten into his carriage. She was bloody but unbowed. They would speak to her today about her future, which could have nothing to do with Lord Treatley.

Miss Stannis, on the other hand, had been listless and uncommunicative. It had been hard to leave her at Dove House, but Mrs. Paul, who administered the property and served as the housekeeper, had told them it would be best. He worried about the condition they would find the young lady in.

"If we need to, I will bring Miss Stannis home with us today, Matthew," Mama said.

They had done so on only one other occasion, when the

woman had needed extra care. He only hoped Miss Stannis would adjust to her new situation.

They arrived, being greeted by Mrs. Paul, who told them, "Lady Treatley knew you would be coming. She is in the parlor and eager to speak to you."

"And Miss Stannis?" Mama asked.

Mrs. Paul shook her head. "I cannot rouse her from bed, Your Grace. She has yet to speak."

"Then we will take her home with us after we speak to Lady Treatley and the others."

They went to the parlor, finding Lady Treatley dressed much better than the shapeless gown she had been wearing two days ago. Matthew could see fire in this woman's eyes and hoped she would not cause them trouble. He would need to make clear to her that she could take no retaliatory measures against her husband. Lord Treatley needed to think his wife still locked away.

"Lady Treatley," Mama said, taking the woman's hands in hers. "It is so good to see you again."

The other woman's eyes filled with tears. "And you as well, Your Grace."

Mama indicated him. "This is my son, the Duke of Reddington. He is the one who arranged for you to have your freedom."

The woman's eyes shone with tears. "Then I owe you my life, Your Grace. You did not share your name with me the other night. Or if you did, I was too distressed to recall it. But I shall never forget your face."

"Please sit," he said. "We have much to discuss, my lady."

As they did with everyone they brought back to Dove Hall, they asked Lady Treatley how she came to be at the private asylum she was placed in. Some told them their story in anger. Some in regret. Some barely could speak, their tears flowed so much. Lady Treatley was in command of her emotions, however, and Matthew thought this session would go well.

He said, "Mr. Larkin, our investigator in these matters, has learned that your husband's gambling is out of control. He owes a great deal to many of the gaming hells throughout town."

"He wanted me to sign papers that would give him access to funds which were protected going into our marriage. When I refused, he had me bound and gagged and dragged off to that horrible place." Lady Treatley shuddered.

"Your situation is different from many of the ladies we try to help," Mama said, slipping her hand about the other woman's in order to comfort her. "Reddington and Mr. Larkin have been in touch with the solicitor who drew up your marriage settlements. They asked him to accompany them to the bank, where your funds are held. Because you were declared incompetent, they learned that your husband has gained access to your funds. He has only taken a small amount from the account so far." She paused. "That will not last. He will become greedy."

"The bastard," Lady Treatley said, disgust in her tone. "How can I stop this? Protect myself from Treatley—and my monies?"

"I will accompany you to town and meet with the banker," he said. "Once he sees you are perfectly competent, we will legally withdraw the funds from his bank and move them to another institution, ensuring Lord Treatley cannot gain access to them." Pausing, he added, "You are fortunate, my lady. Most of the women we remove from these places do not have any funds. They cannot return to their old lives, and their families prior to their marriage do not want them back."

"That is outrageous," Lady Treatley said.

"Your marriage settlements were written up different from most. Many families do not wish to anger the husband, which they would certainly do if the wife returned to her family. As you know, many *ton* marriages are made for the social connections they can bring."

"I only have a sister left. She is a widow, living near Bath."

"I would go to her once you control your monies," Matthew suggested. "I would not be seen in town again. Lord Treatley will come looking for you once he discovers you are gone. Believe me, he will, because he will not be able to pay his gambling debts."

"How did you get me out?" she asked.

"His Grace arranged a substantial payment to the man who ran the asylum," Mama said.

"I will repay you," Lady Treatley said proudly.

"It is not necessary," he replied. "Knowing you are safe and living a better life is payment enough for me."

They arranged for Lady Treatley to be fitted for a few more new gowns, which the seamstress on the grounds would sew for her. She would wear one of those to visit the bank manager and use the other couple to travel to Bath.

"I will place you on a mail carriage to Bath," Matthew told her. "Or if you have adequate funds, you might wish to rent a post chaise to convey you there. Does your husband know of your sister and her whereabouts?"

Lady Treatley snorted. "I doubt it. He would have had to listen to me when I told him of her becoming a widow. She had no children, the same as I, and the new heir wished her to be gone from his estate. Bath was the nearest town, and she has taken rooms there."

"I think it better you travel by mail coach," Mama said. "And take a different name in case any of the passengers speak to you. Lord Treatley could always hire a Bow Street runner of his own and try to track you down."

"That is excellent advice, Your Grace," Lady Treatley said. "I should have enough to purchase a small cottage for my sister and me. We might stay in Bath—or we could go elsewhere. Whatever I do, I shall write to you and let you know where I am." Grim determination filled her face. "I wish to help you in any way I can. If I can donate funds to help you remove women from those abominable places, I will do so. If one needs shelter, I will house her and help her get back on her feet."

"You are more than generous, my lady," he said. "Mrs. Paul will take you to be fitted for new clothes now. I will return in a week's time and escort you to town."

They all rose, and Lady Treatley took their hands in hers,

squeezing tightly. "You have given me my life back, Your Graces. I am forever in your debt."

Mrs. Paul took charge of Lady Treatley, and Mama led Matthew upstairs to the room where Miss Stannis had been assigned. All the rooms at Dove Hall were painted in soft, pastel colors. The house had an abundance of windows, which allowed for quite a bit of natural light to shine inside, giving the house a cheerful appearance.

Mama tapped lightly on the door and then opened it, saying, "Miss Stannis, it is the Duchess of Reddington and her son, who is the duke."

He followed Mama inside, seeing the still body lying on the bed. As they drew closer, he saw Miss Stannis staring at the ceiling.

They took a seat in the chairs beside the bed. In cases such as these, he knew to let Mama do the talking. Many of the women they freed from the asylums were traumatized by the experience and especially terrified of men. Matthew would sit quietly and speak only if Mama signaled him to do so.

Mama quietly began talking to Miss Stannis. She mentioned the weather. What she had eaten for breakfast. The names of the carriage horses which had brought them there. All the while, Matthew could see the young woman listening, not reacting, but she was not so far gone as to be unaware of their presence.

Finally, Mama touched Miss Stannis, placing her hand atop the other lady's. Miss Stannis' body jerked, but she did not pull away.

That was a good sign.

For another hour, Mama talked of inconsequential things. Tasks assigned to the household staff. The recent autumn harvest which had been brought in. How a housemaid had wed a local farmer, leaving Mama to look for a new one to hire. Then she mentioned a new addition in their barn.

"One of our cats has had a litter of kittens," Mama began. "It is not a usual time of year for that to occur, which is why it surprised me. She had four in all. A tortoiseshell. Two tabbies. And one quite nondescript little creature."

"I like kittens," Miss Stannis said, the first words she had spoken since leaving the asylum.

"Oh, so do I," Mama said. "I am so glad we have that in common. You know, you might want to come to Redfield and see the litter."

A few moments of silence. Then Miss Stannis said, "Yes. I want to come." The young woman turned to look at Mama. "It was awful," she whispered.

"I know," Mama said, patting Miss Stannis' hand. "I have been in an asylum myself."

"You?" Surprise was obvious in that single syllable.

"I spent two years in a madhouse," Mama confirmed, her face grim. "I wanted to die."

"So did I," Miss Stannis said, tears leaking from her eyes. "Anything would be better than remaining there."

Mama indicated Matthew, and Miss Stannis finally glanced at him.

"I helped free Mama from her situation. I did the same for you."

Looking puzzled, the young woman said, "Why?"

He kept the vehemence from his voice, knowing she needed a gentle tone. "Because it was wrong to place you there. Mama heard whispers about it during the Season."

Miss Stannis frowned. "When is it? You said something of the autumn harvest."

"It is the third week of October." Then, knowing Mama had heard the gossip last year and that they had been searching for Miss Stannis for over a year, he added, "The year is eighteen-o-eight, my lady."

More tears came now. "I lost over a year in there. Papa had me carted off in June. When I refused to wed that old, fat cow. Lord Burghley."

Her words confirmed everything Larkin had discovered. Miss

Stannis was the only daughter of a viscount who had agreed to sell his daughter in order to gain property adjacent to his country estate. Lord Burghley had to be past seventy, and this young woman, known as a bluestocking, had not been one to go quietly.

"You do not have to wed anyone, Miss Stannis," Matthew assured her. "You are safe at Dove Hall now. You may remain here as long as you like."

Panic suddenly filled the young woman's eyes. "Do you live here?"

"No, we live at Redfield, my son's ducal estate in Suffolk," Mama said. "But His Grace purchased Dove Hall so that ladies such as yourself had a place to go and recover before they decided the next stage of their life."

Miss Stannis grabbed his mother's hands. "Do not leave me here! He will find me. Take me back." She began weeping again. "I cannot go back. I will kill myself."

Those words signaled to them both that Miss Stannis needed extra care. Most of the women they received were in bad shape, both physically and emotionally. A few, however, were fragile and required more.

"You will return with us to Redfield now," Mama said soothingly. "Once you get your bearings, you may come back here to Dove Hall and stay as long as you wish. Some have decided to remain on the estate and help others like them. Some have moved on, taking new names, going to work for a living. You will have all the time in the world you need to decide what is best for you."

"Promise me I will never have to see Papa again. Or that awful Lord Burghley," demanded Miss Stannis.

"I give you my word as a gentleman," Matthew said. He looked to Mama. "Shall we return to Redfield?"

Miss Stannis was wearing a night rail, so Mrs. Paul was called in to help provide a gown for the young lady to wear. He went downstairs and waited while Miss Stannis was dressed and Mrs. Paul found a few other gowns which would work. Miss Vines, their resident seamstress, always had extra gowns made up in a variety of sizes for those who came to Dove Hall. While they might not fit exactly right, it gave the women something to wear other than the usual gunnysack they almost always wore when he brought them to Dove Hall.

Matthew handed up Mama into the carriage and then gallantly offered Miss Stannis his hand. His heart ached, watching her hesitate.

"Take it, my lady. I know it is hard for you to trust any man at the current moment, but you have my sympathies. My own father placed Mama in an asylum. I was able to liberate her upon his death. I have seen in person what dreadful places they are, and I do my best to free women when I can."

Her eyes narrowed. "What did you have to promise to achieve my freedom?"

"I settled upon a certain price with the doctor who ran your asylum," he said, not sharing how much it cost to remove Miss Stannis from the place of horror.

"I refuse to pay you as I did him," she said, anger and mistrust evident in her eyes.

"I expect no payment from you, Miss Stannis."

"He . . . made me . . . pay. Every week."

Since he already knew that the girl's father paid monthly for her to be kept locked away, Matthew had a good idea what the doctor had required of this young woman.

"You are to make every decision for yourself, Miss Stannis," he assured her. "And that includes what you do with your own body."

She bit her lip, tears forming in her eyes. Gently, Matthew took her hand and handed her up. Miss Stannis scrambled to the seat where his mother sat, throwing her arms about Mama and weeping profusely. He climbed into the carriage and sat opposite them, mouthing one word.

Rape.

Mama's own eyes filled with tears. While she herself had not been subjected to it during her own imprisonment, it was something a few of the women they had helped had suffered. Miss Stannis would take even longer to heal emotionally. They would also have to see if she might be with child, which was a possibility. Mrs. Hanson would be called in to examine Miss Stannis. Mrs. Hanson was a local midwife, and she was also skilled in the use of herbs. The women seemed to take to Mrs. Hanson with ease, and she would spend hours in their presence, talking with them, letting them pour out their miseries to her.

Mrs. Hanson would have her work cut out for her with Miss Stannis.

They reached Redfield. He disembarked from the carriage and quietly told a footman to have Mrs. Ridley prepare a room for Miss Stannis. By the time he helped his mother and their guest from the vehicle and into the house, Ridley met them.

"Shall I have tea brought up, Your Grace?" the butler asked, handing Matthew a note. Seeing it was from Hugo, he quickly read and then pocketed it.

"Yes, Ridley," Mama said. "And slices of cake. Miss Stannis is no doubt hungry. And water for a bath as well, Ridley."

"Yes, Your Grace."

The young woman did appear emaciated. Many of the women they helped also had been starved as punishment. Even beaten. Mama would nurse this wounded dove back to life. Hopefully, Miss Stannis' mental condition would stabilize so that she might take a new name and become employable. If not, she would be forever welcome to stay in one of the cottages on the grounds of Dove Hall.

They went up the steps, each of them on one side of Miss Stannis. The footmen knew to give any of these sudden guests a wide berth.

Mrs. Ridley was in the corridor and indicated which guest bedchamber to place Miss Stannis in. They guided the young woman inside, and she collapsed upon the bed.

"Tea and cakes will be here soon," Mama promised. "Then

we shall bathe you."

He witnessed the panic surging through the woman. "No. I do not want anyone to touch me."

"It will only be me," Mama promised. "I shall wash your hair for you and help you to bathe."

"But . . . you are a duchess," protested Miss Stannis.

Mom gazed levelly at her. "A duchess who has suffered as you have. I promise to be gentle."

Miss Stannis began to sob, and Mama moved her hand, indicating for Matthew to leave them alone.

Stepping toward Mama, he quietly said, "Remember that we are to dine with Hugo and Tia this evening. Tia's aunt and two of her cousins have arrived."

"Go without me," Mama urged. "I cannot leave Miss Stannis unattended in this condition."

"Very well," he said. "I will plan to stay the night so I do not have to come back in the dark. I will see you tomorrow morning."

"Thank you, Matthew," Mama said, her own eyes brimming with tears. "You have saved another one."

He nodded, leaving her with their latest damaged dove. These errands of mercy took a lot from him. Matthew was glad he could push today aside and enjoy dinner tonight with his good friend and Tia. Already, he was fond of his friend's wife. Tia had been excited about her cousins coming to visit. It would be nice to return to a sense of normalcy for a while.

At least until the next woman needed help.

Chapter Three

VERINA FELT REFRESHED after her brief nap. Sarie, the maid Tia had assigned to her cousins, was young but seemed dependable. She told Verina that her older sister was Lady Merriman's lady's maid, and that she hoped she, too, could be a lady's maid someday. Verina did not say anything, waiting to get a better idea of the girl's skills with hair and clothing, but Mama had told her that she might have her own lady's maid when the Season started next spring. If Sarie proved to be reliable, Verina hoped she might talk Tia into allowing Sarie to move to their household.

Sarie told her that she could wear the same dress she had changed into for tea, explaining that Lord and Lady Merrifield kept a casual table in the country and that they did not dress in evening wear to dine.

"But a duke and duchess are coming to dinner this evening," Verina said. "I wish to wear a better gown because of that."

"Of course, my lady," the maid said, going to the wardrobe and pulling one out. "How about this one, Lady Verina? This shade of blue would bring out your own blue eyes."

Since it was a favorite of hers, one which she thought would help her make a good impression with the duke and duchess, she agreed. "Yes, that gown will do nicely."

The servant dressed her and then took down Verina's hair. "I have an idea of what to do with your hair. You do have lovely locks, my lady."

She sat at the dressing table in the room, watching in the mirror as Sarie unpinned her hair and brushed it until it shone. Then, she artfully twisted pieces and pinned them in a style Verina had never seen, but she was pleased with the results.

"See, my lady? Simple but elegant. It suits you."

"Thank you, Sarie. I like it quite a bit."

"If you don't need anything else, I'll head across the hall to Lady Justina and help her get ready."

"I will come with you," Verina said, wanting to see how the maid would arrange her sister's hair.

Justina chose to wear the same gown she had changed into for tea, brushing aside Verina's concerns about them dining with a duke and duchess.

"Val and Eden are a duke and duchess. Hugo's friends are people, just as we are, Verina."

Sometimes, she wished she could be more like her sister. More carefree and not as concerned with her future. Yet Verina knew in her heart that she wanted to wed and have children more than anything in the world. She hoped she would find her future husband during her first Season. While she did not care whether he possessed a title or not, she did want him to be respectful of her. She also wished he would become friends with the men in her family. Family meant a great deal to her, and her husband would be seeing quite a bit of hers when they came to town each Season.

She only hoped the man she chose to wed would agree to bring their children to town, as Ariadne had suggested. Ariadne had been the first of the ten cousins to wed, and she and Julian had decided they would always bring their children to town. They had already started doing so with Penelope, their firstborn. Ariadne said she had hated being abandoned by her parents when they went to town each year for months of the Season, and she was unwilling to make her own children suffer in that manner. Moreover, all the cousins liked one another, and Ariadne said it would be fun for them to bring all the children in the family to town so that the new generation of cousins could grow up familiar with one another, strengthening the bonds of family.

This past Season, in addition to Penelope, Lucy and Judson had brought Elizabeth and Val and Eden had brought William to town. Of course, all three babes were still quite young, but it was a practice those three couples intended to keep up. Dru had given birth to Beau this past July, but she and Perry had already decided he would join his other cousins in the nursery come next Season. Lia, who was due to give birth next month, had also written to all the cousins and promised she and Rupert would definitely bring along their little one.

She assumed Tia and Hugo would go along with this plan, Tia and Lia being twins and so close. They now lived on opposite sides of England, so coming to the Season would be very important to them in order to see one another. Ariadne had shared that while she and Julian would attend a handful of events each Season, she would reserve most of their time to spend with the family which came to town.

Now that Con had wed Rowena, Verina assumed the pair would do the same once they had children of their own. Con and Val had been the closest of friends since boyhood, so whatever Val did, Con would surely agree to.

Verina decided to create a list of qualities she would seek in a husband. At the top of that list would be a man who cherished family. If he did so, he would treat her well and do the same with their children. Everything else would be secondary. It would be nice if he were handsome, and she did like to laugh, so a sense of humor would be important. Beyond that, she determined to be open to the gentlemen she would meet at the many events held during the Season.

And prayed she would make the right match.

Sarie finished dressing Justina's hair. Her sister's eyes opened wide.

"Oh, I do like this. I look older, don't I, Verina?"

"You do. And very beautiful," she said. "Thank you, Sarie. That will be all."

"Just ring when you need help undressing this evening, my ladies. I'll be here quick as I can."

After Sarie left, Verina said, "I am thinking Sarie would be a perfect lady's maid for me."

Justina gasped. "You cannot go about stealing Tia's servants," she chided.

"I will not say anything just yet. I want to see how Sarie does over the course of our stay here. Something tells me that Tia would not mind. She has mentioned being pleased with her own lady's maid, which is Sarie's sister. Sarie told me she also has aspirations of becoming a lady's maid."

Her sister nodded slowly. "Yes, I can see how that would work out. But you would have to talk with Mama about it, too."

"Remember, Mama is to come with Tray for Christmas. By then, I will know if I want to hire Sarie or not. If I do, she might even return with us to Traywick Manor. Or Tia could bring Sarie with her to town next spring. I just wanted to get your opinion. Let us go downstairs to the drawing room. I am excited to meet the duke and duchess."

When they entered, she saw Tray and Hugo were already there. They joined them. Hugo was telling a story. He had a deep voice and a very deliberate way of speaking, pausing every now and then. His story had them laughing, though, as Tia joined them.

"Oh, look at the two of you," she exclaimed. "I see Sarie has been hard at work. She is very clever with hair. I quite like how fashionable my cousins look this evening."

"Mama has told me that Verina is to have a lady's maid once we go to town for the Season," Tray said.

"It will be your first time . . . at the Season. Is that correct?" Hugo asked Tray.

Her brother nodded. "I am done with my university studies. I suppose I could have gone to past Seasons, but I was eager to get home to Traywick Manor each summer. Now that I have reached my majority, all decisions are in my hands. It is one of the reasons I am returning to town to meet with my banker, my financial adviser, and my solicitor. While I have been involved in the estate from the time I was young, I do feel the burden of being the earl more heavily now than before."

Hugo turned to her, smiling. "And you . . . will make your come-out."

"Yes, I will be old enough to do so. Justina is also coming to town with us. It would be wrong for the three of us to leave her alone in Cumberland."

Justina sniffed. "I would be perfectly fine, you know. It would give me plenty of time to draw and paint. But it will be nice to see family and visit some of the museums in town."

The butler entered and announced, "His Grace, the Duke of Reddington."

For a moment, Verina was disappointed as a man entered the drawing room. She had been looking forward to meeting the duchess. Still, she put a smile on her face, ready to meet Hugo's good friend.

As he drew near, she thought him lean as a whippet and about six feet in height. He reached their circle, and she was taken with his cornflower blue eyes and mane of blond hair. She had heard of dimples before but never seen one until now. He had one in his chin, and Verina had the strongest urge to reach out and touch it.

"Good evening," he said, greeting their group.

"It is good of you to come, Matthew," Hugo said. "May I introduce Lady Verina Fulton and Lady Justina Fulton, cousins of Tia, as well as Lord Traywick, their brother? His Grace, the Duke of Reddington."

The duke took Verina's hand. Bowing, he brushed his lips across her knuckles, causing a tremor to run through her. Sarie had said evening gloves were not necessary, and so his touch was even more intimate than a usual introduction. She thought all her cousins and their husbands quite nice-looking, but this duke looked as if he had stepped from a fairytale.

"It is good to meet you, Lady Verina."

"Likewise, Your Grace."

The duke greeted her siblings, and then Tia asked, "What of the duchess? I am disappointed she did not accompany you this evening."

"It was a hectic day. We actually wound up with an unexpected guest, and she is attending to her this evening."

"You could have sent a note and canceled," Tia said. "Or we could have made room for your guests at our table."

"No, the duchess encouraged me to come without her. I enjoy my visits to Merrifield, more so now that my friend has wed a lively conversationalist," Reddington complimented.

The butler brought a tray of drinks, and Verina and Justina declined. Mama had said they both might have wine with their dinners each evening, but they were to refrain from spirits the rest of the time.

"Come and sit," Tia invited. "At least until we are called in to dinner."

The duke asked Tray about his country estate, and her brother was only too happy to discuss Traywick Manor.

"You seem to know much about running an estate, my lord," His Grace said.

"I lost my father and brother to a carriage accident when I was ten," Tray revealed. "While a guardian was appointed for me, I knew from that moment I was the head of the Fulton family. I took my duties seriously and learned all I could about estate management."

"We have that in common," the duke shared. "I claimed my title at twelve years of age after my father's accidental death. I had no siblings to care for, as you did. Only my mother. She is a clever woman and helped me learn about my various duties. I would love for you to see Redfield if you have time to do so."

"I will only be here through tomorrow," Tray said. "I am

leaving the day after for various appointments in town, then I will return to Cumberland. I plan on bringing Mama back to Merrifield with me come Christmastime, and we will celebrate our holiday dinner with Tia and Hugo."

"I am disappointed your stay is short, but please plan to come to Redfield when you return," the duke said. "I am ten miles from Merrifield, though Redfield is in Suffolk and not Norfolk."

"Plan on showing me your estate, Your Grace," Tray said. "I look forward to seeing as much as I can of Merrifield tomorrow. I am always looking for new ideas to implement at Traywick Manor."

The duke looked at Verina and Justina. "Even though Lord Traywick cannot visit Redfield, I hope the two of you might come."

"Oh, my cousins would love to meet the duchess," Tia said. "She is such a lovely woman."

"I will ask her and send word to you as to when you might come and visit with her," Reddington said.

The butler called them in to dinner. Hugo took Tia in, and Tray offered his arm to Justina, who was closest to him. That meant the Duke of Reddington led Verina to the dining room. She caught the whiff of a clean, citrus scent, liking it quite a bit.

As they followed the others, he said, "I do not recall seeing you at the Season, my lady."

"That is because I have yet to make my come-out, Your Grace," she replied. "I will do so this coming spring. I am looking forward to all the balls and parties. Mama says life in town is very different from the quiet life we lead in Cumberland."

"It can be a bit overwhelming, but you should have some of your cousins present to guide you through the events. Through Hugo and Tia, I have met a few members of your family. They will be a great help in introducing you to others. And if you seek a husband, they will know the reputations of the men who choose to court you."

They reached the dining room, and Tia had them sit at one

end of the table so they would not be so spread out, making conversation more difficult. Verina listened more than she spoke, still in a bit of awe at dining with a duke. She couldn't help but watch him as he spoke. He was handsome, intelligent, and personable. Though he had just met her family, the duke was at ease and made an effort to include them in the dinner conversation. She tried not to be nervous when he asked a question of her. Most men in his position would have ignored both Justina and her, focusing on Tray since he was a man. The Duke of Reddington was a thoughtful gentleman.

After dinner, they retired to the drawing room again, where Tia asked, "Are you staying the night with us, Matthew?"

She did not think dukes were used to being addressed by their given names. Of course, if he and Hugo were longtime friends, they may have always done so. This duke was friendly enough, so Verina supposed he had requested for Tia to address him informally. That would not be an option for her family, however. Verina would be respectful of this man and his lofty title.

"If you do not mind, I had planned on doing so, Tia. Since it is dark this time of year by the time dinner ends, I hate to ask my coachman to drive with only the paltry light of a lamp."

Tia smiled graciously. "You are always welcome here and you know it. Perhaps you can stay long enough to go about Merrifield with Hugo and Tray in the morning after breakfast."

The duke smiled easily. "I could do so for a couple of hours. I have nothing pressing at Redfield." He glanced at Hugo. "If you do not mind my tagging along."

"Not a bit," Hugo assured him. "Since you are staying, would you mind playing for us?"

She was used to being asked to play the pianoforte and found it unusual that the duke would play instead. That is, until he sat and his fingers danced rapidly across the ivory keys. Verina sat spellbound as he played, wishing she could possess half the talent he held. When he finished playing, she began applauding enthusiastically.

"That was wonderful, Your Grace," she told him. "I rarely hear gentlemen play."

"I try to practice several times a week, my lady. Music has always filled a part of my soul."

"We even had a pianoforte in our rooms at university," Hugo told them. "I arrived at Cambridge, not having any friends, and I quickly ran into Matthew . . . when I stopped for my first meal." He looked at his friend, clear admiration on his face. "Matthew . . . saved me . . . again."

"I would not go that far, old friend," the duke protested.

"I would," Hugo said firmly. Looking to the three Fultons, he said, "I developed a . . . severe stammer growing up. I was bullied . . . because of it. Matthew . . . helped me. He stood up for me. The bullies never came for me . . . after that."

Why Hugo spoke the way he did now made sense to Verina. She had thought him a very measured man, weighing his words carefully. Now, she realized he did that very thing to prevent from stuttering. It was hard to imagine how mistreated he must have been and how other boys must have cruelly made fun of him because of his stammering.

"I had not seen Matthew for several years. He . . . introduced me . . . to the man he shared rooms with." Hugo grinned. "It was my cousin. I had never . . . met him. Anthony stammered, too. Or had. Anthony had taught himself things to do. So that he did not stammer. I moved into their rooms—and found the pianoforte. Matthew played it often."

"We did gather about and sing many a time," the duke agreed. "Anthony had learned that singing helped him keep his stammer at bay. So, I would play, and Hugo and Anthony would join me in song." A wistful look crossed his face. "We had some marvelous times back then."

"Matthew also recites poetry with me," Hugo told them. "Speaking aloud actually . . . helps when one stammers. The rhythm of poetry helps . . . break the words into phrases." He paused. "You might have noticed that . . . I halt as I speak. I must concentrate in order to get out what I wish . . . to say."

"You speak beautifully," Verina told him, impressed with this earl even more than she had been before. He had overcome a great deal, and it was obvious he loved her cousin very much.

Tia placed her hand over her husband's. "Hugo's determination is just one of the things I fell in love with. He sings to me often, and he will recite poetry as we walk about Merrifield."

"I think that quite romantic," Verina said. "I like poetry myself. Perhaps I will find a poetry-spouting suitor once I make my come-out."

Hugo pointed to the duke. "Then you should consider Matthew here. He has memorized more poetry than I have and can recall vast numbers of verses at will."

She felt her cheeks heat. "I do not think his duchess would want me to chase after her husband."

The Duke of Reddington's gaze fell upon her. "I have no wife, Lady Verina."

Confusion filled her. "But . . . you said the duchess could not come for dinner this evening," she protested.

He laughed. "The only duchess in my life is my mother, my lady."

Suddenly, Verina wanted to get to know this man better.

Much better.

Chapter Four

MATTHEW SHAVED HIMSELF and then dressed, having left Barrow back at Redfield. He had done as he had promised all those years ago and hired Barrow away from Harrow School. First, he had Ridley teach Barrow everything about being a footman, and Barrow had served at Redfield in that capacity, taking special care to watch over Matthew's mother during his years away at school. Once he left university, he had made Barrow his valet. He trusted Barrow with his life.

As he readied himself, his thoughts drifted to Lady Verina Fulton. She was uncommonly pretty, someone who intrigued him. Mama had been nudging him the past year to take a wife, but Matthew wasn't certain if that was the path for him. He had his work with the damaged doves. Because of that, he traveled quite a bit across England, seeing what women he could save. He did not think he could have a traditional marriage due to his dedication to these downtrodden women.

And Lady Verina seemed the type to very much want a traditional marriage and life.

Matthew made his way down to breakfast, as comfortable at Merrifield as he was his own home since he visited so often. As he entered the breakfast room, he saw a buffet had been set up and assumed it was because of the Fulton cousins' visit. Hugo was already at the table, along with Lady Verina and Lady Justina.

He joined Lord Traywick at the buffet and asked, "Did you

sleep well, my lord?"

"Surprisingly, I did. I usually do not when I am in a new place, but I think I was worn out after our long journey to Merrifield."

Matthew filled his plate, always one to eat a hearty breakfast, and then he took a seat at the table, Lady Verina to his right. She wore a gown of pale blue, which only made her blue eyes appear bluer and her buttery blond hair gleam even lighter than it had seemed last night. The gown dipped modestly, only showing a small portion of the top of her rounded breasts. He had the urge to trace them with his tongue and fought it off, appalled at what a rakish thought that was, especially regarding a sweet lady such as Lady Verina.

They spoke of people in the neighborhood, and both Lady Verina and Lady Justina seemed eager to meet others while visiting Merrifield. Hugo said he would invite some of their neighbors to dinner to introduce them about and then added, "There is an assembly each month in Merrivale. The next one . . . will take place the first Saturday evening of November. If you enjoy dancing, it would be a good place . . . to mingle and have a bit of fun."

"Both my sisters enjoy dancing," Lord Traywick said. "You must go to this assembly," he encouraged his sisters. "I know you enjoy the ones held at home."

Tia joined them, and Matthew thought she looked a bit pale. He would not be surprised if she were with child. Hugo had spoken with him about their desire to have children as quickly as possible.

"What do you have planned for your cousins today, my love?" Hugo asked his wife.

Before Tia could respond, Lady Verina said, "Justina and I were hoping we might accompany you gentlemen as you go about the estate today. We both want to see it as much as Tray does, and this way, you would only have to take the three of us out a single time."

Tray chuckled. "My ever practical sister," he said, smiling fondly at Lady Verina.

Matthew could see a closeness between the siblings. Having had none, he experienced a quick moment of jealousy, pushing it aside.

"I would not mind in the least," Hugo declared. "We would be happy to have you join us this morning."

Lady Justina turned to Tia. "Would you like to go with us?"

"No, I have a few things I can do here while you are away from the house. That way when you return, we can spend time together. I think it best that the three of you accompany Hugo and Matthew."

They finished eating and went down to the stables. All three Fultons said they were accomplished riders, and the appropriate horses were saddled and brought out for everyone. Matthew helped Lady Verina into the saddle, his hands going about her waist as he lifted her up. He caught the faint scent of peaches coming from her and suddenly wished to nuzzle his nose against the long column of her neck.

He stepped away, shaking his head, trying to rid himself of such a fantastical notion. He had a widow in Redgrove, the nearest village to Redfield, and discreetly visited her a few times a month. Other than that, he had little to do with women, much less the ladies of Polite Society. He had to remind himself that Lady Verina was still not yet out and thrust aside his budding interest in her.

Or so he told himself.

They rode about Merrifield, Hugo pointing out various things of interest to their party. Lord Traywick had several questions, and so did his two sisters. It was obvious the brother was not only solicitous of his younger siblings, but he was eager to hear what they had to say, as well.

At one point, Lord Traywick said to Matthew, "Since I came into the earldom so young, I was always asking questions of other adults around me. Verina and Justina idolized me and followed me about. They, too, have learned quite a bite about estate management, simply by traipsing after me and listening carefully." He paused. "Both will make for good wives. That is, if we can get Justina interested in marriage."

He had thought the young earl was hinting for Matthew to take an interest in one of his sisters, but he was surprised by what Traywick had said about the younger girl.

"She does not wish to wed?" he asked.

Lord Traywick shrugged. "While Verina has looked forward to her come-out for years now and cannot wait to find a husband and start her own family, Justina is extremely independent. She says she has no interest in marriage, but Mama hopes that will change."

"She is still young," he noted.

The earl nodded. "Yes. Barely six and ten—but she is wise beyond her years. If she does wed, her husband will have his hands full since she is so opinionated."

"How old is Lady Verina?" Matthew causally asked.

"Seven and ten," responded Lord Traywick. "She will turn eight and ten the first day of the new year."

"I suppose you will accompany her to the Season and help her find this husband she yearns for."

"That is my plan. Of course, Mama and Justina will come to town with us. Mama is a most amiable woman, and she has made many friends throughout the *ton*. My goal is to see Verina wed—and hopefully, Justina—before I ever consider looking for a bride for myself. What of you, Your Grace?"

"I am five and twenty now. I know it is important for me to provide an heir. The Season has never held much interest for me, however. Yes, Mama and I have attended together the past several years, but no woman has struck my fancy. I wind up going to fewer and fewer events as the Season goes on, finding most of the eligible ladies . . . boring."

"I hope you will find a lady to your liking this year, Reddington. You see how happy Tia and Hugo are. I think all of us long for companionship. Perhaps even love."

Matthew shook his head. "Love is not for me, Traywick. I know your family seems to have made several love matches, but I do not see that in my future. Yes, I want someone who would be suitable as my duchess, but emotions can be . . . messy. I do not wish to entangle myself in something such as love."

They rode by a row of cottages, and Hugo stopped their party, saying, "This is where my tenants live. You can see the common garden they tend over there."

Hugo then pointed out a few of the cottages which needed their roofs replaced.

"This time of year, since the autumn harvest has been collected, is good for repairs such as these. I will assist my tenants in putting these new roofs on next week. We will also make small repairs to other roofs which are in need."

"Justina and I will help," offered Lady Verina.

Matthew chuckled. "You are going to hike your skirts and climb a ladder up to the roof, my lady?" he teased, causing her cheeks to redden.

"No, Your Grace. When Tray replaces roofs at Traywick Manor, we make a party of it. All the tenants turn out, the men removing the old roofs and replacing them with new ones. With so many helping, the task goes quickly. The wives cook a large feast and spread the food out on tables we provide. Mama has instilled in us the idea that we are to care for our tenants' welfare. That means *showing* them we care. Our cook also prepares several dishes, and we take them to this feast. Mama, Justina, and I serve the workers and their wives."

He thought that a very good idea, but while he could ask his own cook to send food to an occasion such as this, Mama would never mix with tenants. She might have done so early in her marriage, but she was still withdrawn around others, due to her past experiences, both with her husband and the madhouse. Perhaps when he wed, his wife would be interested in something of this nature. He liked the idea of demonstrating by his actions that he cared for his tenants.

"Verina and I also take baskets of food to tenants and others in the village when they are ill or if they become new mothers," Lady Justina said. "I do not like holding babes, but Verina is wonderful with the newborns."

Matthew looked at Lady Verina, and something tugged at his heart. It was a feeling he had never experienced before.

And it frightened him.

"It is nice that you are so involved with your tenants, my ladies," he praised, trying to shove the odd feeling aside. Wanting to get away, he added, "I am afraid I must leave you now. I have things to accomplish at Redfield."

"We have seen the entire estate," Hugo declared. "We will ride back with you."

The group cantered to the stables, and he told his coachman to ready the horses for their return to Redfield.

"Would you care to come in for something to drink, Your Grace?" Lady Verina asked. "I am certain you are as parched as I am after our long ride."

He wanted to simply to spend more time in her company, but Matthew decided that would not be wise.

"No, thank you, my lady. I must head home."

"Remember to check with the duchess to see when I can bring my cousins to call upon her," Hugo reminded him.

He did not think it would be a good idea for them to come to his estate while Miss Stannis was present. She seemed spooked enough with Mama and him. Then again, they could ask her to keep to her bedchamber while they entertained guests.

Smiling, Matthew said, "I will let Mama know and have her check her diary. Tell Tia I shall send a note around for when you might visit Redfield." He turned to Lord Traywick. "When you return to the area, my lord, I will extend that invitation to you, as well."

"I am looking forward to it, Your Grace."

He bid them goodbye and mounted the steps to his carriage

while the team was being attached to it.

Should he take a wife? Eventually, he must do so, if only to get an heir off her. While he was not yet ready to pursue Lady Verina as a suitor, it would not hurt getting to know her a bit during her stay at Merrifield. The atmosphere would be informal, making it easier to get to know more about her. If he decided he thought her a good candidate to be his duchess, he could begin a courtship next spring during the Season. That would please Mama to no end.

They reached Redfield, and he left the carriage. Higgins, his head groom, came to meet him.

"A word, Your Grace?"

"Of course, Higgins."

"Her Grace and the new young lady have been in the stables for hours. With the kittens."

Matthew recalled Mama mentioning the kittens, and Miss Stannis had seemed interested in seeing them. Twice, they had actually given a cat to one of the women who remained in one of the cottages at Dove Hall. Giving them a small creature to look after seemed to give them purpose. He believed this would be the case with Miss Stannis.

"I worry about Her Grace being here for so long," Higgins continued. "Maybe you might intervene, Your Grace."

"I will go there now," he assured the groom.

He entered the stables and walked down the row of stalls, coming to the last one, which had its door open. Inside, sitting on the hay, were Mama and Miss Stannis. The mother cat was nursing her litter, which looked to be about six weeks of age to him.

"Good afternoon," he said softly, not wanting to frighten their guest. Still, Miss Stannis startled at the sound of his voice, her body tensing. Her eyes flew to him, wild, and Matthew deliberately remained outside the stall.

"Do you recall me, Miss Stannis? It is Reddington. Mama and I came and helped you leave the bad place."

He never referred to where the women had been kept as an asylum or madhouse, learning early on that it triggered strong—even sometimes violent—emotions. His second mission, that of a Miss Harrington, had driven that lesson home to him. When she had tearfully asked if she were truly now free, he had assured her that she would never be confined to a madhouse again. The very use of the word had produced a wild look in her eyes, and she had lashed out, blackening his eye in her terror. From that point on, Matthew made certain to avoid any term which might cause one of the women to erupt in anger or fear.

She nodded slowly, but he could see she still had no trust in him. Most likely in any man.

Turning his attention to his mother, he said, "Mama, I hear you and Miss Stannis have been here all day. Perhaps it is time you come in and had some tea."

"No!" the young lady barked. "I want to stay here. With the kittens."

His gaze met Mama's, and she shook her head subtly. "I will stay with Miss Stannis, Reddington. She finds petting the kittens soothing. I am thinking she would do a wonderful job if we allowed her to keep one."

A hopeful look crossed the young woman's face. "You would? I could have one?"

"Yes," Mama said soothingly. "You would need to care for it, though. Feed it. Groom it. Play with it. Even love it."

"Oh, I can do that, Your Grace. I can, I truly can!"

"They are too young now to be taken from their mother. Once they are weaned in a few more weeks, then we can talk about you taking custody of one."

Miss Stannis turned her eyes to the litter, biting her lip. "Oh, I do not know which one I should take. They are all such sweet little furballs."

"You do not have to decide just yet, Miss Stannis," Mama assured her. "We shall see which one you bond with. It always seems that a kitten will gravitate toward someone. Why, it is almost as if they choose you, instead of the other way around."

Matthew knew then that Miss Stannis would be with them at Redfield for a few more weeks. This had only happened one other time, a woman so fragile that she could not heal at Dove Hall and needed special care from his mother. He wondered if he should even ask Tia's cousins to Redfield. That decision would be left up to Mama.

Returning to the house, he spent several hours in his study, only emerging at teatime. When he entered the drawing room, he did not see Miss Stannis present.

"Where is Miss Stannis?" he asked.

"She has gone to her room to lie down." Mama smiled. "She told me she would be thinking of which kitten she might like."

"I know a kitten is the prize you are offering her. I only hope the thought of caring for it will help in her recovery. She seems more fragile than most of the others."

"Most of those whom you have helped, Matthew, are older than Miss Stannis."

He realized that was true. She looked young and was probably no more than a year older than Lady Verina. Suddenly, the thought of Lady Verina being placed in an asylum caused a rush of rage to pour through him. The thought of the willowy beauty wedding a man who might one day cast her aside caused a wave of protectiveness to fill him.

Mama frowned. "I do not believe she will be one we can send back out into the world, I am afraid. We need to start thinking of which cottage to place her in. Whether to leave her on her own or to have her live with one of the other women."

The teacart was rolled in, and Mama poured out for both of them.

Accepting a cup and saucer from her, he said, "I think it wise for Miss Stannis to have a human companion. I do not believe she would do herself harm, especially if she has a kitten to care for, but she needs company. Someone to talk with. I suggest Miss Ross."

Matthew referred to Lady Ross, a dove whom they had brought home a little over two years ago. She was in her mid-forties and barren, the reason her husband had her locked away. Lord Ross had even told his wife he sent her to the asylum to die, hoping she did so sooner rather than later. While they had been able to bribe the doctor who ran the establishment she had been placed in, continuing to pay the monthly fee for Lady Ross on top of a generous bonus to release her into their hands, they had learned Lord Ross had died in a racing accident. Matthew had met with the Ross family's heir and solicitor, and the new Lord Ross had given over the monies due to Lady Ross in the case her husband preceded her in death, seeing the marriage settlements were quite clear.

She now lived in one of the cottages at Dove Hall and had Matthew invest her funds for her, insisting that part of them go toward helping other women such as herself. Lady Ross insisted upon going by Miss Ross. She volunteered in the local community and played the pianoforte at the local assembly each month.

"Yes," his mother agreed. "I can see that. Despite never having any children of her own, Miss Ross is quite nurturing. She would look after Miss Stannis. It would not have to be a permanent situation, though. I believe Miss Ross cherishes her solitude. The next time we are at Dove Hall, I will go and see her and discuss the situation."

"When would you like to go to Dove Hall and speak with Miss Ross?" he asked.

"Not for a few days, at least. I do not think Miss Stannis would agree to accompany us there. She is too sensitive. I cannot leave her alone."

"I agree. In the meantime, Hugo would like to bring Tia's cousins to visit with you. Lord Traywick is leaving tomorrow. He has business in town and then will return to Cumberland, bringing his mother back at Christmastime. Tia's cousins, Lady Verina and Lady Justina, will remain until then."

Mama's eyes lit up. "Oh, I would love to meet them, Matthew. Tia is such a lovely young lady. I am certain her cousins are equally pleasant." Then Mama paused, and he knew what was coming next as she innocently asked, "How did you find them?"

"They were quite amiable. Lady Verina is the elder, and she will make her come-out next spring. Lady Justina is a year younger than her sister."

"I see. Let us give Miss Stannis tomorrow to continue settling in, and then we could have Tia and her cousins come visit the following afternoon. I shall send a note to ask them to visit on Friday."

"You will not have Miss Stannis at tea, will you?" he asked, worried how the young woman might behave around guests.

"Oh, certainly not. Miss Stannis is not ready to be around anyone yet," Mama assured him. "She can remain in the stables with the kittens while they are here. They will not even know she is at Redfield."

"I told them an unexpected visitor is what kept you from coming with me yesterday."

"All right. I will keep that in mind in case any of them ask." Mama smiled. "So, tell me more of Tia's cousins."

He did so, talking about all three of them so that Mama would not focus on Lady Verina. Still, he must have given something away as he spoke.

"This Lady Verina seems unusual. Is she someone you might be interested in, Matthew?"

Not wanting to tip his hand, he merely shrugged. "Possibly. I have just met her. I am certain I will see something of her—and Lady Justina—because I go to Merrifield regularly. Hugo and Tia are often here, as well, which will mean seeing these two cousins."

Mama smiled enigmatically. "I am looking forward to meeting Lady Verina."

Matthew knew his mother was like a dog with a bone at times. It would be best not to say anything else, or she would pick up on his interest in Lady Verina.

"I think I will have a slice of the cake," he said affably.

She handed him a plate with the cake and said, "You do not fool me, my boy, even if you think you do. I will respect your feelings and not pry. For now…"

So much for trying to hide the fact that he was intrigued by the young woman.

"I think you will like her, Mama. Lady Justina, as well," he said, before changing the topic.

At dinner that evening, Mama told him that she had sent a message to Lady Tia, asking her and her cousins to spend the day at Redfield on Friday.

Matthew decided he could wait patiently until then.

Chapter Five

VERINA WATCHED TIA closely as the carriage took them to Redfield, thinking her cousin looked a bit pale. Hugo had said the estate was ten miles from Merrifield. Merrifield was located in Norfolk, right on the border where Norfolk joined Suffolk. Redfield was in Suffolk. It would take them about half an hour to reach their destination. She hoped that Tia was not ill and that they would not have to turn back. She decided to watch her cousin closely, however, and suggest they do that very thing if Tia's color did not improve.

"I think it nice that you and His Grace met at university," Justina said. "Especially since you had not seen one another for several years."

"His Grace was brave to stand up to your bullies, Hugo," Verina added. "Anytime a group of boys are in a pack, it can be dangerous."

"The Duke of Reddington was not afraid of anyone. Or anything," Hugo told them. "Of course, I knew who he was. As an older boy who was athletic and frequently won academic prizes, he was someone I aspired to be like. It did shock me, though, when he came to my rescue. He very calmly told the ringleaders that I was not to be touched—or they would have to deal with him."

"And they simply left you alone after that?" Justina asked, wide-eyed.

"That was the power of the Duke of Reddington," Hugo told them. "He had become a duke at an early age, yet he was mature enough to know exactly how and when to wield his power. The troublemakers who led the group of boys against me already understood the pecking order of Polite Society. No one would wish to anger a duke—because a duke could seek revenge at any time. They were smart enough to leave me alone."

Tia snuggled against her husband. "I am glad Matthew stood up for you, my darling. And that he has become your trusted friend for all these years."

"Yours, as well, love," Hugo said tenderly. Then looking to Verina and Justina, he added, "Matthew danced with Tia at the Season. For a while, I thought they might be interested in one another."

Justina made a choking sound, and Verina patted her sister on the back.

"Truly?" Justina got out.

"Hugo is exaggerating," Tia said. "Yes, I did dance with him. After all, he was a duke. Who would not wish to dance with a charming, eligible duke? Especially one who dances as gracefully as Matthew does. But even then, I had my eyes on Hugo here."

"I am glad you won out over the duke," Justina declared. "His Grace seems very nice, but you are more approachable."

Out of curiosity, Verina asked, "Was His Grace seeking a bride last Season?"

Hugo shrugged. "He said he was considering the idea. His mother, I believe, is ready for the pitter-patter of little feet at Redfield. If she is to get those grandchildren, Matthew must wed."

"He is still a bachelor," she mused. "I suppose he found no one to his liking, especially since you swept Tia off her feet."

"Matthew bores easily," admitted Hugo. "He goes to events and then is disappointed by the meaningless chitchat in ballrooms. He usually disappears into the card room at a ball. As last Season progressed, he went to fewer and fewer events."

"He will never find a bride if he does not actively look for one," Justina pointed out.

Verina wondered why the duke became bored so easily.

Perhaps she would ask him.

They arrived at Redfield at noon, and the duke and his mother greeted them outside.

"Please, come in and we can have our introductions inside," the duchess said. "It is far too chilly to do so with today's brisk wind."

They moved toward the large house, one which was very appealing, and entered the foyer. A butler took their bonnets and reticules, but all three women chose to keep their spencers.

The duchess smiled graciously. "My son has told me of your cousins, Tia. I am delighted to meet them."

"Mama, this is Lady Verina Fulton and her younger sister, Lady Justina."

They both curtseyed to the duchess, who took each of their hands in hers, pressing them lightly. "Welcome to Redfield, my dears. It is so good to have you here." She smiled at Tia and Hugo. "And you know I am always happy to see the two of you. Come, let us go to my parlor. It is much smaller than the drawing room and easier to heat. Ridley has a wonderful fire going for us, so we should be perfectly toasty."

They followed their hostess, the duke bringing up the rear. Her Grace took Justina's hand, saying, "Why don't you sit with me, my lady?"

That left Hugo and Tia to sit on one settee, while Verina and the duke took the other. She was a bit breathless, sitting this close to a duke. No, sitting this close to this man. While Mama did some entertaining at Traywick Manor, none of their guests were devastatingly handsome bachelors, much less dukes. Verina felt her heart speeding up as she caught a whiff of his cologne. It was the same he had worn when he had come to Merrifield, a bright citrus, mixed with his own masculine scent, and she found it most appealing.

"I have sent for tea," the duchess said. "With little cakes that our cook makes. I wanted something to warm you after your journey to Redfield, but it is not a full tea."

"It was not a long trip, Your Grace," Verina bravely said, not knowing if she should speak to a duchess without being specifically addressed. "And while it is crisp and cool outside, the carriage was comfortable."

The older woman gazed at Verina a moment, nodding slightly, almost studying her. She could feel her cheeks heat.

"It is good to know that the short journey did not bother you, my lady. Tell me of your interests. I do so love to hear about others new to me."

She swallowed, unused to having attention brought to her. "I enjoy getting outside, Your Grace. At home, I ride quite a bit and walk a great deal. I do all kinds of needlework, as well as some gardening."

"I see." The duchess turned her attention to Justina. "And you, my lady? What do you like to do?"

"At times, I am my sister's shadow, Your Grace. We walk and ride together, oftentimes visiting our tenants or the sick in our village. I also enjoy sketching and painting." Justina paused. "And I abhor needlework. I avoid it like the plague."

The duchess grew thoughtful. "So, you see to your tenants' needs?"

When Justina remained silent, Verina spoke up. "We do, Your Grace. Our mother believes it is not only the Earl of Traywick who is to look after his people. Rather, it is the job of the earl's entire family to do so. From the time we were young, Mama took us with her when she visited tenants or even those in our local village. Sometimes, she would merely stop by for tea and talk with our tenants. Mama has urged us to get to know every family on our estate. We know the parents and their children. Who has lost a tooth and who has skinned a knee. We bring baskets of food to those who fall ill. I have even taught a few of the children to read."

"That is most impressive, Lady Verina!" the duchess exclaimed.

"Not really, Your Grace. My family may own the lands where our tenants reside, but they are as an extended family to us. We celebrate their happiness with every marriage and birth. We also mourn with them in times of loss."

The duchess gazed at Verina a long moment. "I find that very refreshing, my dear. Is this something you plan to continue once you are wed?"

"Absolutely, Your Grace. I hope my future husband will see my role as more than ornamental. While I do love to don a pretty gown and dance or sing, I want to do my part in the new family I become a member of."

"You are quite right to think this," the duchess said. "I wish I had been brought up to do so. When I came to Redfield, I was one of those ornamental brides you mentioned. And my shiny veneer did not last. I have never become involved with our tenants, the way my son has."

The duchess' frankness surprised Verina. She wondered what the previous duke had been like.

"It is never too late," she said gently. "You might be surprised how welcoming your tenants would be if you visited them."

The duchess pursed her lips in thought. "Perhaps you are right, Lady Verina. I will consider the matter."

Talk turned away from her, for which Verina was grateful. She sat quietly, listening to the others, content to be in their company. Justina, on the other hand, was her usual, vocal self, even in the company of a duke and duchess. Her sister freely gave her opinion about several topics. Verina watched as the duke covered his mouth twice, coughing each time, hiding a chuckle.

The second time, she turned to him and quietly said, "Justina means well. She is a bit forward, but she is a sweet girl."

"A very *opinionated* girl," he replied.

She took offense to his tone and hissed, "My sister is intelligent, Your Grace, and not afraid to hide it."

"Forgive me, Lady Verina. I did not mean to sound judgmental."

"Hmph."

She turned her attention back to the conversation, but she noticed the duchess was watching her and the duke. Verina could not afford to alienate such a powerful person in Polite Society. She would do her best to keep her own opinions to herself and not speak with the duke again. His words regarding Justina had irritated her. If anything raised her hackles, it was someone who spoke ill of her family.

It surprised her when he suddenly said, "Would you like to see Redfield, my ladies? Since you both enjoy riding, I thought we could see a bit of my estate while you are here."

"Oh, I was enjoying hearing Lady Justina's opinions about the war with Bonaparte," Her Grace said. "Perhaps you could take Lady Verina out for a ride while we stay in."

Verina looked to Justina. "Do you wish to see Redfield?"

"Actually, I am enjoying talking with Her Grace," her sister replied. "Not many adults take me seriously."

"They should," the duchess encouraged. "You are not spouting things off the top of your head, my lady. It is obvious you have read quite a bit about the war and are most knowledgeable."

"Mark my words," her sister said. "The recent battle at Vimeiro will result in the rise of Wellington's prominence. I believe he has the vision to lead England to victory over the Little General. It may take a few years, but if I were a gentleman and could place bets, my money would be on Wellington."

"Go ahead, Reddington," his mother urged. "We will be fine without your company. Just try to be back in time for tea."

"Yes, Mama." The duke stood. "Shall we go down to the stables, my lady?"

He offered her his arm, and she wasn't surprised to find it hard as a rock. Though lean, he looked very strong, and she supposed he knew how to handle himself with pistols, swords, and fists.

As they left the house and went down to the stables, she asked, "Were you afraid when you stood up to Hugo's bullies? After all, he said it was a group of boys who terrorized him, and you were only one person against them."

"Though that was many years ago, I do not recall being afraid. I only know I saw a wrong—and I had to make things right." He hesitated. "It is something you will learn about me. Injustice of any kind angers me. I cannot sit back and allow it to occur."

"Well, I doubt we will come to know each other well, but it is nice to know this about you, Your Grace."

He halted. "Why do you say that?"

She frowned. "I am not certain what you are asking me."

"You will be here for almost two months, Lady Verina. Surely, we will get to know something of one another during that time."

"Yes, I suppose that is possible. However, over the next two months, how often will we truly encounter one another? It is not as if we will see each other in the local village when we are running errands or stopping for tea. I am sure you will come to see Hugo a few times. He may also come to visit you, but Justina and I would not be with him."

His gaze bored into her, causing a delicious chill to race along her spine. "I think we will see one another more than you think, my lady. I do hope you will come to know something of me."

She smiled. "Well, I have learned that injustice causes you to act bravely. Even brashly."

He chuckled. "There is that."

He began walking again, and they reached the stables.

"I did not mean to make fun of you, Your Grace. I actually admire you for standing up for Hugo—and any other unfair behavior which you witness. As a duke, you have a responsibility to society. You are a man others look up to. If you act, so will they. That is how great your influence is."

"I do not see myself as some grand crusader, Lady Verina.

But I do have causes which I work for. Wrongs that I try to right. Perhaps you would like to hear about that sometime."

He held her gaze for a long moment. Something passed between them as he did, something Verina would later ponder and have no answer for. It seemed as if he opened up a piece of his soul and handed it to her. Why, she couldn't say, only that she believed he trusted her.

And she trusted him, as well.

"Good day, Higgins," he greeted as a man stepped from the stables. "This is Lady Verina, and she rides quite well. Have horses saddled for us both. I am going to take her about Redfield."

"Aye, Your Grace."

They did not speak while the groom was gone, but the silence was anything but uncomfortable. This was something new to Verina, and she would think on this later.

Higgins returned, leading two horses by the reins. "I thought Sunshine would suit Lady Verina."

"I agree. She's feisty but friendly." He stepped to her. "Allow me."

His hands went about her waist, spanning it because they were so large. The first time he had helped her into the saddle, Verina had gone breathless. The same happened this time. It was as if she did not want him to release her. She longed for his hands to remain on her waist, while she put hers on his shoulders. And she desperately wanted a kiss from him.

"Madness," she said under her breath.

Why was this man stirring things within her? True, she had very little experience being around men, other than the ones in her family. Why did this duke cause her heart to palpitate and her insides to flutter?

Verina reminded herself that this man was a duke, far above her station. According to Hugo, His Grace was also one who bored easily. With her limited experience, she would never hold his interest for long, so she had no reason to daydream about him. He was Hugo's friend. That was why he was being kind to her and her family. When next Season came, he might greet her pleasantly and then walk past her. If it were true that he sought a bride, he would look to a lady who was beautiful and sophisticated, not a simple country girl such as herself.

She watched him mount his horse and leaned low. Whispering in her horse's ear, she said, "Sunshine, do not let me down today. Be one with me."

The horse nickered as if she understood Verina.

"This way," the duke said, turning his mount.

Verina followed, forcing herself to keep her focus on riding—and not on his broad shoulders and beautiful posture.

He took her about Redfield, and she asked a few questions as they went. He answered them thoroughly, treating her respectfully and not as some featherhead, which she appreciated.

When they had seen a good portion of his estate, they began trotting back to the stables. The trot became a canter, and then they began racing one another, galloping across a large meadow. They went so fast, she felt a few locks of her hair loosening, flying in the wind.

She reached the stable yard seconds before him, drawing on Sunshine's reins to bring the horse to a halt. Laughing, she slid from the saddle and stroked the horse's neck.

"You flew as the wind, Sunshine. Thank you."

Verina kissed the horse's nose and turned, finding the duke standing next to her.

"You kissed a horse?" he asked, looking perplexed.

"Sunshine helped me outrun you," she explained. "It was my way of thanking her."

The look he gave her was heated. "And what would it take for me to win a kiss from you, my lady?"

His question flummoxed her. She turned away, knowing her face flamed, not from exertion, but from his flirtatious words. Verina took the reins and led Sunshine into the stables, where a groom met her.

"I'll take Sunshine for you, my lady," the boy said cheerfully.

"Thank you."

Higgins took the duke's horse and asked her, "How was your ride, my lady?"

"Sunshine proved to be the perfect companion," she declared, adding, "Better than human ones."

Verina started toward the house, the duke falling into step with her.

"I am sorry if I offended you, my lady," he apologized.

She stopped and faced him. "I have never kissed a man before, Your Grace. I am also not one to play games. If I kissed you, it would be because I wanted to so badly that my teeth ached."

Verina began marching toward the house again, hoping he would leave her in peace.

"Let me know when you have a toothache then," he called after her.

Disgust filled her. The Duke of Reddington might have a strong sense of justice, but she believed it to be inappropriate to ask for a kiss. She did not answer him because she had nothing to say to him.

All she wanted to do now was return to Merrifield.

Chapter Six

MATTHEW REGRETTED TEASING Verina. Being as young and naive as she was—and obviously having never been kissed—she had not taken well to his flirtatious suggestion of a kiss. He was not even certain why he had asked her how to gain one from her, other than the fact that he was attracted to her. It is not as if he went about taking advantage of young ladies. After all, he was a gentleman and behaved as one. Or at least he had until he had met Lady Verina.

So, why had he asked such a thing of her?

They returned to the drawing room just as tea was being served. After the others asked a few general questions of Lady Vernina and her impressions of Redfield, she fell silent for the rest of teatime. He doubted anyone noticed because the conversation flowed well between the others.

Except for his mother.

Mama tried to catch his eye, which Matthew avoided. He continued to be the perfect host for their guests, but he was disappointed in how the day had turned out. He had thought Lady Verina had the potential to be his duchess, but with the way she had turned cold and now silently pouted, she was obviously not the one for him. He needed a woman with more maturity. Even experience.

Still, he liked her idea of service toward tenants. He had always paid for things such as repairing roofs, but he had never actively participated in putting a new roof onto a cottage. Matthew believed that would mean a great deal to the tenants at Redfield if he put in some of the sweat necessary to maintain the cottages.

He looked to Hugo now and said, "When you put those roofs on next week, I would like to be present."

"What?" his friend asked. "You wish to see me laboring?"

"No, Hugo. I wish to participate. I want you to teach me. Because I want to start doing the same here at Redfield."

Mama clucked her tongue. "That is not necessary, Matthew. After all, you are a duke. No one thinks any less of you for not climbing upon a roof and helping to thatch it."

"It is something I wish to learn how to do, Mama." Turning back to his friend, he asked, "May I come to Merrifield for this?"

"You are always welcome at Merrifield," Hugo said affably. "It will take probably three or four days. Come the first day. You are under no obligation to stay after that You should see enough that day to satisfy your curiosity."

Even though he did not want to be around Lady Verina overly much, Matthew heard himself saying, "No, I will be there the entire time. I wish to be a part of the whole process and participate fully. I shall bring those new skills of mine back to Redfield and put them to good use."

"I will let you know when we are to start. Plan for mid-week or later," Hugo told him.

Their guests left after tea. As they watched the carriage roll down the lane, his mother turned to him.

"What did you do to that girl?" she asked harshly.

He had never heard that tone come from her, much less be directed at him.

"I teased her a bit," he admitted, not willing to make her a party to the entire story. "She did not take it well."

"I had high hopes for her. For you. I have told you it is time for you to take a duchess, Matthew."

"Well, it will not be Lady Verina, Mama," he said flatly. "I will see you at dinner."

Matthew retreated to his study and brooded. Thank goodness he would be making a trip to town with Lady Treatley soon. He needed time away from Redfield. Hopefully, he could quickly forget about Lady Verina Fulton.

MATTHEW LEFT REDFIELD at first light, heading to Dove Hall, where he collected Lady Treatley and her small valise. He told her it would take until mid-afternoon to reach London and that her solicitor would be waiting to talk things over with them.

"After that, we will stay the night at my townhouse, then see your banker tomorrow morning. We will then put you on the next mail coach to Bath. I know you have not had time to write to your sister to warn her of your arrival, so I hope she will be welcoming to you."

Actually, Your Grace, I posted a letter to her yesterday. It will arrive in time to give her a day or two's notice before I show up at her doorstep."

"If she will not take you in—"

"No, I assure you, she will. Despite the gap in our ages, we are quite close. I am what you call a change of life babe. My mother birthed my sister, and then for the next twenty years, she had a myriad of miscarriages and stillbirths. When she thought she was too old to give birth, she was surprised late in life with me. There are twenty years between my sister and me. Surprisingly, we are close, thanks to her wedding a local viscount. I saw her frequently growing up."

"It is good you will be able to have someone to go to," he said. "Many of the women we help have no one."

"She, like me, was barren. She was the viscount's second wife, however. His first had given him two sons, so she was able to serve as a mother to them. Unfortunately, both boys died when they were still children, so her husband's nephew claimed the title when he passed last year. That is when she came into her marriage settlements. They lived about forty miles from Bath, and she has always had a fondness for the town, which is why she moved there, hoping to ease her grief and have a fresh start."

"Even if for some reason she could not take you in, Lady Treatley, you will have adequate income to find a place of your own," he assured her. "Have you given any thought to a new name, as my mother suggested?"

"I was Amelia Harper before I became Lady Treatley. I may return to that name."

Matthew frowned. "Though you will have your own funds, there is still a small chance that your husband still may come looking for you. He would give your maiden name to a Bow Street runner. I think you should alter it slightly. Keep the same initials, for instance."

She thought a moment. "I have always favored the name Amanda. I had a childhood friend named Amanda. She was lost to a fever when we were eight years of age. I have never mentioned her to my husband." She brightened. "I shall become Miss Amanda Hall then. You might as well start calling me Miss Hall so that I become used to it, Your Grace."

"I will do so," he told her. "Still, Mama is right. When you book your mail coach ticket and ride to Bath, do not use Amelia Harper or Amanda Hall to make it harder to trace your movements. Again, it is merely a precaution. I would suggest you be Mary Smith for that journey. It is a very common name and would be hard to connect you to it, much less find you once you arrive in Bath."

"Her Grace is a clever woman."

"She is indeed," he said proudly. "Mama survived an asylum, the same as you did, Miss Hall."

"I was only in there for a few months. I cannot bear to think what would have happened to me if you and your mother had not sent Mr. Larkin to save me."

"That is water under the bridge, Miss Hall." He paused. "Shall we make it Mrs. Hall? It would be more appropriate for your age."

She nodded. "I like the idea. I shall create a beloved Mr. Hall, whom I lost, which is why I am now a widow. I will give him all the traits I desired in my own husband, ones he never possessed. My Mr. Hall was kind, loving, and treated me as a queen."

"You have had a good attitude about all this, Mrs. Hall," he praised. "Not every woman does."

He had instructed his coachman to take them straight to the solicitor's offices once they arrived in town. They entered them just before three o'clock that afternoon. The clerk alerted Mr. Damley to their arrival, and the solicitor greeted them and escorted them to his office. Quietly, Matthew told Lady Treatley not to share her new name until he brought it up himself.

"My dear Lady Treatley, it is so good to see you," Mr. Damley said.

"It is thanks to you, in part, that I am able to be here," she said. "You wrote up a very solid marriage contract for me, leaving me access to the monies I will now live off of."

"I am only sorry to learn your husband has touched these funds," the solicitor apologized. "We do have an appointment at nine o'clock tomorrow morning with the bank manager. I have warned him not to alert Lord Treatley."

For several minutes, they discussed the income Lady Treatley would receive yearly and how she would be able to access it.

When Mr. Damley had fully explained her financial situation to her, a wistful look crossed her face. "I only wish I could go to Treatley's townhouse and collect a handful of things. A favorite gown. A cameo my grandmother gifted me upon my wedding. I know that sounds foolish. Material possessions should not hold such great value, yet sometimes, they do."

"I understand," Mr. Damley said sympathetically. "I can do nothing about the gown, but I believe the cameo is amongst what was brought to me."

This was a new development, and Matthew sat up. "What do you mean, Mr. Damley?"

"I wanted us to meet first, so that I might explain Lady Treatley's situation fully. Since we have now gone over everything, including the name change Lady Treatley has requested, I would like us to meet with two individuals in my conference room." He smiled. "You will recognize both, my lady. The first is Mr. Larkin, the Bow Street runner who spirited you away. Along with him is your former lady's maid."

She shot to her feet. "Martha is here! Oh, she was very dear to me."

Mr. Damley rose, and so did Matthew.

The solicitor said, "Lord Treatley demanded that your maid produce all your jewelry after he had you whisked away. Martha told him only you knew where the key to the jewelry box was. The girl is quite clever, my lady. As you were being forcibly removed from the house, Martha went to where you kept your jewelry and hid it. When she said she had no idea where the key was, Lord Treatley grew frustrated and smashed it to the ground, breaking it open. Of course, he found nothing inside it. He dismissed Martha, without references, on the spot, blaming her for the missing jewelry."

Lady Treatley gasped. "Oh, it is just like him."

"Martha brought the jewels to me for safekeeping, not keeping anything for herself. She recalled accompanying you to my offices when the marriage settlements were signed. She told me how you were forcibly removed from your home. I was looking into where you had been taken when I was approached by Mr. Larkin and informed of the work His Grace does. Your jewels are safely at the bank we will visit tomorrow, my lady."

Tears welled in her eyes. "I must speak with Martha now."

They went to the conference room, and both mistress and maid burst into tears upon seeing one another, clinging to each other. Lady Treatley thanked the servant for her quick thinking and good heart.

"I know not what household you went to, Martha, but I am leaving town, never to return. Would you come with me?"

Matthew noticed how Lady Treatley did not name where she was going. She was just as canny as her lady's maid. What Mr. Damley did not know, he could not reveal to others.

"I haven't found work yet, my lady. Without references, it's almost impossible to find a decent position. Mr. Damley here was kind enough to give me a reward for bringing your jewels to him, something to tide me over. I knew he would keep them safe for you. You always spoke so highly of him. I knew he could be trusted."

Lady Treatley turned to Mr. Larkin. "I must acknowledge your role in my escape from that madhouse, sir. I cannot thank you enough for what you did for me."

"Happy to do so, my lady," Larkin said easily.

Matthew said, "I think that concludes our business for today. Mr. Damley, meet us at the bank tomorrow morning at a quarter till nine. Larkin, keep to your current investigation and notify me when you have something to share."

They left the offices, and Matthew said to Martha, "We will go to where you are staying now. You are to pack your things and come with us. Do not speak to anyone."

His carriage took them to a neighborhood where ducal carriages were rarely seen. He told Lady Treatley to remain inside the carriage, and Matthew went inside with Martha, watching her pack her meager belongings.

"Go directly to the carriage. I will speak to your landlord."

He paid the landlord a healthy amount, which covered Martha's rent until the end of the year, adding five guineas on top of it.

"If anyone comes looking for Martha, she left for a new position. You do not know where it was, but you think it might have been in York. I am a duke—and I will know if you share what you shouldn't." He paused. Almost whispering now, he threatened, "I will come and find you. And make you pay."

"Yes, my lord," the nervous landlord said, pocketing what amounted to a bribe buying the man's silence in case anyone came looking for the lady's maid.

He did not think Lord Treatley would manage to hire someone to track down his wife anytime soon, much less her lady's maid. If an investigator did find this is where Martha had stayed, Matthew felt certain the landlord would reveal nothing, leading to a dead end.

In the carriage, they explained to Martha how Lady Treatley would no longer go by that name. He told Lady Treatley not to use her alias or share it with Martha until they were safely at their destination. He made certain not to mention it. The less the servant knew about where they were headed, the better. He did tell Martha that Lady Treatley would be traveling as Mary Smith tomorrow, and Martha was to refer to her employer as Mrs. Smith.

"Do I get to have a new name, too?" she asked eagerly.

"You may take one on the mail carriage, but do not share it unless specifically asked," he cautioned. "When you reach your final destination, it is up to you whether or not you wish to remain Martha or become someone new."

They returned to his townhouse in Mayfair. By now, his servants knew not to ask questions about sudden guests. The new arrivals shared a room and took their dinners on a tray in that room. The less contact his servants had with the two women, the better.

The next morning, Matthew escorted them to the bank, telling Martha to remain inside the carriage. Both women brought their valises with them since they would leave straight for the mail coach after this morning's appointment.

Mr. Damley met them in front of the bank, along with Lady Treatley's physician. Matthew wanted the doctor present in case Lady Treatley's mental status was called into question.

They entered the bank. Matthew gave his name, and they were immediately taken into the office of the man who managed this branch. He had been made aware of the topic of discussion by Mr. Damley.

"I find this highly unusual, Your Grace," the man began.

Staring coldly, Matthew said, "And I find it highly unusual that you would begin handing over funds to Lord Treatley which do not legally belong to him."

"But . . . but . . ." the bank manager sputtered. "He is Lady Treatley's husband."

"Legally, he was never to gain access to those funds," Matthew said. "Yet you gave him access to those funds."

He reached out a hand, and Mr. Damley handed him a copy of the marriage settlements, which Matthew slapped onto the desk.

"This copy is for you. Read the marked passages," he demanded.

They sat in silence while the bank officer perused the contract.

"I see," he said when he had finished. "But Lord Treatley said that Lady Treatley had been placed in an asylum. That she no longer had her faculties and could not make decisions regarding these funds. He even brought a doctor with him, attesting to her condition. As her husband, naturally, control then fell to him."

"You have yet to look at me," Lady Treatley said haughtily. "Do so. Now," she demanded.

Reluctantly, he met her gaze.

"Do I look mad to you? This was all a ruse so that my husband might get his hands on what was not his. He is a gambler and a liar. Treatley cannot be trusted. You took his word, not that of *my* physician."

She looked now at her doctor, and he cleared his throat. "I have treated Lady Treatley for several years, and I find her perfectly sane. You should have asked many more questions than you did, sir, before acting so rashly and putting those funds at Lord Treatley's disposal. Whoever Lord Treatley paid off to come here and tell you that his wife had gone mad is a liar and a disgrace to the medical profession." He sniffed. "That is, if he was even a doctor."

Lady Treatley took command of the conversation again. "How much has my husband removed from my account?"

The bank manager consulted a document on the desk and named a figure. It was not excessively large, and Mattthew knew that was usually the case in these instances. Once access had been gained to an account, withdrawals were slow at first, testing the waters. Then they came rapidly after that.

"Lord Treatley told me he took the funds for your care. That is all," the manager said, sounding defensive.

"What he removed is ten times what he was paying for my supposed care," she said bitterly.

He spoke up. "I expect the bank to make good on these missing funds. Immediately. Else I shall go to the newspapers and give them the entire story, as well as take the matter to court."

His threat hung in the air a moment.

Visibly trembling now, the bank officer said, "Of course, Your Grace."

"We shall now remove Lady Treatley's funds. See to the missing money being replaced and a transfer now." He named a bank which had a branch in Bath, and the manager excused himself, leaving them in his office. Matthew also told the physician his presence was no longer needed, and he, too, left the office and bank.

"The funds will be in Lady Treatley's name. I do not believe anyone at this bank will reveal to Lord Treatley where the funds were transferred once he returns here to dip from the account." Matthew looked to Mr. Damley. "When we conclude our business here, you are to go to the new bank. Meet with its chief officer, explaining this delicate situation. As we mentioned earlier, Lady Treatley will be living under an assumed name, and she will need to access her funds using it. Have the change made to the name we shared with you today so that when she arrives at her destination, she will be able to access them."

"I will do so, Your Grace," the solicitor promised. "I will be as discreet as possible."

Matthew provided Damley with the new name, swearing the solicitor to secrecy. Then he said, "If you have any trouble in arranging this, make use of my name. If that is not enough, send word to my townhouse. I will stop by the bank and make certain things are accomplished to my satisfaction."

"It would be good to have something from Lady Treatley's hand," Mr. Damley suggested. He went to the desk and removed a sheet of paper. "Sit here, my lady. Write just a brief note, using both names, and signing as each. I will take it with me."

She did so, and shortly after, the bank manager returned.

"It is done," he said, his face pale. "I used a discretionary fund to replace the missing monies from Lady Treatley's account. Her account here is now closed, and her banknotes have been transferred to her new bank." He swallowed. "Is there anything else I can assist you with, Your Grace?"

"No," Matthew said flatly, not bothering to thank the man.

They left the offices, dropping Mr. Damley at the new bank. Lady Treatley insisted on going in with the solicitor, afraid the letter she had penned would not be enough. Matthew joined them. Their business was quickly handled, and they parted from Mr. Damley.

"Write to me, my lady," the solicitor said. "I wish to know you are safe."

"I will do so, Mr. Damley. Thank you for all your assistance."

Matthew's coachman took them to the nearest location, and he had the driver purchase the pair of mail coach tickets to Bath. It would be too noticeable for a duke to do this. The coachman returned, handing the tickets over to him through the window.

"The next coach leaves in half an hour, Your Grace."

"Very good."

He gave the tickets to the new Mrs. Hall, saying, "Here you are, Mrs. Smith. I also request that you write to me once you are settled."

"I will do so, Your Grace," she promised, leaning over and brushing a kiss upon his cheek. "You are an angel."

Mrs. Hall and her servant left the carriage, carrying their valises and joining the line his coachman directed them to. The gown Miss Vines had sewed for Lady Treatley was plain and serviceable. She would not stand out in the crowd. Matthew waited until he saw them board the vehicle before he tapped on the roof, signaling his driver they could now leave.

He returned to his townhouse, telling the coachman they would head for Redfield in the morning. As he closed his eyes that night, Matthew fell into a deep, satisfying sleep, knowing he had helped another damaged dove.

Chapter Seven

Verina was sitting with Tia, both women working on embroidery. Verina had packed a tablecloth when she left home, a project she had been working on for months now. She thought by the time Mama arrived in December that it would finally be finished. Tia worked on a sampler for Hugo's office.

Since Justina refused to pick up a needle, she had volunteered to go to the kitchens to check with Cook regarding the food they would be taking with them to the tenants' cottages. They would be leaving in half an hour, and Justina had said she would see the wagon loaded. Tables had already been brought to the area for the wives to begin setting out food as their men worked on the new roofs for several cottages.

Though she didn't want to think about him, all Verina could picture was the Duke of Reddington, his coat and waistcoat discarded, his sleeves rolled up, revealing muscular forearms. She couldn't help herself. Despite his inappropriate remark after their ride, all she had thought about was the duke. Why, she couldn't say. She had felt out of sorts ever since that day. Even Justina had asked what was wrong with her.

"Ouch!" she said, pricking the pad of her finger with her needle. Quickly, she pulled her hand away from the tablecloth, not wishing to have drops of blood stain it. She sucked on her finger a moment, trying to draw the blood from the small puncture.

"You must be woolgathering," her cousin said. "I find sometimes I do that when I pick up my needle. The motion of moving up and down tends to lull me. And I—"

Tia gasped, dropping her sampler, her hands flying to her mouth. Her eyes grew round, and Verina knew her cousin was about to be sick. Quickly, she leapt to her feet, dashing to retrieve a vase. Ripping the flowers from it, she hurried back to where Tia sat and held it close to her. Tia placed her hands over Verina's and yanked the open end of the vase to her mouth, spewing into it.

Then she released Verina and sat back, her head falling to the back of the settee.

Worry filled her. "You became sick so suddenly, Tia. Shall I send for the doctor?"

Lifting her head, Tia shook it. She pulled a handkerchief from her sleeve and dabbed her mouth. "No. There is no need to do so. I am not truly ill."

Verina set the vase on the ground, the putrid smell rising from it, making her feel a little queasy. "I do not understand."

"I did not myself. Until this morning. It struck me that my courses had ceased." Tia paused. "I am with child, Verina."

"Oh!"

Tia dabbed her lips again. "Lia—and Ariadne—had already told me some of the signs. A sudden nausea can be part of it. Why, Ariadne was so ill when she carried Penelope that she had chamber pots placed in every room. And even on the landings of the staircase!"

"Why do you become sick?" she asked, fascinated now since she knew nothing about how a woman came to be with child, other than it had something to do with lying with your husband. Mama had addressed the topic with her a few months ago, telling Verina that before she made her come-out, they would have a long talk about men, women, and the making of babes.

Her cousin shrugged. "I am not certain why. Maybe it is because the babe is something new inside me, and my body is having to get used to it being there, growing and taking up room. Ariadne told me most women have bouts of nausea during the first few months they are increasing. Sometimes, you feel ill. Sometimes, you actually lose anything you have eaten. She said it is worse in the mornings upon arising. Now, I understand why I have been so tired and out of sorts."

"Have you told Hugo yet?"

"No, I was waiting to be certain, but after what happened just now, I know I must be increasing. Lia, too, has told me about being ill. She also said her breasts grew tender early on, and mine have grown the same way these past two days." Tia smiled. "Hugo is going to be so pleased."

She placed her hand over her cousin's. "He will be. I think the two of you are going to be wonderful parents." She paused. "Do you wish for a son—or daughter?"

"I could not say. This is all so new to me. Getting used to the idea that I carry a babe within me is . . . hard to think about. Of course, Lia is due to give birth in mid-November." Tia paused. "Shall I share a secret with you?"

"Please do so," Verina encouraged. "I will keep it."

"Lia thinks she is carrying twins," Tia confided. "It makes sense since we are twins, and they are said to run within families. Lia told me that she has grown quite large, much larger than usual. The midwife also believes that she is carrying two babes. If that is the case, she may deliver earlier. I pray for her health and the babes each night."

"Wouldn't it be wonderful if you both had twins?"

"I will think about that later." Sadness filled Tia's face. "Oh, I wish I could be with Lia at this time. I know Rupert is with her every step of the way, but we have always done everything together."

"Lia will bring her babe—or babes—to town next Season, won't she? We have been told that is the family tradition, one which Ariadne has started."

"Yes, Hugo already knows about it. Since Lia and I are living so far apart, it is impractical to visit one another. Meeting in town each spring, and bringing our children along, will be the ideal way to spend time together, as well as allow our children to get to know one another. Their other cousins, too. Just think of all the fun we would have had if our parents had brought all of us to town for the Season each year."

"I would have liked that. Especially after Papa and Lucius were gone. Though I had Justina—and Tray would come home from school each June—it was always a bit lonely when Mama was gone for months at a time. She has always looked eagerly to going to town each spring, especially since she is so close with Aunt Alice."

"Yes, Mama so appreciated when Aunt Agnes came to stay with us after Papa's death. She had your mother, and Lia and I had you and Justina to help us through that time, as well."

Verina hugged Tia. "Thank you for sharing your news with me. I will not tell a soul. Not even Justina."

"I promise you will not have to keep the secret for long. I plan to tell Hugo tonight when we are alone. Then I will share it with Justina. I think I will keep the news to only that small group for a while. I know sometimes things can go wrong in the early months. Lucy told me to wait until I believed I was three months along, and then I should tell all the cousins."

"That is a sound plan," she agreed. "In the meantime, you should see the midwife. She might be able to tell you more, especially when your babe might be arriving."

"That is a good idea, Verina. But I will write to Lia and tell her of my news. Even if things go astray, I want her to know what is happening with me."

"Do you feel well enough to go and serve food?"

Tia laughed. "Actually, now that I have emptied my belly, I feel as normal." She paused. "I did not like the smell of the fish last night, though. I may have to avoid fish for the near future. We shall see. This is all a new experience to me."

Verina chuckled. "I plan to learn what I can from you. While

Mama has promised to discuss these matters with me, something tells me I shall learn more about the entire experience from you." She picked up the vase. "Let me go and rinse this and replace the flowers which are strewn about. If Justina sees them this way, she will certainly know something is afoot."

Quickly, she took the vase with her and cleaned it, returning to Tia's parlor and rearranging the flowers. Less than a minute later, Justina returned, her cheeks pink.

"I have been helping load the food baskets into the wagon. It is time to go. I asked for your spencers and bonnets to be brought downstairs," Justina told them.

"Is the wagon full?" asked Tia.

"There is room for one of us to sit in the bed. Another can drive the wagon, and the last of us can share the driver's bench."

"I think I shall play the lady of luxury and sit in the wagon bed," Tia volunteered.

"Then I am happy to drive," Justina said.

They slipped into their spencers and bonnets and cut through the kitchens. A footman helped Tia into the wagon, and another one assisted the Fulton sisters onto the driver's bench. Justina took up the reins.

"I am glad we rode the estate with Hugo and His Grace," her sister said. "I have a good idea how to get where we are going because of that."

The day was chilly, but thankfully, there was no wind. They reached the area where the tenants resided, and Verina saw the tables already set up. Some of them bore dishes of food, and women were bringing more from their cottages. Justina stopped the wagon, and they had abundant help in taking the food they had brought and setting it out.

Verina made certain to assist Tia from the wagon, and her cousin said, "I am not some delicate creature, though my condition is considered delicate. I hope to continue to walk and ride for as long as I can."

"Let me know if you tire while we are serving the food," she said. "You mustn't overexert yourself."

"I know." Tia sighed. "Once Hugo finds out, he is going to hover over me like a mother hen does her chicks." Then she smiled. "And I will enjoy every minute of his attention."

Now that the food had been situated, Verina's eyes turned to the work at hand. Her eyes skimmed the rooftops.

And landed upon the Duke of Reddington.

He was much as she had imagined. Though the day was cold, he had removed both coat and waistcoat. His cravat had also been discarded, leaving his throat exposed. His sleeves were rolled to his elbows, and even from a distance, she saw his beautiful forearms.

Bloody hell. A man wasn't supposed to be beautiful. Especially his forearms.

Yet something stirred within Verina at the sight of him. She tightened, as a coil might, waiting to spring open. She dug her nails into her palm, trying to compose herself, but her heart beat as if she had run all the way here.

All from watching him from a distance.

This alone told her he was dangerous. Somehow, she had fallen under his spell, and she vowed not to be susceptible to his charm. Yes, he was handsome. Yes, he was a duke. Yes—other than asking what it would take to win a kiss from her—he seemed to be a decent sort of fellow.

Verina decided she could not possibly avoid him, either today or during the rest of her stay at Merrifield. To survive, she would have to harden her heart to his many charms. That is when it hit her.

She should treat him as she did Tray. As a brother. She could be familiar with him, or at least as familiar as a person could be with a duke. After all, Reddington was a family friend. He would be afoot during the next few weeks while she and Justina were here. He would come around again once Tray returned with Mama since it seemed to her that they had taken a shine to one another. She would merely close off any feelings he stirred within her and act as though he were a brother. Verina had loved to play pretend when she was young. This would be the grown up version of pretend.

She only hoped that she could pull it off and not get lost in his cornflower blue eyes or swoon when she inhaled his marvelous citrus scent.

"I can do this," she said under her breath, willing herself to be stronger than she suspected she might be.

Being a person who enjoyed organizing things, Verina was soon directing the wives, changing some of the placement of dishes and keeping others. Since not every farmer was atop one of the cottages, she had them bring out tables and chairs from various cottages so that they would have places to sit while eating. She also began assigning roles to various women, having some acting as servers, others distributing plates and silverware, and a few pouring mugs of ale, setting them out on the tables so the men could drink something once their work came to a halt and they lined up for their meal.

She dashed across to the cottage where Hugo worked and shouted up, "How long until you can stop?"

He looked about at the progress and told her, "Two minutes."

Nodding, she went back to the tables of food. "We have two minutes," she told the others.

Verina said things would go more quickly if they dished up plates of food and handed them out, so she prepared a sample plate.

"Let us start with this much food," she explained. "We want to make certain that every man working on the roofs is fed first—and well. Then we can have the other men line up. After that, the women and children can be served. Lady Merriman and Lady Justina will help us do so."

"You will need help, my lady," one woman said.

"No, you have worked very hard preparing all this food, and you will have already served the men. Let us do this for you."

A loud whistle sounded, and she realized it came from the duke. Things came to a halt, and men scampered down ladders resting against the walls of various cottages. A few women stood nearby with buckets of water, allowing them to wash up as they headed to the tables, downing their ale in a large gulp. Verina indicated for those at the ale stand to refill the mugs, and she helped direct the workers to the line.

"Roofers first, then others who are helping them on the ground line up next," she shouted. "Then the rest of the men may fall into line."

Once she saw they lined up according to her instructions, she hurried back to the tables, supervising as plates were dispersed. At one point, she sensed eyes upon her and guessed it was the duke, but she kept her focus on the tasks at hand.

After all the men were served, she encouraged the women and children to line up. She, Tia, and Justina filled plates with food as quickly as they could, and those served took their food to the tables, sitting amongst the men.

When the last of them were served, she shouted, "If you wish for more, it is available."

Hugo stood, raising his tankard of ale high. "We have accomplished much today. So much that I believe by the end of tomorrow, we will finish our work. I want to thank my lovely wife, as well as her cousins, Lady Verina and Lady Justina, for helping to organize this feast today."

A loud cheer went up, and she felt pleased that things had gone so well.

"We will repeat this tomorrow, a new crew of roofers atop the remaining cottages. My thanks to those who prepared today's food and those who will do so again for us tomorrow."

Verina encouraged Tia and Justina to take a plate and sit, saying, "I will be here to help anyone who wishes to be served again."

She wanted Tia off her feet and gave her cousin a pointed look. Tia obviously received Verina's unspoken message and picked up a plate, handing it to Justina and then taking one for herself.

Several men came to her, asking for seconds, and she gave them whatever they asked for. Three-quarters of an hour later, the men had finished eating and went back to work. The women and children followed soon after, and Verina helped organize crews to wash the dishes in a nearby stream and had others return the tables and chairs to the appropriate cottages. The tables which had been brought from Redfield would remain for use tomorrow.

"You must be exhausted."

She looked up, seeing the Duke of Reddington had joined her. His face and throat glistened with sweat. Through the thin lawn of his shirt, she could see his muscular chest. She averted her eyes, having glimpsed those beautiful forearms up close, which made her knees go weak. Then she recalled how she was supposed to treat him.

"What are you doing on the ground, Your Grace?" she teased lightly. "You are supposed to be atop a cottage, seeing to its roof and gaining experience."

He frowned a moment, seemingly surprised by her light-hearted tone. "I thought that you should eat, my lady."

"I will do so later. I need to go to the stream now and see how the washing of dishes is coming along."

"I will walk with you." His tone brokered no protests would be accepted.

She began heading toward the stream, and he fell into step with her.

"You did an excellent job organizing this for Hugo. While he and his steward may have broken the men into groups for efficiency, your skills in readying the meal made things go smoothly and efficiently, allowing the men to get back to work quickly."

"I suppose I should put my skills to use and join His Majesty's army then," she quipped. "If England had more competent officers such as Wellington and myself in charge, that dog

Bonaparte would run back to France with his tail tucked between his legs."

"Who *are* you?" he asked, looking bewildered.

"Lady Verina Fulton. Though I do believe we have met, Your Grace."

She liked the tone she had taken with him. She felt in charge of the situation. And Verina couldn't but be a bit pleased that the duke seemed slightly off-balance.

They reached the stream. "Thank you for accompanying me, Your Grace. I advise that you get back to work now."

A slow smile teased his lips, turning the corners of his mouth up. It continued to spread until it was absolutely breathtaking, and that dimple in his chin looked so very appealing. Verina placed a hand against her belly, trying to keep the butterflies which were exploding from causing her to turn giddy. She told herself to be careful and not show any sign of weakness around this man.

"You have surprised me, my lady." Reddington paused. "And that is *very* hard to do so."

"Have I surprised you because I am a woman—or because I am young?" she demanded.

"Both. Today, you have convinced me that the weaker sex might just be the stronger one. And that I should not discount someone merely because of their youth."

"I am glad I am a woman, Your Grace, and I think character is more important than age. While I do agree that maturity is important, too often others overlook the very young. I may be just under eight and ten, but I am as sharp and clever as those twice my age."

"And modest," he said, causing her to giggle.

"See, you made me giggle. Now I sound half my age. Go away, Your Grace. Go back to the roofs."

"Goodbye—for now—Lady Verina."

She watched him walk away, admiring his broad shoulders, her eyes focused on how his tight breeches molded to his buttocks and legs. When he was out of sight, she let out a sigh.

Verina felt she had won this round between them.

But if today were a battle, who was to claim victory in their war?

Chapter Eight

Verina allowed Sarie to dress her, excited about tonight's assembly in Merrivale, the local village. She felt that she and Justina were settling into life at Merrifield. Hugo and Tia had held a dinner party in their honor that week, inviting a dozen guests for them to meet. Four had been couples, while two had been eligible bachelors from the neighborhood, and the other two single ladies. While Miss Chambers was nearing thirty and firmly settled on the shelf, she had been a delight to be around. The other, Miss Kannady, had made her come-out last Season, and Verina could not wait to spend more time with her, asking about various aspects of the social whirl. It was one thing for Mama to tell her about the Season and quite another for someone close to her age to describe all the events and people.

"You look lovely, my lady," Sarie said, having guided Verina to the dressing table so she might style her hair.

While she had no ballgowns yet, Verina had brought a few nicer gowns to wear for events such as the recent dinner party and tonight's assembly. Sarie had dressed her in a midnight blue gown, which was a perfect contrast to her blond locks.

The maid finished dressing Verina's hair. "I'm off to ready Lady Justina," the maid said cheerfully, leaving the bedchamber.

That gave Verina some time alone to think.

Naturally, her thoughts strayed to the Duke of Reddington.

He had been present all three days new roofs had been placed on various cottages or old ones mended to withstand another year. The duke was an extremely hard worker, and even Hugo had mentioned how having his friend helping had made everything run more smoothly. Hugo had also complimented Verina for helping set up the mid-day meal for the three days. That third day, the workers were able to linger over the feast since their work had been completed. She had been encouraged to join the others as they ate. The entire time, she sensed the duke's eyes on her. They had not spoken since that first day, but she was more aware of him than ever.

Thankfully, Tia had not invited him to the dinner party since he did not live in this neighborhood, nor would he be attendance at tonight's local assembly. She would have the freedom to dance with whoever asked and merely enjoy herself without worrying if Reddington would ask her to dance or what they would talk about.

She thought to change into a satin pair of slippers which she had brought for a special occasion, and then she went across the hall to watch as Justina was readied for the assembly. Her sister might not like the idea of marriage, but she—like Verina—absolutely loved to dance.

"I like what Sarie has done with your hair, Verina," her sister said.

She patted her hair. "I do, too. I think Sarie is going to make for a wonderful lady's maid when the right opportunity arises."

"Thank you kindly, my lady," the servant said.

Verina had already decided she would speak with Tia about hiring away Sarie. Now might be a good time to do so.

"I am off to see what Tia is wearing," she said brightly. "I will see you downstairs."

She went to the rooms which she had learned her cousin only used for bathing and dressing. Tia actually stayed the night with her husband, sleeping in his bed. Verina knew that was out of the ordinary. Even her parents, who had loved one another deeply, slept in separate bedchambers. When she had asked Tia about it, her cousin had blushed prettily and said she and Hugo needed to be together.

Tia had told her husband of the coming babe. Justina, too, had been invited to share in the good news. While nothing had been said to anyone else, including servants, Verina knew most of the household was aware that their mistress was increasing, simply because they were having to clean out chamber pots which Tia regularly spewed into.

She knocked and then entered Tia's bedchamber, seeing that her maid was almost finished dressing her mistress' hair. Other than the fact that her cousin appeared a little tired, no one could tell by looking at her that she was with child. It made Verina wonder if Lia had already had her babe. Or babes. It would be exciting if Lia did give birth to twins. Every day when the post came, Tia eagerly went through it, disappointed when no letter from her own twin had arrived. Verina had reminded Tia that Lia was not due for another ten days, but she, too, was ready to hear news from Crestwood. Perhaps if she did not find a husband this first Season, she could go and spend next autumn with Lia, Rupert, and their little one.

Verina watched as Tia's maid put the final touches on her hair. "There you go, my lady. You look wonderful. I hope you enjoy the assembly this evening."

"Thank you," her cousin said, dismissing the maid. She then turned her attention to Verina. "I see you are wearing blue again this evening. You seem to favor the color."

"I have always been fond of shades of blue." She smoothed the skirt of her gown. "Justina always tells me no matter which hue of blue I wear, it makes my eyes stand out."

"She is right. It is good you have learned what color flatters you, Verina. You will have to let your modiste know when you go to town. Do you know which one Aunt Agnes will be using for your wardrobe?"

"Mama said that Ariadne insists that I use Madame Laurent."

Tia nodded. "Yes, several of us in the family go to Madame. I think you will enjoy working with her. Her designs are original, and Madame listens more to her clients than most modistes do." Tia smiled. "If there is a disagreement between you and Aunt Agnes, Madame Laurent will always come down on your side."

"I look forward to meeting her and attending the Season." She paused. "That is something I wish to discuss with you, Tia."

"I know we have not talked much about the Season yet, and I am certain you have many questions about it. You must be curious. Because I have done my own come-out, we should talk at length about yours. If you think it might bore Justina, we can find time for just the two of us to do so."

"I have something to ask, and I hope it does not anger you. I have enjoyed having Sarie attend to me during my stay at Merrifield. Mama has told me that once I go to town, I may have my own lady's maid."

Tia nodded in understanding. "And you believe you would like to steal Sarie from me."

"Oh, I had no intentions of doing so—and I have yet to say anything to Sarie—but she is so genial and has done such a nice job taking care of Justina and me. She is a wonder with hair. Sarie has shared her ambitions of becoming a lady's maid. Since you seem happy with her sister as your lady's maid, might you consider Mama hiring Sarie?"

"I know Sarie has been very happy working with the two you. She has told me so," Tia shared. "I can easily find another parlor maid and replace her. Yes, Cousin, Sarie can be yours if she chooses to leave Merrifield."

"Oh, thank you, Tia!" she cried, embracing her cousin. "I do not truly need her until I go to town, though. You would be able to keep her until spring."

Tia laughed. "Thank you for your generosity," she teased. "Let me be the one to approach Sarie and discuss the matter with her. If you speak to her first, she may feel an obligation to me. I want her to know I am perfectly comfortable with this decision. Of course, if you do take her on as your lady's maid, not only would she attend to you in town, she would also go with you to your new household when you wed. That would be two different moves for her. The choice should be up to Sarie."

"I agree, Tia. I am thankful that you will allow Sarie to consider it."

"Shall we go downstairs? Hugo is certain to be waiting for us by now."

Hugo and Justina were both in the foyer, and the four of them went out to his carriage. It was but a short ride into Merrivale. They had yet to go into the village, other than attending Sunday services at the local church, where they had heard Hugo's cousin deliver the sermon.

"You might wish to come into Merrivale this coming week," Hugo said.

"Yes, I need a new pair of gloves," Tia said. "I could take my cousins to the milliner's. We could also visit a few of the other shops and even have tea while we are in the village."

Hugo took his wife's hand and tenderly kissed her fingers. "Let me know if you need my escort, love. And by no means are the three of you to walk all that way," he declared. "You will be driven in the carriage."

"You have become so protective of me, Hugo."

He placed a hand on her belly. "Not just of you, love, but of our son or daughter."

Verina saw the tenderness in Hugo's eyes. For a moment, she thought she was wrong. That she should consider a love match. But she was not her cousins. Her practical nature knew the likelihood of another love match within their family was against the odds. Besides, it was perfectly possible to have a successful marriage without love, and that would suit her. She would look for a gentleman who brought out the best in her, and she hoped that she would do the same for him.

They entered the assembly room and were greeted by many as they made their way about the room. She had learned local assemblies were quite informal and that no dance programme would be issued. If a gentleman wanted to dance with her, he would simply ask before a number was played. And if they ran short of gentlemen, Tia had told them ladies would even dance with one another.

She spied Miss Kannady, and she and Justina and went over to visit a few minutes with their new friend.

"I am so happy you were able to come this evening," Miss Kannady said. "Do either of you enjoy dancing, or do you prefer to watch the dancers?"

"We both love dancing," Justina said brightly. "I am hoping to dance every set this evening. Oh, there is Miss Chambers. I would like to go and speak with her a moment."

Justina excused herself, leaving the two of them alone.

"Mama and I would love to invite you to tea, Lady Verina. Of course, Lady Merriman and Lady Justina are also welcome. I so enjoyed our conversation in the drawing room the other night, and you play the pianoforte beautifully."

"We would be honored to come for tea. Please send a note to my cousin."

"Is any day better than another?" Miss Kannady asked.

"Tia has not mentioned any specific plans, so we should be open to visit any day next week. We have discussed coming into Merrivale and doing a bit of shopping one day, however."

"Oh, that would be wonderful to meet up and do so together. I will speak to Lady Merriman and see if Mama and I might join the three of you on your outing."

"If you will excuse me, Miss Kannady, Tia is calling me over. Let us speak later this evening with both your mother and Tia present. Perhaps we could firm up our plans then."

Verina rejoined Tia and Hugo, as did Justina, and they introduced the two of them to several others new to them. As always, she thrived when meeting others, and several of them mentioned sending invitations to them over the next few weeks. It seemed as if she and Justina would be quite busy during the rest of their stay at Merrifield.

"It looks as if the dancing will soon commence," Tia remarked. "I know Lord Vallow was asking after you, Verina. Ah, there he is, heading our way now."

Lord Vallow was a newly-minted viscount who had attended the dinner party. He was very tall and had a wonderful sense of humor. Verina had been drawn to him and was happy he now might ask her to dance.

He bowed, greeting them. "Lady Verina, I heard that you enjoy dancing. Would you do me the honor of partnering with me for the first set?"

"I would be happy to do so, my lord."

The center of the room was crowded as they lined up opposite one another. The musicians struck up a tune, and she was caught up in the music. Dancing was one of the chief reasons she looked forward to the Season. Mama had told her there could be between fifty and sixty balls each Season, and she thought of all those nights where she might dance until the wee hours of the morning.

Verina was out of breath by the time the set ended, and Lord Vallow asked if she might care for some punch. She agreed, and he guided her to one of the tables where punch was being served. He retrieved a cup for each of them, and they moved to a corner of the room, sipping the cool drink, which was a bit too sweet for her tastes. Still, it was refreshing, and she drained her cup.

"I am so glad you have come to visit your cousin for a bit," Lord Vallow told her. "I do not recall having seen you at the Season before."

"I am to make my come-out this next spring, my lord."

He smiled. "Then I am happy I have already made your acquaintance even before next Season begins. Let me return you to Lord and Lady Merriman. Perhaps we might even dance together again later this evening."

She smiled up at him. "I would enjoy that, my lord."

Verina took the arm he offered, and they moved across the room, returning to where Hugo stood. Surprise filled her.

The Duke of Reddington chatted with him.

She stiffened, and Lord Vallow asked, "Is something wrong, my lady?"

"I am simply worried. I do not see my cousin with her husband," she lied. "Perhaps Tia has gone to the retiring room."

"I am returning Lady Verina to you, my lord," the viscount told Hugo.

Before she released Lord Vallow's arm, she smiled up at him. "Thank you for the dance, my lord. I look forward to dancing with you again this evening."

The viscount departed, and Verina maintained her composure, reminding herself to treat Reddington as she might Tray.

"Whatever are you doing in Merrivale, Your Grace? Do they not have assemblies where you reside?"

"They do, Lady Verina, but I recalled both you and Lady Justina mentioning how much you enjoyed dancing. I do, as well, and thought I might come and see if I could have a dance with you both."

"Matthew is an excellent dancer, Verina," Hugo told her. "You could not be in better hands."

"I am so glad you came tonight, Your Grace," she said, causing one brow of his to arch. "It has been wonderful getting to know Hugo since we came to Merrifield. It is as if Justina and I have claimed a new brother." She smiled sweetly. "And I am coming to view you the same way."

He scowled at her. "I am not your brother."

Hugo chuckled. "Relax, my friend. I believe Verina merely means she is comfortable in your company."

"Yes," she said. "Just as if you were Tray. Or Hugo."

She saw he didn't take kindly to her words.

"We should dance, my lady," he said abruptly, stepping to her and taking her hand, placing it on his sleeve. "Come to the dance floor."

He guided her, and she said, "That was more a command than a polite invitation to dance," she pointed out.

They reached the center of the room, and squares began forming.

"Are you trying to rile me?"

Verina gave him an innocent look. "Now, why would I wish to annoy you, Your Grace?"

Before he could answer, the music began. She allowed him to move her about the floor. Oh, he did dance divinely. He moved with an athletic grace, effortlessly keeping to the rhythm of the music. Dancing with the Duke of Reddington was like dancing on air.

She reminded herself that she did not like him much, however, and so when the set came to an end, she moved back to Hugo and Tia, the duke trailing after her. Justina was also there.

"Ah, there is my sister, Your Grace. I know you were eager to dance with both of us. Justina, His Grace would like to reserve the next dance with you."

Her sister's face lit up, and Verina turned away, being asked by a new gentleman to dance. As she did so, she hoped the Duke of Reddington was done with her for the night.

Because despite her dislike of him, he stirred feelings within her that she was not ready to confront.

CHAPTER NINE

MATTHEW SHOULDN'T HAVE come tonight. He had lied to his mother, telling her that he was going to Dove Hall to check on a few things. She asked if any new women had arrived or if any news was on the horizon regarding locating a new one. He had told her no, but that he hoped to hear from Larkin soon regarding another. He then mentioned having other plans, saying he would not be home for dinner. She had given him a knowing look, aware of the widow he saw in Redgrove. The widow no longer held any appeal.

Because he could not get Lady Verina out of his mind.

He told himself she was all wrong for him. That she was young and immature. That was a lie, however. Yes, she was about to be ten and eight soon, but many eligible young ladies on the Marriage Mart were that age or even younger. And as far as being immature, he did not think someone of that nature could have pulled together the wonderful feast during the days Hugo and his tenants had worked on repairing the roofs of the cottages. Lady Verina had taken charge with ease, organizing where people and items should go, ever watchful when something need to be changed or done.

From his vantage point, high on a roof, he had been able to witness her efficiency and friendliness. She did not put on airs. Rather, she was willing to work just as hard as those around her, perhaps even more so. Matthew could tell she did not feign her interest in the tenants, their wives, and their children. She had a true sincerity about her. He could not think of any young ladies he had meet within Polite Society who would have done the same.

"Damnation," he said under his breath as he watched her skirts twirling as she danced with some man who had claimed her for a set.

All right. So she was organized and efficient. Kind and friendly. Those were certainly qualities he would seek in his future duchess. Lady Verina also was very pretty. He could tell she was still growing into her looks. As she matured, she would become downright beautiful—and maintain that beauty for many years to come.

But she seemed to have pushed him aside. He knew, in part, it had been his rakish remark about kissing her which had turned the tide against him. At first, she had been distant and cool to him. Now, however, she seemed to take things in stride, wanting to treat him as a brother.

Brotherly affection was the last thing Matthew wanted from her. Instead, he truly wanted to kiss her. Hold her. Get to know more about her. More importantly, for the first time in his life, he wanted to share with her about his clandestine work. He needed her to know what he did for these women. Not because he wanted credit for his actions. Heavens, that was the last thing he desired. What he wanted to see was how Lady Verina reacted to him doing that kind of work. Would she approve? Be repelled? Find it altruistic? Interesting?

While Larkin did a good deal of the groundwork in investigating, Matthew did his fair share. He was used to traveling—sometimes with Mama, often without her—and spiriting away a dove from her place of torture. Lady Verina had not hidden her interest in marriage and wanting children.

Would she be able to take to a marriage which was so unconventional?

No, he was putting the cart before the horse. He had to first get Lady Verina to like him more. To think of him not as a brother, but as a potential suitor—and husband. Only then would he share with her a small portion of the work he did. Work which he could not stop because too many women suffered at the hands of tyrannical husbands. He might only be able to save a few each year, but that was more than if he sat back and did nothing.

The question was how to change her view regarding him. Matthew believed he had made a good first impression on her, up until his remark about a kiss. He supposed the only way to alter her opinion was to spend time with her and prove he was more than some rakish fellow trying to steal kisses.

The music ended, and he watched as she accompanied her latest partner to the punchbowl. Her face was flushed with the exertion of dancing, and she was more than pretty. In fact, the more he saw her, the more attractive she grew in his eyes.

"Admiring the view?"

Turning, he saw Hugo had come to stand next to him. Matthew shrugged. He was not ready to say something about Lady Verina to his dearest friend.

"She would make for a good duchess," Hugo said.

"Who?"

His friend snorted. "You do not have to pretend . . . with me, Matthew. You came tonight… to see Verina."

"What if I did?" he countered, frustrated that he was so easily read.

Hugo studied Verina. "She is like a wild colt. Full of enthusiasm. Hard to restrain. She is young, but she has a good head on her shoulders. She also has a kind heart. Just look how she is already looking after my tenants, and she has only been here three weeks."

"She is clever. And pretty. I will grant you that."

"Verina is a young lady of good character. She would never bore you. I have seen your eyes glaze over at a ball, and then you disappear into the card room. Or go home. Yes, she is young, but you could guide her. Teach her how to become a wonderful duchess. Your tenants would adore her, as would your servants."

"Her family is full of love matches, Hugo. She does not love me. Why, you heard her. She thinks of me as a brother."

"Does she?" his friend pressed. "I think you need to spend more time in one another's company. I am not saying make any kind of commitment now. Just get to know Verina better while she is at Merrifield. That would give you a leg up, come the Season. She will be meeting a large number of eligible bachelors. Yours would be a friendly face in a sea of strangers."

"Very well. Why don't you come for dinner? Tonight is Saturday. Shall we make it Monday night? You could arrive by teatime. Have dinner. Stay the night if you wish. And leave the following day. That would give me the opportunity to be in her company."

"I will tell Tia we are engaged for Monday and part of Tuesday," Hugo said. "It is a good thing because all our neighbors are besieging us with invitations. It seems you are not the only one who wishes to know Verina."

Matthew glanced about. "I think I will ask Lady Justina to dance."

He marched off, asking the youngest Fulton to dance a second time. She readily agreed, and they had a marvelous time during their dance. Lady Justina was lively, an eager dance partner.

"Oh, thank you for asking me to dance again, Your Grace. By far, you are my favorite partner of the night."

"Your joy in dancing is obvious, my lady. The pleasure was all mine."

She looked at him pensively. "You like Verina, don't you?"

"Your sister is very nice."

"No," she said, shaking her head. "It is more than that. I know I am biased, but Verina would be a good match for you. She does not fawn over you because you have a grand title."

"You do not think she is like other women?" he challenged. "I cannot think of a woman of my acquaintance who would *not* wish to be a duchess."

"Titles mean nothing to my sister," Justina insisted. "She also is not one to demand love from her betrothed."

"She isn't?" he asked, surprised to hear this.

"Verina has shared with me that she believes marriages can be successful if a husband and wife care for one another. If they are friends. Verina is looking for companionship, as well as a man who will take an active role in raising his children. From what I gather, not many men in the *ton* see much of their children. My cousins and their husbands are different. Verina wants a gentleman who will be kind to her and put family above all else. Could you do that, Your Grace?"

He did want children desperately. Being an only child, he had longed for siblings. As an adult, a duke with a vast fortune, he knew he could have as many children as he liked. He was not one to hand them off to servants and rarely see them. He wanted to be close to his sons and daughters. It seemed as if Lady Verina were looking for many of the same things he did.

"I am beginning to think about marriage, Lady Justina. Whether to your sister or another remains to be seen."

She studied him a moment. "I think you might have a chance with her. You would certainly challenge her." Then she smiled at him. "Thank you again for the dance, Your Grace."

Lady Justina left him, not seeking an escort. She was quite the independent creature. Opinionated. Likeable. Outspoken. Pretty. Idly, he wondered if he should wait for her to mature and seek her hand in a few years. But his head told him Lady Verina would be a better match for him.

And Matthew was doing his best not to listen to his heart.

Emotions got people in trouble. Although he would like to make a love match, he already found his emotions hard to deal with at times. He had seen incredible heartbreak in his work. His energy was better spent helping women find a new life. If he could find favor with Lady Verina, he believed she possessed several good qualities which would help make him a better duke, while providing him with the children he yearned for.

It was time for him to take the initiative and see if he could change Lady Verina's stance toward him.

VERINA FINISHED HER cup of punch and excused herself, needing to find the ladies' retiring room. She did so, taking care of her business and even splashing cool water on her face. Though they were into the first week of November, she had grown overheated with all the dancing. The cool water felt good on her skin.

A servant handed her a cloth, and she dabbed her face dry, ready to enjoy the rest of the evening. The dancing had been spirited tonight, and she had not lacked for partners. Of course, her best one had been the Duke of Reddington. It shouldn't surprise her that he danced so effortlessly.

As she left the retiring room, she found none other than the duke himself standing nearby, looking as if he waited for her. He smiled as she came toward him.

"There you are, my lady. I was hoping to have a few minutes to speak with you."

He was certainly handsome. She would give him that. Verina decided Reddington had simply had a weak moment in mentioning how to win a kiss from her. That had been his only faux pas around her. She thought of how he had stood up to Hugo's bullies and how solicitous he was toward his mother. He had also helped Hugo in overcoming his stammer. There was much good in this man, and she should not play games with him.

"What about, Your Grace?"

He hesitated. "I hope you are not one to hold a grudge."

"No, I am not. Do you believe I hold some resentment toward you?"

Shrugging, he said, "I am not certain. I did say something most inappropriate to you, and I regretted it the minute it left my lips."

Why did he have to talk about his lips? Her eyes immediately strayed to them. They were firm. Sensual. Her own lips began to itch, wondering what it might be like to share a kiss with him.

"I am sorry I teased you, my lady," he apologized. "I know you are above reproach and would not go handing out kisses, especially to gentlemen you had just met. I regret my words, and I hope you will forgive me."

She saw sincerity shining in his eyes. "I believe you are sorry, Your Grace. And there is truly nothing to forgive. Your remark merely caught me offguard. I will be better prepared when the Season arrives. I have very little experience in the company of men, other than my own family. Something tells me you will not be the last to tease me about kissing."

His mouth grew stubborn. "If a man insults you during the Season, you must tell me of it, my lady. I will see to him."

"No. You will not," Verina said firmly. "First, it is not your place to rush about, pretending to be my protector. I will handle any wayward gentlemen. My tongue can be sharp and my morals high. If a man cause me further problems after I have addressed the issue, I will simply tell my brother and the other men in my family. They are a fierce lot, Your Grace, and would broker no nonsense from some rake who behaved untoward to me."

"I see you have thought this through."

"As I said, I was unprepared for your flippant remark. I now know you were playfully vexing me. I will be more prepared come the spring."

He gazed at her admiringly. "I believe you will be, my lady. Good for you."

Verina grew warm, hearing the praise come from him. From those sensual lips. From this tall, handsome man. She reminded herself not to fall into any kind of trap.

"We should return to the dancing," she told him.

"I agree. Would you dance with me again, my lady?"

She had already been told by Mama that if a gentleman asked for a second dance in the same evening, he was showing his express interest in you. This, however, was Norfolk, far from town and the glittering balls of the Season. What harm could come in dancing again with the most handsome man present tonight?

"I would be happy to engage in another set with you, Your Grace."

CHAPTER TEN

VERINA WENT DOWN to breakfast, a spring in her step. Almost two weeks had passed since the assembly they had attended in Merrivale, and every day had been filled with new adventures. The neighborhood had been so welcoming to Justina and her, and they had received several invitations. They had dined with prominent members of Polite Society in the area. Gone to tea with others. They had been riding and walking and even ventured into the village twice with Miss Kannady, her mother, and Miss Chambers for shopping and taking tea. All in all, this had been a delightful visit. Verina would be sad to see it end.

This afternoon, they would be heading to Redfield again. The duke had asked them to come for dinner on the night of the assembly, but they had been flooded with other invitations and put off dining with him and his mother until today. They would leave mid-afternoon, taking tea with the duchess, as well as dinner. They would stay overnight and then return to Merrifield tomorrow morning.

She had not seen Reddington since the night of the assembly, although he had been to Merrifield. Both times, she, Justina, and Tia had been out, and Verina thought it a good thing. She had been so busy that she had hardly had time to give the duke a second thought.

Or his very kissable lips.

Verina wondered what a kiss was like. She had engaged in

kissing her pillow on a few occasions, pretending it was the duke. Oh, she knew she was foolish to do so. He was not the one for her, but she could not help but be intrigued by him—and the thought of kissing him. She supposed he kissed women all the time. Men that handsome would.

But he had wanted to kiss her. Of that she was certain. Verina was glad she had stood up to him, however. It wasn't often a duke was told no, and she was rather proud of herself for doing so.

She reached the breakfast room and found she was the last to arrive that morning. Although Tia was still retching some throughout the day when nausea struck her, their various cousins had sent advice to her of how to keep it to a minimum. Ariadne, Eden, Lucy, and Dru had all given birth and were more than willing to share advice with Tia. Looking at her cousin, Verina thought Tia would make for a wonderful mother. She had such a spark about her. Hugo, too, would be an excellent parent. Now that she knew about his stammering, she understood why he spoke in such a slow, measured way. Hugo would exercise great patience and care with the children they had, and he would love them completely, just as he did his wife.

After she greeted the others, Hugo reminded them that they would be leaving at half-past two for Redfield.

"Fortunately, it looks as if the skies will be clear for our trip," he said. "Hopefully, the same will be true of tomorrow."

Verina knew travel became substantially more difficult with rain. The roads could easily clog, making even their short journey to Redfield difficult.

Halfway through breakfast, a footman arrived with the post, and Tia eagerly accepted it. Verina doubted she and Justina would receive anything today. A letter from Mama had come only yesterday, talking mostly about Mrs. Walters, the widowed cousin Mama was helping to care for in town. Tray had written to them recently, and they had received that letter two days ago.

"Oh!" Tia exclaimed. "Lia has written to me!"

With trembling fingers, Tia broke the seal on the letter, quickly skimming it for news. She broke out in a brilliant smile.

"Lia has safely delivered twins. Mother and babes are healthy."

Inwardly, she breathed a sigh of relief. Childbirth was hazardous, and many women were lost during it. It was hard enough to carry one babe—much less two—and Verina knew how terrible it would have been for Tia to have lost her twin.

"Read it aloud to us, love," urged Hugo.

"I will in a moment, my darling," Tia told him. "I wish to savor it myself first."

After a few minutes, Tia set the letter on the table and pulled a handkerchief from her sleeve, wiping away the tears on her cheeks.

"Everything is fine," she assured them. "I am simply relieved to have finally received word." Tia cleared her throat. "Here is what Lia has written."

My dearest Tia (and Hugo, too!) –

It has taken me three days to write to you about the events which have changed our lives. I have been tired, but it is the best kind of tired in the world.

I birthed twins!

We have named them Mary and Edward. Mary came first, squalling and red-faced, claiming our attention. Her brother followed, and he is a much more placid sort. That has continued to be true in the three days they have been with us. Mary is demanding, wanting to be fed and held, and crying and growing red until she gets what she desires. Once her simple needs have been met, she is the sweetest girl on earth.

Edward has remained, for the most part, a calm, quiet babe, studying us with large eyes. I know they say that babes do not smile for a few months, but Edward smiles. Not only with his sweet mouth, but his eyes. Rupert says that Mary will be a handful, while Edward will always know how to pacify his sister. Even now, as they lie in their crib, Edward will reach for Mary's hand, and she becomes serene at his touch.

We had suspected there would be two of them, and so we were prepared with a couple of names for girls, as well as two for boys. These two just looked like an Edward and a Mary. We will save the names which were not used for the future if we are so blessed. And no, my dear Tia, I am not going to share them!

Rupert had already proven to be wonderful with children, thanks to his relationship with Celia, and I also think he takes after Julian. He holds one infant and I the other. We have spent hours, merely holding our newborns and smiling at them and each other. Creating life is a true miracle. I already can see bits of each of us in our twins. It will be such a pleasure to watch them grow and change over the years to come.

Please share this wonderful news with Verina and Justina. I know you are enjoying their visit to Merrifield. I cannot wait to see both of them—and you and Hugo—come next spring. Ariadne is right. There is no way we could leave Crestbrook for town without bringing our two bundles of joy with us. I cannot wait for Edward and Mary to meet their other cousins, both young and old, and I especially cannot wait for my dearest, sweetest twin to hold her niece and nephew. You are the person above all whom I wish to introduce these babes to.

I hope this letter finds you in good spirits and health. It was wonderful to receive the news that you are increasing, Tia. I pray that you will not suffer too greatly in these early months.

I plan to write to Mama now. I know she will share my letter with Val and Eden. Eventually, I will write to all our cousins when I have a chance, but if you are sending them a letter anytime soon, you have my permission to share this good news with them.

I love you so very much, my darling twin, and I think of the bond we share. How Mary and Edward will also have that connection between them. It will be nice to have another set of twins in our large, extended family.

Write to me soon, dearest Tia.

All our love,
Lia, Rupert, Celia, Mary, & Edward

Verina found herself reaching for her own handkerchief, dabbing her damp eyes. She and Justina had grown close to Lia during the months they had spent together both at Millvale and Traywick Manor. It was lovely to hear that her cousin had safely borne her babes.

Tia smiled brightly. "I am glad my letter finally reached Lia and she knows that I am with child. Oh, it is wonderful to learn about Mary and Edward." She touched her belly. "And to think that life now grows inside of me, as well."

After breakfast, they retired to write several letters. Since Lia would write to her mother—and Val and Eden would receive the news that way—Tia said she would write her sister to let Ariadne and Julian know of the twins' arrival. She would also notify Con and Rowena about the twins' birth. Tia asked Verina to write to Lucy, Dru, and Aunt Charlotte, while Justina would send letters to Tray and their mother. That would ensure that everyone in the family would be informed.

That afternoon, they boarded Hugo's carriage and took the half-hour drive to Redfield. The butler greeted them and told them the duke and duchess awaited them in the drawing room. Verina could not blame them for waiting inside since the day was chilly. She had even used a lap robe in the carriage on their journey here, trying to stay warm.

The duchess was most welcoming, and Verina found herself continuing to like the older woman quite a bit. Her Grace exhibited a natural poise and possessed a quiet beauty. She was everything Verina thought a duchess should be. The duke would need to wed a woman as regal and confident as his mother, not someone such as herself.

He did not direct any specific questions to her during tea, for which she was grateful. She found herself a bit shy around him, which was unlike her. Still, she fully participated in the conversation, and the time passed quickly.

After tea, the duchess asked if they might like a tour of the house, and Verina and Justina readily agreed, both curious about the grand residence. Since Tia had already seen all of it, she remained with Hugo and Reddington.

It took over an hour for them to see the entire house, which was twice the size of Traywick Manor. Then again, it was the country seat of a duke.

"This is where Reddington spends most of his time when we are not in town, but my son also has several other estates scattered about England. Even one in Scotland."

"Does he visit them very often?" she asked. "It must take a good deal of time to do so."

"Matthew is a man conscious of his ducal duties, so naturally, he does go to his various holdings when he can. It is difficult when he is gone so much. I do miss him a great deal."

"He has been the duke a long time, hasn't he?" Verina asked, already knowing the answer to her question, but she enjoyed hearing the duchess speak.

Sadness washed over Her Grace's countenance. "Yes, he was only ten and two when the title was foisted upon him. It was as if he grew old overnight. Matthew wanted to learn everything he could about his responsibilities, and he has taken them seriously ever since."

"It is good he had you to help guide him, Your Grace," she said.

The duchess' gaze met hers. "I believe he is the one who guided me, my lady."

She supposed Her Grace had been in mourning for the husband she lost and that her son had been of great comfort to her.

They went to the duchess' sitting room, and she had a servant go and bring Tia to them, allowing the men to have time on their own. Most of the talk centered upon Lia and her newborns, and Her Grace promised to embroider something for each of the babes.

That evening, they went in to dinner, and Verina found herself sitting on the duke's right hand. He asked her several questions about Traywick Manor and her life there, as well as what she had been doing the past two weeks since they had seen one another. She found herself relaxed in his company and hoped things would remain cordial between them for the remainder of her visit at Merrifield.

After dinner, they retired to the drawing room, where she and Justina were asked to play the pianoforte. Verina readily accepted, going first. Then Justina played as the two of them sang a duet. As usual, her sister was slightly off-key, but the others still applauded politely when they finished.

"I would like to hear His Grace play again," she said boldly. "You did so when we first met."

Smiling, he said, "I am always happy to play for others."

He played two pieces for them, and she was astounded at the depth of his talent.

"I will never be able to play as well as you do, Your Grace," Justina told him. "Then again, I am certain you practice more often than I do."

"Shall we sing together a bit?" he asked.

They gathered around the pianoforte, and she enjoyed hearing his rich tenor, as well as Hugo's deep bass. After two songs, the women asked for only the gentlemen to sing for them, and they obliged.

When the duke finished playing, he said, "I spent many a time at my pianoforte at university, singing along with this fellow."

"Singing is one of the things which helped save me," Hugo said earnestly. "It was providence . . . meeting up with you in the pub that day. As well as getting to know my cousin."

"How is Anthony these days?" His Grace asked. "It has been a while since I have seen him."

"Busy as ever," Hugo replied. "He came home . . . with us. Last Sunday. Spent the afternoon. Anthony says Verina and Justina have become . . . new favorites of his."

Her Grace said, "I am ready to retire. Do not let me stop you from having a bit of fun without me."

Tia also rose. "I find myself tiring easily these days. I believe I will also retire."

Hugo stood and took his wife's hand. Verina knew it would be inappropriate for her and Justina to remain with the duke, unchaperoned, and so she said, "Justina and I will also head to our bedchambers."

Sarie had come with them, and she helped Verina undress and don her night rail.

"Go and assist my sister," she told the maid. "I can unpin my own hair and brush it out."

The servant left, and Verina collected her pins, happy that Sarie would be coming with her. Tia had spoken to the girl, and Sarie had leapt at the chance to become a lady's maid. If Tia could find someone in the village to replace Sarie as a parlor maid, she had said Sarie could return to Traywick Manor when they departed. If not, Tia promised to bring Sarie to town with her come the spring.

Verina wasn't really tired, and so she donned her dressing gown and decided to sit and read a bit. She opened the book she had brought with her and had only read a few pages of it when she thought she heard something in the corridor. It was . . . someone whispering?

She went to the door and opened it, and something brushed past her leg, causing her to squeak. She only hoped it was not a mouse.

Suddenly, a young woman appeared. She was close to Verina's age and wearing a dressing gown. She seemed wild-eyed. Her hair was shorn close to her scalp.

"Did Patches run in here?" she asked, clearly distressed.

Having no idea who this woman might be, Verina asked, "Patches?"

"I think she ran in here when you opened your door." The woman pushed past her, entering the room, moving about the room, her eyes searching.

"Under the bed!" the woman cried.

She glanced down and saw the tip of a small tail sticking out.

The young lady dropped to her hands and knees and reached under the bed, pulling out an adorable black and white kitten. She rose, kissing its head, and then came toward Verina.

"See? Patches did come in here. I call her Patches because . . . well, you see . . . she has patches all over her." Hesitantly, the woman asked, "Would you like to hold her?"

Wanting to calm this stranger, since she still seemed very excitable, Verina said, "Please," and stretched out her hands, taking the kitten. She brought it close, nuzzling her nose between the kitten's ears.

"How old is Patches?" she asked.

The woman frowned, thinking a moment. "Hmm. She was about six weeks when I got here. I think I have been here four weeks or so. Anyway, I should be going to the cottage tomorrow."

"The cottage?" Verina prompted, trying to keep the conversation moving, as well as understand it and more about this woman.

"I am to live with Miss Ross. Of course, she is not truly Miss Ross. She is actually Lady Ross—but she does not want anyone to know that. His Grace has told me I might like to take a new name. Because I am starting a new life."

"What is your name now?" she asked gently, handing the kitten back to the woman, who brought it to her chest.

"Miss Stannis." Then her eyes grew wide. "You mustn't tell anyone about me, though. No one is to know I am here. Or at Dove Hall."

"I am not familiar with Dove Hall," said Verina. "Is it nearby?"

"Yes. They brought me first to Dove Hall, but my mind was muddled. I was still confused. You know, after my time . . . there."

She remained quiet, deciding to let Miss Stannis share more only if she wished to.

"It was awful. At the asylum. Every day was horrible. It jumbled my mind. I am still not thinking quite straight, but I am getting better."

"I have heard they are terrible places. Why were you at the asylum?"

Miss Stannis leaned close, her eyes large. "Because I would not marry that old goat, Lord Burghley. He must be seventy or older. I refused—and Papa had me put away."

Pity filled her. Verina could not imagine her mother or brother forcing her into a marriage with someone decades older than she was. Miss Stannis looked to be no more than a year or two older than herself.

"How did you come to leave that . . . place?" she asked.

The words spilled rapidly from Miss Stannis. "Their Graces help others. Ones like me. I was a bluestocking, which Papa disapproved of. I do not see why he cared because he only said a handful of words to me after Mama died a few years ago. I did not think I would make a match last Season, but I was taken for a new wardrobe and sent out with a chaperone, some cousin of Papa's who is a widow. The next thing I knew, Papa told me I would wed Lord Burghley. I *laughed* when he said that, thinking he was teasing me."

Miss Stannis touched her cheek to the kitten's head. "He was not. He told me I had to wed his choice. Or else." She grimaced. "I found out what that choice was. At first, I said no and was confined to my room, only given bread and water. Then I was starved for a few days. Finally, Papa told me if I continued to be disobedient, I would be sent away."

"To the asylum."

Miss Stannis shuddered. "I did not know where. I thought my chances wherever he placed me would be better than wed to a man more than three times my age." Tears filled her eyes. "I should have gone through with the ceremony. When Lord Burghley died, I would have had my freedom. But I didn't. I was foolish. If His Grace had not saved me, we would not be having this conversation."

"The Duke of Reddington saved you."

Nodding, the other woman said, "Yes. He helps women such as me. Her Grace also helps. They bring those they help to Dove Hall. Some stay. Some go and have a new life." Miss Stannis' mouth trembled. "I am not as strong as I thought, so I will be one of the ones who stays. I will live with Miss Ross. And Patches. I am to care for Patches."

Verina placed a hand on Miss Stannis' shoulder. "I am glad you gained your freedom. And that you have Patches to look after. Shall I help you back to your bedchamber?"

"I need to return Patches to the stables. The rest of the litter is there, and she sleeps with them and her mother every night. Tomorrow, though, she will come with me. That is when I move in with Miss Ross."

"I will go with you," Verina said.

She took Miss Stannis' elbow and led her from the room, going down the corridor and to the stairs.

"It will be quicker if we cut through the kitchens," Miss Stannis told her, leading the way.

The night was cold as they stepped from the house. Both women only wore their night rails and dressing gowns, so they scurried to the stables. A groom met them.

"Got Patches for me, Miss Stannis?" he asked, obviously familiar with the woman and kitten.

"Yes, here she is. I will be back for her tomorrow. She is coming with me to Dove Hall."

"Good for you, my lady," the groom said, collecting the kitten. "I'll see she's safe and sound with her litter. Go back to the house, Miss Stannis. You can't stay the night again."

Verina pulled on the woman, leading her back outside. They raced across the yard and hurried inside the house, not speaking until they were back at her bedchamber.

"It was nice to meet you, Miss Stannis."

"Likewise, my lady. Who are you?"

"Lady Verina Fulton. I am here visiting my cousin, Lady Merriman."

"Oh, His Grace said he and Lord Merriman are great friends."

"They are," she agreed. "Shall I go with you to your bedchamber?"

"No, I will go myself." Miss Stannis paused. "You were very kind to help me with Patches, my lady. Enjoy your stay."

"I hope you and Patches like your new life, Miss Stannis."

The young woman cocked her head, thinking a moment. "Call me Miss Ross. Or at least I think that may be who I am in the future. I shall ask if Lady Ross—I mean Miss Ross—would like me to be her sister."

"It might be confusing with two Miss Rosses living in the same place."

Worry filled the other woman's face. "You are right. Then I shall be . . . Miss Brandon. Yes, Miss Brandon. It sounds like a strong name for a determined person. And I am determined never to go back to my old life." Her mouth hardened. "I hope Papa rots in hell."

The new Miss Brandon took Verina's hands in hers. "Thank you again for your assistance, Lady Verina. I hope that we meet again someday."

Miss Brandon moved down the hall until Verina could no longer see her shadow. She entered her own bedchamber and removed her dressing gown before climbing into bed. As she pulled the bedclothes over her, she wondered exactly how the Duke of Reddington had gotten into the business of rescuing women from madhouses.

Verina decided she would ask him tomorrow.

CHAPTER ELEVEN

MATTHEW ALLOWED BARROW to shave and dress him for the day. He wished he would have been able to make better use of his time with Lady Verina, but there had been no way to sequester her from the others. He had done his best at dinner, however, to speak with her at length. He believed she had become more comfortable in his company now, and he would build from that foundation.

"Thank you," he told his valet and then left his bedchamber to head to breakfast. He did not know if Lady Verina were one of those ladies who breakfasted in her room or came to the table. He hoped it was the latter so that he might have a chance to talk with her a bit more before Hugo gathered his family to return to Merrifield.

As he rounded the stairs and came to the final landing before reaching the foyer, he paused.

Lady Verina sat on the top stair.

She must have heard him because she turned and rose. "May I speak with you a moment, Your Grace?"

"Of course, my lady. What might I do for you?"

She wet her lips, causing a surge of desire to race through him. He had not been to see the widow in some time now and realized he had not visited her since he met Lady Verina, knowing his taste for her had left him. A thought struck him, one which surprised him.

He might be in love with this woman before him.

Since she had yet to speak again, he asked, "What is it you wish to discuss?"

Her gaze me his. "I would like to know more about Dove Hall."

Her words were unexpected. "What are you talking about?"

"I am not quite certain, Your Grace. But I did meet Miss Stannis last night, and she mentioned Dove Hall. Along with you."

"Discussing Dove Hall is more than a brief conversation, Lady Verina," he began.

"I wish to see it," she said boldly. "I want to learn of the . . . work you are doing."

He nodded. "Let me escort you to breakfast."

Matthew offered her his arm. They went down to the breakfast room. Mama was already present, sipping tea.

"Here is the buffet, Lady Verina. You are to help yourself this morning."

He left her there and went to Mama, bending and brushing his lips against her cheek in greeting. Whispering to her, he said, "She knows of Dove Hall. I want to show it to her. Can you find a way to help me do so?"

Mama smiled up at him. "Good morning to you, my son."

Leaving her side, he returned to the buffet, seeing that Lady Verina had not been shy about placing food upon her plate. He was used to too many Polite Society beauties who ate like birds, wasting food he brought to them from midnight buffets at balls.

He made a plate for himself and joined the two of them at the table. A footman poured coffee for him as Hugo and Tia appeared, Lady Justina accompanying them.

"We are casual this morning," Mama said. "You may take whatever you would like from the buffet."

The other three soon joined them, and they spoke of inconsequential matters. Matthew was afraid Mama was not going to say anything as the meal wrapped up, but he told himself to trust her. Sure enough, she came to his rescue.

"Are you leaving directly after breakfast?" Mama asked.

"Yes," Hugo replied. "A guest should never overstay his welcome."

Mama smiled sweetly. "You could never do so, my lord." She turned to Lady Verina. "I would like to have your company for a bit longer, my lady. Would you care to remain behind at Redfield? We could spend the day together. My son could have you back at Merrifield by teatime or just after it."

With no hesitation, Lady Verina said, "I would be happy to visit with you today, Your Grace." She looked to her cousin. "If that suits you, Tia."

"You may stay, Verina. It will give Justina and me time to ourselves. Perhaps we might go riding together."

Concerned, Hugo asked, "Should you be on a horse now, love?"

"I have spoken to the midwife about that very thing," Tia said. "She told me I could continue to ride for a couple of months, as long as I do not gallop at breakneck speed. I am feeling more myself and would like to be outdoors today."

"I am happy to ride with you, Tia," Lady Justina said.

"Then it is settled," Mama declared.

Breakfast concluded, and they all went downstairs to see his friends off. Lady Verina kissed her cousin goodbye, promising to see her later this afternoon.

Once the carriage rolled down the lane, Mama turned to them. "Come to my sitting room with me."

They went straight to it, and Mama said, "I suppose you have met Miss Stannis, Lady Verina."

"Actually, her name is Miss Brandon now, Your Grace. She told me she was in need of a new name, and that is the one she settled upon. Along with Patches for her kitten's name."

"I see," Mama said, pursing her lips a moment in thought. "Miss Brandon is supposed to leave for Dove Hall this morning. Since she seems to trust you, perhaps we all might ride together and see her settled into her new home. I only ask that you do not quiz her, my lady. Once Miss Brandon is safely tucked away at her cottage, you may ask any questions of us that you choose. Do you agree to do so?"

"Certainly, Your Grace."

Half an hour later, the four of them were seated inside the ducal carriage. Lady Verina sat opposite him, Miss Brandon next to her. The young woman placed the basket she had brought with her between them. Opening it, she removed the black and white kitten she had chosen and settled it upon her lap.

"Patches is going to be such a wonderful companion to me. And Miss Ross, as well."

"You believe you are ready to live with Miss Ross?" Mama asked.

"As ready as I shall ever be, Your Grace. I have imposed upon your hospitality these last few weeks. Know that I am extremely grateful for having this extra time to think about everything."

Miss Brandon fell silent, and the others followed suit. Not another word was spoken until they reached the group of cottages on the estate.

Miss Ross came out to greet them, Miss Vines with her. He knew the two women had grown close ever since Miss Ross's arrival and placement in the cottage.

"Welcome to your new home, Miss Stannis," Miss Ross told the newcomer.

"It is actually Miss Brandon now," the young woman said, looking more confident and calmer than Matthew had ever seen her since they had met.

Miss Brandon held up the basket she carried. "I have also brought someone with me." Opening the lid to the basket, she stepped forward, allowing Miss Ross and Miss Vines to peer inside.

"Oh, what an adorable kitten," Miss Ross said. "Does he have a name?"

"He is a she. I have named her Patches."

"Well, you and Patches are both welcome, Miss Brandon," Miss Ross said. "This is Miss Vines. She is the lady who has made your new gowns."

"Why, I am ever so happy to make your acquaintance, Miss Vines," Miss Brandon said. Then indicating Lady Verina, she said, "This is my new, good friend. Her name is Lady Verina."

They exchanged greetings, and then Miss Ross asked Miss Brandon to come see her new home.

Mama turned to him. "I believe that I will stay with Miss Brandon and help her find her footing. I will see the two of you back at Dove Hall."

The new Miss Brandon turned to Lady Verina. In a gesture which surprised Matthew, she embraced the younger woman and said, "Thank you, my lady. I hope someday you might come and call upon us."

"I would very much like to do so, Miss Brandon," Lady Verina said. "Enjoy your new home."

The four women turned and went into the cottage, leaving Matthew with Lady Verina.

He looked up to the coachman. "Go to Dove Hall. We will be leaving for Redfield mid-afternoon."

"Aye, Your Grace," the driver replied, flicking his wrists and driving off.

"Walk with me, my lady."

Matthew showed her the various cottages on the property, naming the inhabitants of each which were occupied. She listened patiently, not asking any questions of him yet. He led her from the area and struck out for Dove Hall proper at a slow, thoughtful pace.

"I do not know exactly what Miss Brandon told you. I shall start from the beginning to give you a clearer understanding of my work."

They walked another few minutes as he collected his thoughts, and then Matthew said, "My father was a very bad man. Family seems so important to you, and it is because you have the love and support of a large family. It was only Mama and me—and we were at the mercy of the previous duke."

Gradually, he painted a picture of his and Mama's life at Redfield while his father was alive.

"I was just a boy, but I lived in anguish, not being able to help my mother. The duke's cruelty to her was great. His words, used as weapons, were bad enough, but the times he beat her, leaving her bruised and battered, made me feel utterly helpless. Then one day, I came home to find her . . . gone."

For the first time in several minutes, Lady Verina spoke. "He had placed her in a madhouse, hadn't he?"

Matthew nodded. "I did not know that at the time. I only knew she was gone, her absence explained by a weak story which couldn't possibly be true. The duke had friends staying at Redfield when I came home from school for the summer. I was twelve—and Mama had been gone for two years by that point."

Lady Verina winced. "Two *years*?"

"I will not go into the particulars. Just that my father, deep in his cups, fell to his death. I witnessed it from the shadows that night. No one knew of my presence. His so-called friends quickly scattered, leaving Redfield before they might be questioned about the circumstances surrounding his death. I had Ridley summon the constable and told him what I had seen occur."

He came to a halt, turning and facing her. "The first thing I wished to know was Mama's location. Servants know so much about the lives of those they serve. I was told of the asylum Mama had been taken to. It was not all that far from us. I went straight to it, demanding her release."

"How old did you say you were?"

"Ten and two," he said brusquely.

Suddenly, her fingers found his, lacing through them. The gesture brought comfort to him. A warmth rushed through him, filling the emptiness which had lived inside him for so long. They began walking again, slowly, and he continued his story.

"The conditions at the madhouse were deplorable. Mama

was a ghost of herself. I took her home to Redfield and nursed her back to health that summer. I did not want to return to school, but she encouraged me to do so. It took several more months for her to fully recover her health. Several years before she regained her confidence."

"You would never know by looking at her that she had suffered so greatly."

"Mama has an inner strength, unlike anyone I have ever known. It is because of her that I do the work. Saving as many women as I can."

"How do you go about doing so?" Lady Verina asked.

He explained how he retained Larkin, a Bow Street Runner, who did much of the investigating.

"As a duchess, Mama speaks with everyone in Polite Society. She also listens to the gossip. The rumors. If she finds that a lady has suddenly gone missing from her family, we put Larkin on it. Sometimes, it is a younger woman, such as Miss Brandon. Her father wished to marry her off to a man who was decades older than she was. Miss Brandon has a fine mind. She was known as a bluestocking. She was not going to go quietly into this marriage, and so her father left her in an asylum."

"She seems very fragile."

"She is," he agreed. "These places quickly break a person's spirit."

"Miss Brandon is so young. Barely older than I am." Lady Verina shuddered. "I cannot imagine being placed in one."

"Some women we have helped are much older. They are wives who have not pleased their husbands in some way. Sisters who have displeased their brothers. Young ladies who threaten the balance of a family's social connections. Even though Parliament passed several acts late last century regarding the procedure for a person being placed inside a madhouse, it is still far too easy for a man to commit a female relative to one, especially the private houses."

"How are you able to help them?" she asked. "You have no

connection to these women. Why would they release them into your care?"

"I have found almost everything in life boils down to greed, my lady. Oftentimes, I pay a large sum to the man who is running the asylum. Those who are committed receive no visitors. As long as I am willing to pay more than the lady's relative who put her there, they will keep their mouths closed. Of course, I cannot convince these men in charge of a facility to let me bring every inmate back with me. We only take a handful of ladies each year and bring them to Dove Hall. Some live in the cottages you just saw. They are the ones who either wish for a very quiet life, or they cannot handle creating another life out in the world. Miss Ross is the former, while Miss Brandon is the latter."

"I assume these women remain at Dove Hall while they are making this transition."

"That is usually the case. Miss Brandon was extremely upset. The conditions in the asylum affected her more than most. That is why Mama and I brought her home to Redfield."

"And you gifted her with the kitten so that she would have something to care for. Something which needed her."

Matthew nodded. "You are astute, Lady Verina. Giving her the kitten gives her something to live for. It gives her control, something stripped away in an asylum."

He cleared his throat. "We have had a few success stories. While these women can no longer return to the lives they once led, some have changed their names and gone on to be productive members of society. A handful have become governesses and one a lady's companion. One is now a milliner in York, while another is a seamstress. Miss Vines, who was with Miss Ross, remains in one of our cottages and sews new gowns for all those we bring to Dove Hall."

"My admiration for you has grown ten-fold, Your Grace," Lady Verina said solemnly. "You are no shallow, haughty duke. You are providing a service to others."

"It is never enough," he said, his voice full of anguish. "Yes, I tend to my tenants and other ducal responsibilities, but I can never give enough to these women."

She squeezed his hand, and for the first time, Matthew thought of continuing his work with someone other than Mama by his side.

"It is very important that you do not speak of this to anyone else, my lady."

"Not even Hugo and Tia?"

"No," he said solemnly. "Much as I would like to share what I do with them, I cannot chance word getting out regarding what I do. I fear if it did that it would be more difficult to bring those women back to Dove Hall."

"I like that you named it Dove Hall," she said, her eyes shining with unshed tears. "Doves are a sign of peace. Here is a place where they can regain their equilibrium and find tranquility."

"They are," he agreed. "If you research ancient history and mythology, doves also are signs of hope, renewal, and transformation. Even love." He paused. "You now have heard about my work."

"Why did you trust me?" she pressed. "You have not told your very dearest friend in the world, yet you deem me trustworthy enough to keep this great secret."

"I sense a deep empathy within you, my lady. While you will never experience what these women have gone through, I believe you respect not only what I am doing—but also the women themselves."

"I most certainly do," she said vehemently. "You are a champion, Your Grace, and these women should not be judged by the horrors which have befallen them. You have found your life's work, inspired by your mother's unfortunate circumstances."

"While you might have a question for Mama, feel free to ask it—but do not, under any circumstances, bring up her time in the asylum. It has taken her years to cast aside her experiences. The times she goes with me to liberate a woman, she has nightmares for days afterward."

"I will never speak of this to her, Your Grace. That is my solemn promise."

Matthew saw the compassion in her eyes. "Thank you for being so understanding. For being empathetic with Miss Brandon last night. She came to us and remained in a precarious state of mind at Dove Hall. That is why we brought her to Redfield, to keep a close eye on her as she began to heal. Neither of us can tell how strong she will grow to be."

"Again, you have placed her with someone who can serve as a companion to her. I think it wise, as well as giving her the responsibility of caring for Patches."

He pulled his hand from hers, far too comfortable having held it for so long.

"Let us go now and see Dove Hall itself."

As they continued toward the house, Matthew wondered what Lady Verina's opinion of him was now.

CHAPTER TWELVE

THEY REACHED DOVE Hall, which was a rather large manor house. Matthew explained to Lady Verina how he had purchased the property shortly after leaving university.

"Even back when I was a young boy and brought my mother home, I knew I would need to help other women who were in a similar situation. I had asked my solicitor to remain in touch with a local land agent so that I might buy a property in the area. Dove Hall is in a convenient location. I can reach it within a quarter-hour of leaving Redfield. It is also halfway between my estate and Hugo's."

"It must have cost a great deal to purchase an entire estate," she said. "The house and land. The cottages."

He shrugged. "I did sell one of my unentailed estates to help pay for Dove Hall and its expenses. I can afford to take in these women."

"Do you think Miss Brandon is going to be all right?" she asked, concern written across her lovely face.

"Miss Brandon was a bit more fragile than other women we have taken in, but I believe she has an inner strength that will surprise her in the days and months to come. Whether she remains on the grounds of Dove Hall for the rest of her life or chooses to leave will be up to her. No decision is ever final. She may enjoy a peaceful existence on the grounds of Dove Hall for the rest of her days. Then again, she might find in several years that she longs for a new kind of life. Either way, we will always be here to help guide her and support whatever decision she makes."

As they reached the front door and entered, he asked, "Shall I give you a tour?"

"Please do so."

He took her through the house, introducing her to Mrs. Paul, who was both housekeeper and cook and handled the administration of the women, including their placement in the cottages or elsewhere. Once they had seen the entire place from top to bottom, which was void of any residents at the moment, Matthew took her to the drawing room, where Mrs. Hanson brought them tea.

After she left, Lady Verina said, "Both Mrs. Paul and Mrs. Hanson have spent time in asylums, haven't they?"

"You are astute, my lady. They have. How did you know?"

"They have an air about them. A serenity. And there is something in their eyes which told me they had escaped from a different life. They both seem quite content."

"Mrs. Paul could not boil water when she first came to us," he revealed. "She was the first of the doves which we brought here. She has made herself indispensable. I could not do what I do without her help. Mrs. Hanson was the second who came to us. She helps Mrs. Paul with whatever is needed, including supervising the two girls from the local village who serve as maids."

"It is nice they can give back to women who were in similar circumstances. They have a unique perspective, one which other servants would not," she observed.

"Mrs. Hanson also is the closest thing we have to a doctor on the grounds. Many of the women we bring here are so traumatized that they cannot be around a man. Mrs. Hanson already knew quite a bit about herbs. She has spent time learning all she can about how to tend to the women. She creates salves and ointments to put on cuts and bruises. She knows how to mend broken limbs by putting plasters around them. She is a very calming presence to the women who are brought here."

He did not reveal to her that Mrs. Hanson also served as a midwife. Two of the women had been with child when they had been recovered. One had miscarried shortly after she had arrived. The other had delivered a babe which she had wanted nothing to do with, so Larkin had seen to the child's placement at a farm. Matthew could not talk about the sexual abuse some of the women had suffered to this young woman.

"Have many doves have you helped, Your Grace?" she asked.

"In all honesty, I cannot give you a number, my lady. I keep no records, either at Dove Hall or back at Redfield. If anyone were to discover where Mr. Larkin and I spirit the women to, they might also want to see records of where they are now. I have a man who serves in a general capacity on the grounds here. The women rarely see him, but he is here to protect them, especially those who have remained with us in the cottages."

His mother entered the drawing room, and Matthew rose to greet her.

"Shall I ring for some tea for you?" he asked.

"No." She patted his cheek. "I have had my fill of tea with Miss Ross and Miss Brandon."

"How is Miss Brandon?" Lady Verina asked anxiously.

"Surprisingly, she is doing better than I expected. I believe that eventually, Miss Brandon will become restless and wish to leave Dove Hall. She is quite bright. We could help her find a position as a governess or even a lady's companion. As a duchess, I have all sorts of connections within Polite Society. We have helped a few of our doves find gainful employment, usually as a governess. They live far from town, so there is no chance of them being discovered by the relative who had committed them to the asylum."

"We ask that they write to us once a year," Matthew explained. "We want to know how they fare. If they are happy. If they wish to return to Dove Hall or if they seek a different position."

"So, Lady Verina, what do you think of Dove Hall and my

son's work?" asked Mama.

He watched her carefully, wondering how she would respond after all she had learned.

"I think His Grace is most heroic. I have heard of the existence of asylums, but I thought it was truly those who were mad who were placed in them. I had no idea that men put away their loved ones in those places, especially for such petty reasons. Frankly, it has caused me to lose a bit of faith in my fellow man."

"That is because you are from a loving family," Mama told the young woman. "Be grateful for that—and be very careful of the gentleman whom you wed."

"The men in my extended family have looked after the women, especially when it comes time to take a husband. I have all sorts of cousins and their husbands, as well as my own brother, who will look into any suitor who shows interest in me. They will help me in making the most important decision of my life."

"It is quite obvious by watching Lord and Lady Merriman that they are a love match," Mama noted. "I have also witnessed others in your family making the same kind of marriages. Is that what you are interested in seeking?"

Lady Verina said, "While I am happy for my cousins, Your Grace, I do not see myself in a love match. I am a woman with a practical nature. As long as I wed a man of good reputation, one who will devote himself to our children, I will be happy and view my marriage as a success."

"What of his title?" Mama asked.

"I have never been one to be swayed by titles, Your Grace. After all, I have a cousin who is a duke, and Millbrooke is as down to earth as any fellow you might meet. No, I am looking for a man of good character. Character is what is most important to me." Lady Verina smiled. "And perhaps a sense of humor."

"Laughter is important in a marriage," Mama agreed. "That is, in a successful one. I was not so fortunate as to have that for myself."

Lady Verina reached and took his mother's hand in hers. "I

am sorry you suffered as you did, Your Grace. Thank you for raising a son who not only was willing to do everything it took to bring you home, but a man who is interested in removing other women from such an abominable situation."

With her words, Matthew's heart told him that Lady Verina Fulton was the one for him.

The doors to the drawing room flew open, and Larkin raced across to them. Matthew was not scheduled to meet with the Bow Street Runner, and so he knew there was something of grave importance by this sudden appearance.

"Have a seat, Larkin." He saw the investigator glance to their guest. "You may speak freely. Lady Verina is privy to our work and that you are a part of it."

"Very well, Your Grace." Larkin turned to the duchess. "I have finally found Lady Adams, Your Grace."

"Oh!" exclaimed Mama. "Thank you so much, Mr. Larkin." She looked to Lady Verina. "Lady Adams is a good friend of mine. Her husband passed a little over two years ago. I sent a letter of condolence to her in Cornwall when she wrote to me of the news, and I did not see her the following Season since she was in mourning. I wrote to her several times, but she only responded to the first letter, which was certainly not like her. When the Season began this past April, I confronted the new Lord Adams regarding her absence. He was the nephew and gained his title because Lady Adams never bore an heir."

Mama's face turned to stone. "He was most brusque with me, saying his aunt had no reason to attend the Season ever again. That she had moved to the dower house on his estate and wished to lead a quiet life. When I asked if my letters had been delivered to her, he shrugged." She paused. "I knew he was lying. From that moment on, Mr. Larkin was tasked with finding my friend."

She turned her gaze back to the runner. "Where is she? I would like to go with you and Matthew to bring her back to Dove Hall. Even better, I will have her come to Redfield."

A pained expression crossed the investigator's face. "She is actually nearby, Your Grace." He hesitated a moment. "I found her. At Throckmorton."

A sound of distress came from Mama, an eerie keening which wounded Matthew to his very soul. She began weeping profusely, and Lady Verina wrapped her arms about his mother, trying to comfort her.

"Go and tell my coachman we leave for Throckmorton at once," he commanded. "I will be there as soon as I can."

"Yes, Your Grace," Larkin said, hurrying from the room.

Mama broke away from Lady Verina, tears streaming down her face. Her gaze met his.

"I cannot go there," she whispered. "You must bring Lady Adams back here, Matthew." She began rubbing her wrist, and he knew exactly why she did so.

"It will take me half an hour to reach Throckmorton. I hope to retrieve Lady Adams without much fuss. I will return here with her, then I must see that Lady Verina gets back to Merrifield."

"I am sorry I cannot go with you," his mother said, her voice hoarse. "I can . . . never set foot in that place again."

"I will go with you, Your Grace," Lady Verina said, her gaze steadfast.

"No," he said harshly. "You should not be exposed to something of this nature."

"I will go with you," she repeated, determination filling her face. "Lady Adams may be disoriented. Frightened. In need of a woman's presence. I will be there to give her comfort until she is reunited with Her Grace."

Rubbing her wrist more noticeably now, Mama said, "Let her go with you, Matthew. She is right. We do not know what state of mind you will find my friend. Having a woman with you will cause Lady Adams to trust you more."

"Then let us go at once, my lady."

He bent and kissed his mother's cheek. She clung to him for a moment and then whispered, "Go."

They left the drawing room and stopped by his study, where he kept a safe with funds used to bribe those so that the doves might be released to him. Matthew took out a good bit of gold from it, placing it in a pouch. Then he slipped a pistol from the safe into his pocket, wanting to be prepared. He had vowed never to return again to Throckmorton, but he knew Mama would never rest easy until he brought Lady Adams to her.

They went outside to the waiting carriage. Larkin sat next to his coachman. Matthew handed up Lady Verina and climbed in after her. The vehicle went into motion immediately.

"Her Grace was rubbing her wrist," noted Lady Verina. "I have never seen her do that before. Not until Throckmorton was mentioned."

"You are observant. Mama always wears long sleeves no matter what the weather. She does so to hide the tattoo she was given at Throckmorton. They do not call women by their names. Instead, the patients are given a number and marked with that number. It is the way they are addressed, further dehumanizing them."

Tears brimmed in her eyes. "I cannot imagine what Her Grace endured. What all these other women endure. I wish you could help them all, Your Grace."

"I do what I can. Some administrators who run these places can be bribed. Others cannot. Mr. Larkin has worked with me ever since I left university and started these missions of mercy. He is the true hero in this endeavor, my lady. Mama and I turn over what little information we can gather from conversations with members of the *ton*. Larkin takes those breadcrumbs and finds the trail."

He paused. "Well, not always, but a good deal of the time."

They rode in silence for several minutes and then he took her hand in his, threading their fingers together. "Thank you for wanting to come today. You are right. Although Lady Adams knows me as Mama's son, sometimes the women in these places find their minds broken by their ill-treatment. Oftentimes, they have been subjected to cruelty beyond measure, mostly done to them by men. Your presence will be of great comfort to Lady Adams."

"I am happy to help in any small way I can, Your Grace."

She did not pull her hand from his, allowing him to continue to hold it until they reached their destination. When the carriage came to a halt, a sick feeling washed over him. Matthew had been in several asylums over the past few years, but returning to the one where his own mother had been imprisoned was proving difficult for him.

Glancing out the window, he saw a man at the gate. Larkin must have tossed down a coin to him because he opened the gates for them. The carriage continued on for a few more minutes before coming to a halt again.

Turning to Lady Verina, he said, "Stay here. It may take some minutes before I am able to free Lady Adams."

He squeezed her hand and started to pull away, but she held fast to him.

"I am going with you, Your Grace."

Though he wished to protest, he saw grim determination in her eyes.

"There are things that once you see them, my lady, you can never unsee them."

"I understand," she said resolutely. "Let us go."

He exited the carriage and handed her down, going to the front door. His heart began racing, scenes from that awful day years ago flashing in his mind's eye.

As they approached the entrance, he cautioned, "Stay close to me. I do not want anything untoward happening to you."

With that, he pushed open the door.

And was greeted by the horrors of the past once more.

Chapter Thirteen

Verina's heart beat rapidly as the duke opened the door without knocking. He entered and she followed, adhering to his advice to keep near to him.

The first thing that assaulted her was the terrible smell which permeated the air. Having been nearby when Tia had been sick frequently, she was accustomed to the scent of vomit. This was mingled with other things that made her belly tighten. Urine. Sweat.

And fear . . .

She had never thought that a palpable scent. Why, she could not even recall the last time she had felt fear, but it lingered in the air—along with hopelessness. She swallowed, wishing to run from this building, but knowing her presence was necessary to help spirit Lady Adams away.

A large man, one who was several inches taller than the duke and outweighed him by two stone, approached.

"I must speak with Dr. Cheney," Reddington said.

The man's eyes narrowed. "I've seen you here before."

"Yes. Many years ago."

The man nodded to himself. "You're that one. He's still scared of you, you know."

Verina wondered who the man meant. Perhaps this Dr. Cheney?

"Take me to Cheney now," His Grace instructed, his voice

firm and uncompromising.

Turning, the man strode away, the two of them following him. As they went up a staircase, she could hear screams. Moans. A shiver ran along her spine. Her heart began pounding violently.

They reached the next floor, and the man turned. Shock ran through her as the strong smells of human waste permeated the air. She saw benches on both sides of the hall. Women of all ages sat on these benches, their hair shorn as Miss Brandon's had been. They were ghostly pale, wearing gunnysacks that lacked in color. Their feet were bare. As they passed, she saw bruises of varying shades along their limbs. What shocked her was not a one looked up as they walked by. Surely, these women were curious about visitors?

Another scream sounded. Not from these sitting women, who kept their silence. They passed an open door, and she glanced inside the room, seeing a woman tied to a bed. She let out a long, eerie wail, causing Verina's insides to go cold. An attendant stood over her, scissors in hand, shearing the woman's hair close to her scalp.

Verina realized she had paused and rushed to catch up to the duke. She asked, "Why do they cut off their hair?"

"These places are filthy. Lice gets in the patients' hair. Also, they sell it. There is actually a market for it."

She shuddered, biting her lip, continuing to walk beside him. The man leading the way stopped at a door.

"He's in there."

The duke pushed open the door without knocking. A very thin man sat behind a desk, spectacles in one hand, the fingers of his other hand massaging the bridge of his nose. At the interruption, he donned the spectacles again and looked up, frowning at them.

"You do not have an appointment," he said, his gaze landing on her. "Is this the chit you wished put away?" he asked dispassionately, as he rose.

"No!" she said angrily. "We are here to take Lady Adams with us. And you should be ashamed of yourself. This place is terrible."

He pushed his spectacles against the bridge of his nose. "You are making a mistake not leaving this one with me, my lord."

"It is Your Grace, Cheney. We have met before." The duke paused. "I am Reddington."

Immediately, fear filled the doctor's eyes. "You! What are you doing here? You have your mother back. You should not be here!"

"You heard why we are here. We have come for Lady Adams."

Stubbornness filled the man's face. "Well, you cannot have her, Your Grace."

"Name your price," Reddington said, his voice so cold that Verina shivered. "And it is not as if Lord Adams will come looking for his aunt. I know for a fact that his country estate is in Cornwall, far away from here. He will never return for her. He left her to *die* here."

Verina found herself trembling. With anger—not fear. She wanted to speak out again, but she did not want to upset the duke or interrupt his negotiations.

"How much?" he demanded again.

Dr. Cheney named a price, a staggering sum, but the duke merely pulled a purse from inside his coat and tossed it upon the desk.

"That is far more than you asked for. Are you to notify Lord Adams when his aunt dies?"

"He said to do so. Only so he would stop paying the monthly fee," the administrator admitted.

"Then mark this down. Wait five years—and then notify him of her passing. Keep the blood money that he sends you in the meantime, along with what I have given you. And never speak of this again."

"I will—only if you never return, Your Grace."

The look in the duke's eyes frightened Verina, and he said, "If I come back again, it will be to kill you."

And she knew Reddington meant it.

He turned, facing her. "Come. Let us retrieve Lady Adams. I recognized her sitting on one of the benches as we passed."

She found she could not speak and merely nodded. His fingers found hers, and she held fast to them as they left the office. They returned to the corridor, lined with benches, women silently sitting, hunched over. He paused in front of a woman. How the duke had recognized Lady Adams was hard to imagine, for she did not look up, even with them standing directly in front of her.

"Lady Adams?" the duke gently asked as he knelt before her. "It is Reddington. Mama sent me to bring you to her."

Slowly, the woman's head began to rise until her gaze met the duke's. "Reddington," she whispered. "Reddington."

He rose, taking her elbow and helping her to her feet. "Come. Let us go. This is Lady Verina. She came to help."

Lady Adams looked at Verina, her face devoid of emotion. She would have thought the woman might have smiled joyfully. Then again, they had yet to leave the premises. If their positions were reversed, Verina would not have felt safe until in the carriage, far away from Throckmorton.

"The carriage is waiting for us, my lady," she said gently. "Might I assist you?"

Verina took the older woman's other elbow, and Lady Adams shuffled along for a few steps. Then she stopped.

"Miss Baird. You must find Miss Baird." Tears filled Lady Adams' eyes. "Please. Help her."

The duke shook his head. "I have only come for you, my lady. It was difficult enough getting Cheney to give you up. He would never agree to me taking another woman."

Swallowing, she said, "Then leave me. Take her. I am old. Miss Baird is young. They have not broken her yet." She paused. "She suffers greatly, Reddington."

Lady Adams' anguish touched Verina. She looked to the duke and then back to the noblewoman. "We paid enough for two,

Your Grace. Tell me where Miss Baird is, my lady. I will fetch her."

Lady Adams began trembling. "In the water treatment room. Go up a flight of stairs. You will find her there. On the right." She swallowed. "Listen for . . . the screams."

Larkin appeared, and Verina said, "Get Lady Adams to the carriage. We will be there shortly."

Then before the duke could stop her, Verina dashed down the corridor and up the stairs.

She continued down the new corridor, following the shouts and screams she heard. When she reached a room on the right and glanced into it, she saw a young woman close to her own age, tied to a chair, her body bucking. Two men hovered over her. One dumped a bucket of water over her head, causing her to sputter. The other drew back his fist and slammed it into her belly. Fear caused Verina to freeze a moment. Then without regard for her own safety, she hurried inside the room, knowing she had to intervene.

"Stop that at once!" she commanded. "Untie Miss Baird. She is coming with us."

Both men stared at her, a hungry look in their eyes. It made her flesh feel as if ants crawled over her.

Before she could cry out, one of them latched onto her elbow and yanked her close. She could smell stale beer on his breath.

"Looks like we have a new toy to play with."

Verina spat in his face.

He drew back a hand to slap her, and she squeezed her eyes closed, waiting for the blow.

Then a voice said, "Release her now. Or you will never see another sunset."

Opening them, she saw the Duke of Reddington only a few feet away. He held a gun in his hand. The attendant's grasp began to loosen, and he backed away from her. So did the other man.

Free now, she went to the woman in the chair, who trembled from the cold. The room was freezing, and Miss Baird looked like a drowned rat.

"Miss Baird, I am Lady Verina. This is the Duke of Reddington. You will come with us."

"I most certainly will," the young woman said, fire in her eyes. "The one on the right has a blade in his left boot. Take it and slice these cords."

The duke continued to aim his pistol at the two men. Verina went and lifted the trouser covering the attendant's leg, removing the knife. She went back to Miss Baird and cut through the restraints, helping her from the chair. The young woman shivered with the cold.

"There are warming robes in the carriage," she said. "You will be fine."

They hurried past the duke and went to the stairs. Miss Baird needed assistance going down them.

"I have not eaten in a good while," she apologized. "I am so weak."

Then Reddington was there. He scooped Miss Baird into his arms and said, "Hurry."

They raced down the stairs to the ground floor. Verina tuned out the cries and screams as they opened the front door and hustled to the waiting carriage. Mr. Larkin was standing beside it, and he opened the door. The duke climbed the steps, Miss Baird still in his arms. The runner assisted Verina into the carriage, and it took off quickly.

She sat beside Miss Baird, leaning down and picking up one of the robes. She wrapped it around the shivering young lady, whose teeth chattered violently. Verina wrapped her arms about Miss Baird, hoping to warm her.

"Thank you," Lady Adams said. "Thank you, my lady. You are very brave."

"It is His Grace and Mr. Larkin you should thank," she told the older woman. "Mr. Larkin tracked you down. Their Graces have been looking for you ever since your husband's death. Their persistence is what led us here today."

Verina rubbed her hands up and down Miss Baird's arms. "We are not far from Dove Hall. It is a place of refuge for ladies such as yourself. Ones who have been placed in asylums against their will."

Miss Baird cried now, anger still sparking in her eyes. "You must not tell my father I am freed," she insisted.

"That is not how it works," the duke told her. "Dove Hall is a place where you can acclimate yourself to the world again. Mama and I have helped several others in your position, Miss Baird. We know time helps in healing. You may remain at Dove Hall as long as you wish. Some stay permanently, and there are cottages on the estate if you wish to do so. Others—"

"You must notify Lord Hampton that I am freed," Miss Baird interrupted. "We are in love."

Though she still shivered, the story came spilling out. Miss Baird had fallen in love with Lord Hampton, but her father, who had numerous gambling debts, had sold her to another viscount. Instead of wedding the man who paid off her father's gambling debts, Miss Baird had sneaked out of the house on what was to have been her wedding day. She and Lord Hampton had left London, eloping to Gretna Green.

"My father caught up with us," she said, bitterness in her voice. "When I told him I would never speak my vows with anyone but Lord Hampton, he had me taken to that terrible place." She paused. "My father's men beat Lord Hampton. They would not have killed him, but I know he was incapacitated so that he could not follow and see where I was taken."

"I know of Hampton," the duke said. "His country estate is in Kent, isn't it?"

"Yes, Your Grace."

"Then you will go to Dove Hall and wait for him there. I will write and tell him you are safe. My advice, Miss Baird, would be for him to purchase a special license for you to wed. Once you are married, you will have the protection of his name, and your father will not be able to bend you to his will."

"Thank you, Your Grace," Miss Baird said, tears freely falling down her face.

"Thank Lady Adams," he responded. "And Lady Verina. Neither of them would leave Throckmorton without you."

"My thanks to you both," Miss Baird said fervently. "I owe the three of you my life—and my sanity. I do not know how much longer I could have held out."

They reached Dove Hall, and both women were brought inside, where Her Grace was waiting in the drawing room. The two older women fell into one another's arms, weeping profusely.

"I am so sorry for what you went through," Her Grace said.

"Thank you for looking for me. I cannot imagine what resources you used to find me," Lady Adams said. She looked to the others. "Come, Miss Baird. Meet Her Grace, the Duchess of Reddington." To the duchess, she said, "I could not leave Throckmorton without her."

As the three women starting talking, Mrs. Paul appeared. "I have hot baths coming for the two ladies, Your Grace. Miss Vines has been summoned, and she will see they have new clothing. Miss Brandon and Miss Ross also have come to help in settling these two new doves."

"Thank you, Mrs. Paul."

He moved to the three women. "Mama, I must see Lady Verina back to her cousin. We had promised she would be there by teatime or shortly thereafter. If we leave now, she will arrive just after tea."

Miss Baird came toward Verina, the soggy robe falling to the floor as she embraced her.

"You are an angel, Lady Verina. I hope I will see you again." Giving her a shy smile, she added, "I would so like it if we could be friends."

"I would like that, as well, Miss Baird. Will you retire quietly to the country with Lord Hampton after you wed?"

"Certainly not," the young woman boldly declared. "I plan to attend the Season next spring as Lady Hampton. And if I see my father, I will give him the cut direct."

"I am to make my come-out next spring," she shared. "We shall meet up again then."

"I will have you to tea, Lady Verina. By then, we will have much to catch up on."

Lady Adams came and embraced Verina, as well. "You are so brave, my dear. Thank you again. For everything."

She bid the duchess farewell and accompanied the duke downstairs. Inside the carriage, she said, "Well, I certainly had a most interesting day."

He grinned. "You asked about my work. Now you have seen it, firsthand. It is not often the pieces fall into place so quickly. Usually, it takes Larkin months to find a woman. Then he and I—and sometimes Mama—travel to where the madhouse is located as we attempt to retrieve them."

"Have you ever failed?"

"Not yet," he said grimly. "I know the law of probability says at some point, we will. Thankfully, it was not today."

She gazed up at him. "I know you cannot help them all, but I am grateful that you allowed us to go back for Miss Baird."

His cornflower blue eyes darkened, seeming almost deep purple. Her breath hitched. She was aware of how close they sat. The heat of his body.

Then his mouth descended to hers, their lips meeting. He brushed his slowly against hers, causing sensations to spring within her. His palms cupped her face, and she inhaled his scent. Felt his warmth. He kissed her slowly, softly, his lips leaving hers only to return again. One kiss turned into many, and they became longer. Firmer.

His hands slipped to her neck, cradling it, his lips still on hers. The kiss was exciting. Riveting. And deep within it, she felt it spoke of promise.

He broke it, his forehead resting against hers, his thumbs moving up and down her neck in a gentle caress.

Their breath intermingling, he said, "I will not kiss you again until you ask me to do so, Verina."

His use of her given name caused a thrill to shoot through her. She lifted her head, staring up at him.

"Why did you kiss me, Your Grace?"

He smiled wryly. "Is it not enough to want to kiss a pretty girl? One who so bravely followed me into a place of danger and stood her ground."

"I was afraid the entire time we were there," she admitted.

"I was, too," he shared. "I always am."

"But you continue to help those women. That is very brave."

"I am glad you think so."

He kissed her again, gently, and then ended it as the carriage slowed.

"We are at Merrifield," he announced. "I cannot stay. I must get back to Dove Hall. Go along with the white lie I will tell."

Opening the door, he climbed from the carriage and offered her his hand. Verina took it and descended down the stairs a footman must have placed there for her. The duke closed the carriage door, and they headed into the house, the butler opening the door.

Hugo appeared. "You just missed tea." He frowned. "Where is Her Grace?"

"She is in the carriage. She wanted to come inside, but she began sneezing on the way here and fears she might be coming down with a cold. She did not want to expose Tia to it, especially in her condition."

"That is most thoughtful of the duchess," Hugo said. Looking to her, he asked, "Did you have a good day with Her Grace?"

"We learned quite a bit about one another," she said. "I enjoyed being in her company. And His Grace's, as well."

"I must get back to Mama." Reddington looked down at her. "Thank you for agreeing to stay today, Lady Verina. I know Mama and I look forward to the next time we see you."

"Tell Her Grace to go to bed with a hot water bottle when

she gets home. I hope she feels better soon," she told him, understanding now that it would have been inappropriate for the duke to have brought her home with just the two of them inside the carriage. If it were known they had been alone together—much less that he had kissed her—then she would have been ruined.

Unless he agreed to wed her.

Verina did not want to be placed in a position of forcing a man to save her reputation by doing that. She wanted to choose her groom and have him choose her without being told they must wed.

"I will do so, my lady. My best to Tia and Lady Justina," the duke said.

He left the house, and Hugo placed an arm about Verina's shoulders. "Come upstairs. Tia is eager to hear about your day with the duchess."

Quickly, Verina thought of the additional white lies she would need to tell. Reddington had not confided in Hugo of the work he did, and he would be displeased if she did so now. She did not want to upset him, much less prevent him from keeping on with what he did to help others. She pushed aside all thoughts of that very promising kiss as they entered the drawing room.

But she planned to reflect on it at length.

Chapter Fourteen

VERINA HAD NOT seen Reddington for two weeks. She had kept busy with Tia, though. Her cousin was quite popular in the neighborhood, and they were continually receiving invitations to tea or dinner. Tia was looking and feeling well these days. Her nausea had subsided, and she seemed like the Tia of old.

At breakfast that morning, she and Justina had received a letter from Mama. Mrs. Walters was doing much better, her plaster being removed, and Mama was eager to come to Merrifield to be with her girls. Mama had also written to Tia, and her cousin said she would write Aunt Agnes immediately and tell her to come to Merrifield at her earliest convenience.

"Why don't I go . . . and collect your aunt Agnes?" Hugo asked. "I am happy to do so. Write to her. Tell her I will escort her to Merrifield."

"Are you certain you do not mind going?" Tia asked. "I would go with you, but I am only starting to feel myself again. Riding all day in a carriage to reach town and then turning around and coming back the next day has no appeal to me."

"I will miss you," Hugo said, taking Tia's hand and kissing it. "But it will give me a chance to visit with my solicitor. I can travel to town one day. Do my business the next. Then collect your aunt the following day and return to Merrifield."

"Why don't I come with you?" Verina asked. "You have yet to meet Mama since she did not come to town this past Season."

"I had not thought about that," Hugo admitted. "Your mother might be . . . more comfortable with you present. After all, I am a stranger to her."

"She will come to adore you, just as Justina and I have," she assured him. "Besides, I was thinking that Mama and I might see a modiste while I am in town. I could have her take my measurements, and we could commission a few gowns from her now, while it is a slow time of year. That way, when we do come to town, I should have several gowns close to being finished."

"That is a brilliant idea," Tia declared. "I will write to Madame Laurent and tell her you will be in town soon and ask for an appointment. My letter will introduce you to her."

"Do you want to come along, Justina?" she asked her sister.

"Not really. I hate carriage travel. I wish I were a witch and could fly on my broomstick to whatever destination I chose. It would be so much faster—and more fun—than being trapped inside a boring carriage that bumps along."

"Well, we will have plenty to do here while Hugo and Verina are gone," Tia said. "Why don't you call at Redfield and see if Matthew needs to go into town? He is always good company and would make the journey go faster."

Verina thought about the last time she was in a carriage with the duke.

And that kiss . . .

She was very conflicted about the Duke of Reddington. On one hand, she was intrigued by his philanthropic efforts to help mistreated women. She had asked him how many he had helped, and he had not given her an exact count. She thought the duke merely modest. He was too humble to take credit for removing ladies wrongly sent to asylums. She knew that between his missions of mercy and the running of his various estates, he must be quite busy.

On the other hand, she was hoping to find a husband come the next Season. While Verina admired his efforts, she was torn between respecting all he did for the downtrodden and her own desire for a conventional marriage. That meant having a husband who spent his time at home with her and their children, not one who went traipsing about England, heading willingly into dangerous situations. As the duke had said himself, the odds meant that sooner or later, he would run into trouble since he hadn't so far.

She did not want to wed a man who, even though he showed an unselfish concern for the welfare of others, was rarely at home—and put the well-being of total strangers above that of his family.

Shaking her head, Verina knew she was getting ahead of herself. She and the duke had only shared a kiss in his carriage. Once. No declarations were made, nor was there any mention of an understanding between them. She still had much to learn about him, as well as he had to know more of her before she could seriously entertain any kind of offer from him. Just because they had kissed did not mean he cared for her. Or was wishing to commit to her for a lifetime.

Especially if she asked him to set aside the work he did.

Actually, now she thought about it, the duke would not make for a good husband. While he had a kind heart and was most handsome, he would always have a driving need to help women who had been placed in the same position as his mother. The Duke of Reddington might be a man of fine character, but she did not think him husband material.

"That is a good idea, love," Hugo said. "I will send a note to Matthew, telling him that we will leave for town the day after tomorrow, and he is welcome to accompany us."

Verina now regretted volunteering to go to town with Hugo to fetch Mama. Then again, it was not as if she would be in the carriage alone with the duke for all those hours.

Two days later, they called at Redfield. Hugo had received a response to his note, and Reddington would accompany them to town. Her Grace walked out to the carriage with her son, kissing him goodbye.

From the carriage, Hugo asked, "I hope you are feeling well, Duchess. Matthew told us that you believed you might be coming down with a cold."

She saw the duchess looked surprised and quickly said, "I am glad you stayed in the carriage when you and His Grace brought me home the other day, Your Grace. It looks as though you are the picture of health now, however. It is good to see you looking so well."

The older woman quickly caught on. "Why, I am feeling just fine now, Lady Verina. In fact, an old friend has come to call upon me. I will enjoy her company while my son is away."

"I hope your friend will take good care of you, Your Grace—and you of her, as well," Verina said.

"Oh, she is in fine spirits, my lady. Perhaps on your way home from town, you might call upon us. I am eager to meet your mama. Better yet, head straight for Merrifield and allow her to rest a bit. Then I will invite you to tea. Lady Adams, my friend, should still be with me."

"That is very kind, Your Grace. I will tell Mama about your invitation."

The duchess met Verina's gaze. "I also have another friend who happens to be in town now. She will wed by special license. Perhaps my son can introduce the two of you. I believe you would have much in common."

Verina was happy to hear that Miss Baird was already in town and that Lord Hampton had already arranged for the special license. The sooner Miss Baird was wed, the better.

"I hope that will be the case, Your Grace."

"Mama, we must be off," the duke said. "You and Lady Verina can speak another time."

"Be gone then!" the duchess said good-naturedly. "It was lovely seeing you again, Merrifield."

"Likewise, Duchess," Hugo replied.

The duke kissed his mother goodbye and climbed into the carriage. Verina had been sitting across from Hugo, and so

Reddington chose to sit next to her. It made sense. Hugo was a very large man, at least three inches over six feet, but the duke sitting next to her only made Verina aware of him in a way a woman is aware of a man.

And she would be sitting next to him for a good six hours or more today.

For a few hours, the two entertained her with stories of their university days, including tales involving Anthony, Hugo's cousin who held the living at the local parish. Anthony had been to dinner twice during their stay at Merrifield, and she thought him amusing and intelligent. She actually liked the sermons he delivered because Anthony used a bit of humor in them.

When they stopped to change horses, the duke led her inside the changing station.

"We should purchase something to eat," he told her, taking her arm as Hugo watched the team being traded out.

"Tia's cook sent a basket with us, Your Grace," she told him as they walked away. "We can eat from it. I believe she sent some cold chicken legs. A round of cheese. Some fruit."

"I saw the hamper," he said as they moved out of Hugo's earshot. "I wanted to tell you about Miss Baird."

"Oh, please do so," she said eagerly. "I am so happy she is already in town and preparing for her wedding."

"No one except Lord Hampton knows she is there. I wrote to him, briefly explaining the situation, and promising to have her brought to town. He replied, telling me he would head to town and go to Doctors' Commons for the special license."

"What does it allow?" she asked.

"A couple may wed any time of day and at any place of their choosing," he informed her. "No banns need be called. I have known several couples to wed with one of these licenses. They allow for a more private, intimate wedding than the parade of people one sees at a wedding held at St. George's in Mayfair. They also require no waiting period." He paused. "Sometimes, a couple wishes to wed quickly, as in this instance."

"Do we know where Miss Baird's father is? Hopefully, not in town."

"Mr. Larkin escorted Miss Baird to town. While there, he learned from one of the viscount's servants that he is at his country estate. Most members of the *ton* are this time of year."

Verina frowned. "Where is Miss Baird staying?"

"At my townhome. Do not worry," he added when she sucked in a noisy breath. "My servants are tremendously discreet. They will not breathe a word to anyone that Miss Baird is in town, much less that she is staying at the residence of a duke. Her reputation would be in tatters if word got out."

"She is going to have a hard time of it next Season, married or not. If she were supposed to wed another man, the banns would have been called and guests would have been invited to her wedding. For her to have stood up that groom, a man of her father's choosing, and then arrive in town as Lady Hampton? I shudder to think what the gossips will make of that."

"Fortunately, that is only partially the case. Larkin found out that while the banns had been called in her home parish, her father had not sent the news to the London newspapers, so nothing of the upcoming nuptials was printed in town. Miss Baird's father, Viscount Ayles, lives in Durham, far from London, in the north of England."

"And the wedding guests?"

"Miss Baird told Mama and me that the ceremony was to be held the afternoon after the third and final reading of the banns. Only a handful were supposed to be in attendance."

"It seems as if she will be safe in town then, especially with so many of the *ton* at their country estates this time of year."

"Yes. I asked her not to leave my residence, though she does have the run of it. I also called in Mama's modiste, and she came directly to the townhouse. Lord Hampton is paying for a new wardrobe for his bride since she only had a few gowns which Miss Vines sewed for her once Miss Baird reached Dove Hall. I will pay for her wedding gown, however, and have been asked to be one of the witnesses to the ceremony."

The duke's gaze pierced her. "I know Miss Baird would be delighted if you could attend, Lady Verina. She thinks a great deal of you."

"Will it take place while we are in town?"

"Yes. Tomorrow, as a matter of fact. I was already planning to come to town when I received Hugo's message."

"I am surprised that Her Grace did not come."

"She is still tending to Lady Adams. The poor woman's health was broken in that place. Mama is nursing her back to good health."

"What will become of Lady Adams?"

"I believe she will stay with Mama as a companion of sorts. She will not attend any of the social affairs of the Season with Mama, but rarely do companions do so. They were friends before, but I see a closeness between them, as if they are now sisters."

"And you welcome Lady Adams into your family?"

"I am happy to do so." He paused. "So, would you be willing to attend the wedding ceremony? It is scheduled for ten o'clock tomorrow morning. A wedding breakfast will follow."

She thought a moment. "Hugo is due to see his solicitor sometime tomorrow morning. I suppose I could go. I hate not telling him the truth, though."

"Why don't you tell him that you received a letter from an old friend who was to wed? That you had not thought about attending the ceremony because you thought you would be at Merrifield. Mention it—and I will offer to escort you. He will not object."

Verina very much wanted to see Miss Baird again, so she agreed to the plan.

They returned to the carriage. She waited until after they had stopped again to change out the horses and were back on the road again.

"Why, what is the date?" she asked.

The duke told her, and Verina, doing her best playacting, said, "It must be fate. My friend Miss Baird is to wed tomorrow in town."

"A wedding, you say?" asked Hugo.

"Yes. I have known Miss Baird a good while now. When she wrote to me to tell me of her betrothal, she shared the wedding date with me. Of course, I replied and told her I would not be able to attend because I would be at Merrifield. But with this sudden turn of events, I find myself in town."

She paused and beseeched, "Might I go to the wedding ceremony tomorrow, Hugo? Only a few family and friends will be in attendance. It is to take place at ten o'clock."

He frowned. "I meet with my solicitor at half-past ten. I suppose I could try and move the appointment so that I might accompany you."

"I do not mind escorting you to the wedding of your friend, Lady Verina," the duke offered. "You know how fussy solicitors are, Hugo. If you try to push the appointment for later in the day, he might not have any openings available. And you are only going to be in town and able to do business tomorrow."

"That is true," Hugo mused. He looked at Verina. "Would you mind Matthew taking my place?"

Verina turned her gaze upon the duke. "If you truly do not mind, Your Grace, I would appreciate it. So would Miss Baird."

"I am more than happy to take Lady Verina to her wedding."

"Perhaps you both can come for tea tomorrow afternoon," she said. "Surely, your business would be completed by then, Hugo."

"It will be."

"I am afraid I cannot come for tea, my lady," Reddington said. "I have an appointment tomorrow afternoon which will not allow me to do so."

She did not know if he had another engagement or not. It did not matter.

Verina was going to a wedding—with the Duke of Reddington as her escort.

Chapter Fifteen

THEY DROPPED REDDINGTON at his townhouse, and Hugo had his driver go to his townhouse afterward.

"I hope you do not mind that we are not trying to see your mother after our long journey today, Verina."

"No, Hugo, I am perfectly happy with the decision to wait and see Mama and Mrs. Walters tomorrow afternoon. His Grace has said he would take me to the modiste Tia has recommended after my friend's wedding, and we can send word for Mama to meet me there. I can then spend the rest of the afternoon with her and her cousin."

She paused and then added, "It is very kind of His Grace to offer to escort me to the wedding since you are otherwise engaged."

"I have more than a meeting with my solicitor," he said. "You must keep this in confidence, Verina."

"Of course. What do you wish to share with me?"

"I have decided that with each child Tia bears, I am going to gift her . . .with a piece of jewelry. First, I will begin with a pair of earrings. I have already written to the jeweler whom I purchased her wedding band from. He has. . . a few pairs for me to see tomorrow morning."

"That is a wonderful idea, Hugo! Tia will be so pleased at the thought you have put into this."

"I thought . . . that she might wear each piece until . . . each child is ready to wed. Our daughters could then inherit the piece from their mother. Our sons could take the jeweled piece … and give to their wife on their wedding day."

Tears sprang to her eyes. "You are a most thoughtful man, Hugo. I just may allow you to pick out my husband for me. That is a lovely tradition to begin. I might even steal the idea from you."

He laughed heartily. "You are welcome to do so, Verina. I do . . . want to keep it a secret, though. At least until Tia has given birth."

"Do you know what kind of gem you wish to purchase this first time?"

"I may go with a sapphire. To match her azure eyes. Then again, it will depend upon . . . what the jeweler has."

After they arrived at the townhouse, Verina asked for a tray to be sent to her bedchamber. The day had been long, and she wanted to eat a bite and then retire. Reddington had told her that they would make an early start of it tomorrow morning. He would be at Hugo's townhouse by half-past eight. When she had asked him why so early, he told her that with no lady's maid to help prepare her, Miss Baird might need Verina's assistance. She would be happy to do whatever she could to make certain her new friend looked lovely for her wedding to Lord Hampton.

Awakening refreshed, she again asked for a tray in her room and ate breakfast while servants brought hot water up for her bath. Hugo's housekeeper helped bathe and dress Verina, and she wound her hair into a simple chignon since she had left Sarie behind at Redfield.

Going downstairs, she found the Duke of Reddington waiting in the foyer for her. He looked quite handsome in his wedding finery, and once more, she wondered if she should allow herself to develop feelings for him or if she should merely remain friendly with him.

"I hope you have not been waiting long, Your Grace."

"Not at all, my lady. You are right on time. I, on the other hand, have a tendency to be early to everything. There have been many times I have either sat in my carriage for several minutes or gotten out and taken a walk around the block before I attended some *ton* event."

She liked his refreshing honesty. And Verina could not help but think that she liked *him*. Not the Duke of Reddington, but Matthew Keaton, champion of downtrodden women.

And a man who kissed extremely well.

They went out to his carriage, and he told her, "I do not live far from Hugo."

"Then we should have walked, Your Grace," she gently chided. "There was no need to have your team readied just to drive me a few blocks."

He looked at her as if she had sprung an extra nose. "Walk? You would have walked?"

Verina laughed. "I am a country girl, Your Grace. I walk everywhere when I am at Traywick Manor, and I have done my fair share of walking while visiting at Merrifield. Why, you must recall when we went to Dove Hall that we walked from the cottages to the hall itself, and that was a fair distance."

"I suppose we did. I should have asked if you wanted to walk that far. I suppose I had other things on my mind that day."

"If I had not wanted to walk that far, I would have spoken up, Your Grace."

A few minutes later, they arrived at a beautiful square. It contained only three houses. Two sat opposite one another, with a park between them, while the last one sat opposite the entry to the square. Verina had been too tired to notice anything about the duke's residence when they had dropped him off late yesterday.

They got out of the carriage, and Verina could not help but be taken aback by the sheer size of the townhouse. As they entered it, she was enthralled with its grand foyer. Several large paintings were on display, and the magnificent staircase was a thing of beauty in itself. She could picture future guests lining up along that staircase in a receiving line, waiting to meet the Duke and Duchess of Reddington.

A woman appeared, and he introduced Verina to his housekeeper, saying, "Please take Lady Verina upstairs to Miss Baird's bedchamber. She is going to help the bride prepare for her wedding."

"Of course, Your Grace," the housekeeper said, leading Verina upstairs.

The woman tapped lightly on a door and then opened it, ushering Verina inside. "Let me know if you have need of anything, my lady."

"Thank you," she said, closing the door and crossing the large bedchamber.

Miss Baird sat at a dressing table, while a trim woman fussed over a gown lying across the bed.

"Lady Verina!" Miss Baird cried, leaping to her feet and rushing to Verina, throwing her arms about her. "I had no idea you would be attending my wedding."

"I found that I was going to be in town for a day or two, and His Grace told me of your plans. He did not think you would mind if I came to witness the ceremony."

"Mind? I am thrilled you are here. I have told Hampton all about you and how brave you were."

Miss Baird bit her lip, and Verina knew she did so to keep from giving away anything about her past predicament. Turning, Miss Baird indicated the woman. "This is Madame Laurent. She is a modiste Her Grace sent to me."

"A pleasure to meet you my lady," the modiste said. "I believe this is a happy coincidence. Are you the Lady Verina which Lady Tia wrote to me of? That is, Lady Merriman?"

"Yes, Madame Laurent. Tia told me she would write to you and ask for an appointment for this afternoon. I planned to leave the wedding breakfast and meet my mama at your dress shop."

"What are you interested in, my lady?"

"I will be making my come-out in a few months' time. I

thought as long as I was in town, I might have you—or one of your assistants—take my measurements. Even put in an order for a few gowns before the Season begins."

"You are wise to do so, my lady. I create the gowns for several women in your family. They are all such a pleasure to work with. I was about to help Miss Baird into her wedding gown," Madame Laurent said.

"Let me know how I might assist you, Madame."

They lifted the gown over Miss Baird's head, and it fell like a waterfall about her. Madame Laurent smoothed it here and there and then stepped back, looking pleased.

"Yes, Miss Baird. This suits you quite well."

Miss Baird went to the full-length mirror in the corner and smiled. "Oh, Madame, it is like a dream. But what am I to do with my hair?" Then she looked at Verina. "I like the simplicity of the style you are wearing, my good friend. Would you mind terribly if I copied it?"

"I do not mind in the least," she replied. "In fact, I will do your hair for you." She looked at the modiste. "I believe your work is done here, Madame Laurent. I will see you in a few hours."

"I already have a few ideas for your gowns, Lady Verina. I will sketch them and also choose some bolts of fabric for you and your mother to look over." The modiste smiled. "I think we will have a marvelous time working together."

After the modiste left, Verina brushed Miss Baird's locks until they shone. Then she twisted her friend's hair up, pinning it carefully.

Admiring herself in the mirror, Miss Baird said, "Oh, I am so very happy. To be here. With you. Marrying the man I adore. When I think of—"

"Do not," Verina commanded. "That episode in your life is over. Do not waste another precious moment thinking about it or the cruelty of your father."

"He was so certain he could control me," Miss Baird said.

"But how could I wed another man when my heart belonged to Hampton?"

Miss Baird's words struck Verina. Suddenly, she could not see spending the rest of her life with anyone *but* the Duke of Reddington. Should she tell him this? Encourage him? He said he would ask for no more kisses from her. That she would need to be the one who asked for one from him.

Nerves flitted through her now. She was not ready to declare anything to him. She might only be thinking of him favorably because he was the first man outside her family that she had truly gotten to know. She told herself that she deserved a Season before she made up her mind.

They talked of the Season then, with Miss Baird telling Verina little details that Mama had not mentioned.

"It is so good to have you as my friend," she told Miss Baird. "I am so comfortable in your company."

"Since you are to make your debut come the spring, Lady Verina, know that my husband and I will do everything we can to help introduce you to eligible bachelors."

"I greatly appreciate that, Miss Baird."

A light tap sounded on the door, and Verina answered it. It was the housekeeper.

"The vicar and Lord Hampton have arrived, Miss Baird. If you are ready, you may come to the drawing room with me."

Miss Baird clasped Verina's hands in hers. "If this is a dream, promise you will not wake me from it, my lady."

They went arm in arm to the drawing room. The vicar stood with a gentleman who beamed the moment he saw Miss Baird. The duke stood by the man's side, and she knew this must be Lord Hampton. No one else was present.

She and Miss Baird crossed the room and went to stand in front of the vicar. Miss Baird slipped her arm from Verina's and allowed her groom to take her hands in his.

"Are we ready to begin?" asked the vicar cheerfully.

Verina had been to a couple of weddings in Kidsgrove, their

local village, but she had been more caught up in what the bride wore and how the church was decorated. This time, she carefully listened to the vows the couple spoke to one another.

And imagined saying those same words to the duke . . .

She had been watching the bride and groom throughout the entire ceremony, but now she looked over the groom's shoulder, her gaze meeting that of His Grace's. He gave her an enigmatic smile, causing an odd sensation to wind its way through her. Once more, she fastened her gaze upon her new friend and the groom, listening as the vicar completed the ceremony with a prayer. Then the clergyman announced the couple were now as one, and Lord Hampton lightly brushed his lips against his bride's.

For a moment, Verina closed her eyes and recalled what it was like when the duke kissed her. She opened them, only to see him staring at her, a knowing smile on his sensual lips, as if he read her mind and knew what her thoughts were. Her cheeks heated.

Lord Hampton thanked the vicar, who said he was not able to stay for the wedding breakfast.

As he left, Lord Hampton turned his attention to Verina and said, "I have already profusely thanked His Grace for his role in saving my one true love. I knew not where she had been taken and was despondent, afraid I would never see my beloved again. My wife tells me that you, too, played a large role in the recovery effort, Lady Verina."

"You must not forget Lady Adams' role in this," she reminded the couple. "We had come for her. We knew nothing of Miss Baird and her situation. It was Lady Adams who insisted we locate Miss Baird within the asylum and bring her with us. In fact, she even said that if we could only take one with us, she was willing to remain behind."

Tears welled in Lady Hampton's eyes. "I did not know that," she said, her voice shaking with emotion. "Lady Adams was so good to me. That place was a chamber of horrors. Lady Adams was the one bright spot within it."

"What has happened to Lady Adams?" Lord Hampton asked. "If she has nowhere to go, she is welcome to remain in our household."

That one statement alone told Verina that Miss Baird had chosen very wisely, falling in love with a man of remarkable character.

The duke spoke up. "My mother and Lady Adams were friends when Lady Adams' husband was alive. I believe she is going to remain at Redfield as a companion to Mama."

"Then you will be able to meet her, Hampton," the new Lady Hampton declared.

"Yes, I am certain Mama would like to have the both of you to tea when we return to town for the Season. Lady Adams would appreciate that, as well. She will not be mixing in Polite Society again. We do not want her nephew, who claimed her husband's title and had her locked away, to know that she has been liberated from the madhouse."

The duke cleared his throat. "Might you like to go into your wedding breakfast? I asked for it to be laid out in the actual breakfast room. It is the most pleasant room in the household, and we are a small party."

Lord Hampton turned to his bride. Offering his arm, he said, "My dear Lady Hampton, might I escort you to the breakfast given in our honor?"

The former Miss Baird's smile was blinding as she gazed upon her groom. "Lead the way, my lord."

Reddington gave Verina his arm, and he took them to the breakfast room. As they ate several courses, they all complimented the duke on his cook. At the end, a small cake was brought out, along with flutes of champagne.

His Grace stood, holding the flute high. "To Lord and Lady Hampton. I hope that you have many good years together and that the four of us remain steadfast friends."

Verina lifted her own champagne flute and smiled at the newlyweds. Sipping from it, she couldn't help but wonder if she might one day be the hostess of this grand house.

Chapter Sixteen

THEY WERE TO leave Merrifield tomorrow morning and return to Traywick Manor.

And Verina had not had the opportunity to ask the duke for another kiss.

Today was Christmas Day, and Reddington, his mother, and Lady Adams were coming to celebrate with them. They would share the holiday meal at mid-day so that the servants might have their own celebration in the servants' hall later that afternoon.

Verina paced her bedchamber, not ready to go downstairs just yet. She looked back over the past few weeks and how she had grown to enjoy the duke's company more and more. He had an affability about him, a quality which put others around him at ease. She already knew what a good duke and son he was, as well as the tremendously important work he did. While she still longed for a more conventional marriage, she had decided that being wed to the Duke of Reddington was something she wanted. True, he would not always be present, off helping other women, but she believed when he was at home with her, she would have his full attention, as would their children, and that was what was most important.

She knew he wanted children because he, Hugo, and Tray had had a conversation about that very thing only a few days ago. Tray had arrived and spent a good deal of time with the duke at Redfield. Reddington had also come to Merrifield to see her brother. Verina had gone to the library to choose a book to read and found the three men talking there, discussing the fact that Hugo would be a father come this new year. It wasn't as if she eavesdropped upon them. They spoke openly and freely in front of her as she perused the shelves for a book.

What she heard, though, let her know that the duke was cut from the same cloth as the men in her family—whether they were born into it or had married into it—placing a high value on family.

Was that what had finally helped her to make up her mind about him? Or was it that kiss, the one which she could not seem to forget? All Verina knew was that her opinion of the duke was high, and her admiration for him seemed to grow daily. Having never been in love, she did not know if this *was* love, but she believed the friendship which had sprung up between them would be a strong foundation for a successful marriage.

That is, if he had marriage on his mind. With her. He never indicated his feelings to her. Oh, she knew he liked her and was comfortable in her company, but sometimes, he was difficult to figure out. While the women had talked at tea one day, Verina had listened to a conversation between Hugo and the duke. Reddington admitted to his friend that it was hard for him to let down his guard around others because he did not know if they liked him for himself or the fact that they enjoyed being in the presence of a duke.

Verina could not relate to that. Yes, her father had been an earl, but she did not think others befriended her because of her social status. She could see how that would happen in the case of a duke, however. Not many men held such a prominent title. She wondered how hard it had been on him, coming into his dukedom at such a tender age, having to go against the world alone. He had told her it had taken a good while before his mother was more like her old self after he had brought her home from Throckmorton and that he'd had to rely on only himself.

Suddenly, a wave of tenderness for this man overcame her.

She wanted to hold him. Talk with him. And yes, even love him.

Leaving her bedchamber, she went to the drawing room, finding Tia and Mama there. It had been so good to have Mama at Merrifield the past few weeks because she had missed her mother terribly. She wondered what it would be like when she permanently left Mama's household.

Mama had helped Verina in selecting several materials for Madame Laurent to use in making up new gowns for her. The modiste's designs had been clever, and Verina knew they would flatter her figure. Madame had talked of other women in their extended family, ones she had dressed, and Verina knew she was in excellent hands with this modiste.

As she joined them, Tia asked, "Are you all packed for your departure tomorrow?"

"Almost," she replied. "Sarie has left out a traveling gown for me to wear tomorrow morning, as well as a night rail and my dressing gown for this evening."

Tia had been unable to find a parlor maid to her liking, so Sarie would remain behind at Merrifield and come to town when the Season began. Mama had praised how Sarie had styled both Justina's and Verina's hair, and Verina had assured Mama that Sarie was just as talented at caring for her wardrobe.

Tray joined them, followed by Hugo and Justina, and they talked while they waited for their guests to arrive. The duchess had told Verina that Lady Adams would remain with her from now on, telling Verina that while they had been friends previously, the experience they had both shared at the madhouse had bonded them for life. Lady Adams would not be taking a different name, as other damaged doves had. She would not appear at any *ton* events during the Season, but she would accompany Her Grace to town. The duchess had also told Verina that she had always longed for a sister, and that is what Lady Adams had become to her.

The trio arrived and were shown into the drawing room. Tray enthusiastically picked up his conversation with the duke, and Verina couldn't help but smile, liking the fact that her brother enjoyed Reddington's company so much.

Then Anthony arrived, and Mama told him how much she had enjoyed his Christmas sermon this morning. They had attended the service earlier, and Anthony had told them he would come to Merrifield as soon as he had completed his duties for the day. She liked Hugo's cousin very much. Anthony was warm and friendly, and she found it hard to believe that he, too, had stammered as a child, the same as Hugo. While Hugo spoke in a very careful manner, taking frequent pauses, Anthony's words seem to easily roll from his tongue. He had confided in her that he still had to practice daily in order to deliver his sermons without stuttering. Anthony regularly read aloud, sang, and recited poetry. She knew Hugo also did those very things, as well.

Since the two cousins were from the same family, Verina wondered if any child Tia and Hugo had would suffer from the same impediment. If he or she did, she knew the child would be showered with love and patiently guided in speech.

The butler announced that Christmas lunch was ready to be served, and they made their way to the dining room. The duke, taking her arm, escorted her there. No seats had been assigned, and she was happy when he took the place on her left.

Talk was lively throughout the meal, with Mama, Her Grace, and Lady Adams telling the younger people of Christmases past, when they were children. Mama even spoke some of the first Christmas when she and Papa had been newlyweds, wiping away a few tears as she did so. Her mother always spoke of Papa with great fondness, and Verina was aware that amongst the older generation in the family, her parents had been the only love match.

Papa was now gone, as was Uncle Charles and Uncle Arthur. The new generation of men—Val, Con, and her brother—had now taken up their titles and would guide the family in the years to come.

They finished eating their Christmas goose and pudding and

Anthony thanked Tia and Hugo for hosting him, saying he needed to return to the vicarage. He had a few elderly members of his congregation that he wished to call upon this afternoon, ones who had been unable to attend the services, and he wanted to bring them some Christmas cheer. They bid Anthony goodbye and retired to the library, which was cozier than the drawing room.

Tray said, "I do not know about the rest of you, but I am feeling terribly sluggish. Is anyone up for a brisk walk?"

"I would be happy to join you, Traywick," the duke said. "While the day is cold, there is no wind to speak of. Anyone else up for the adventure?"

"I am," Verina said, not wanting to pass up the opportunity to spend time with him. "I will need to don my pelisse, though."

"We will come, too," said Tia, taking her husband's hand and rising.

That left only Justina, and she shrugged. "Oh, all right. I will join you and not nap as these older ones are bound to do."

They went upstairs and as Verina started down the corridor to meet the others in the foyer, her sister joined her.

"I shall do what I can to see you paired with His Grace," Justina said.

"What?"

Justina gave her a shrewd look. "Do not tell me you do not have feelings for the duke, Verina. I know you too well. And I have watched His Grace watching you. Not just today—but ever since the two of you first met. I know you have always been all about having your Season, but I think you should open your eyes and see the man right in front of you."

Shock ran through her. "You truly believe he is interested in me?"

Her sister giggled. "I would say he has the look of a hungry wolf wanting to devour a lovely little lamb every time he gazes upon you."

Justina left her, hurrying down the stairs. Verina followed at a slower pace. If it were obvious to Justina, was it to the others? Or was it because her sister knew her so well? Either way, she was glad to have it confirmed that the duke did show an interest in her.

She was the last to arrive in the foyer. As she did, Justina slipped her arm through Tray's.

"Brother, you must tell me everything that has been happening at Traywick Manor and in Kidgrove."

They sailed through the doors, Hugo and Tia following them.

That left her with Reddington. He took her hand and slipped it through the crook of his arm.

"It is a pleasure to walk with you this Christmas Day, Lady Verina."

Their group walked at a leisurely pace, so she saw no need to try and catch up with the others.

"I am glad we decided to walk," she said. "If not, I fear I would already be napping by the fire now."

"Would that be such a terrible thing?" he asked, smiling at her. "Especially if you are next to good company."

Neither of them said anything more after that. Verina simply relished being in his company, leaning into his warmth. Contentment filled her, and she hoped it did the duke, too.

After an hour of strolling about Merrifield, Hugo turned them back in the direction of the house.

As they reached it, Tia said, "I would ring for tea to warm us, but the servants are all celebrating now. I do not wish to inconvenience them."

Hugo said, "I would make tea for you, love, but I have not a clue how to do so."

"I confess I do not know how to, either," Tia said. "Does anyone?"

"I do," Reddington said, surprising them all. "Do you not recall how I used to make tea for us in our rooms at university, Hugo?"

"That is right. You did!"

"I can do so now so that we do not disturb your servants. However, it should not be tea for six. We should go ahead and make enough for the others, as well." He glanced down at Verina. "My lady, would you be willing to assist me?"

Verina knew this would finally give them a few moments alone together, and she said, "I am happy to do so, Your Grace. Simply tell me what you need me to do."

"Only tea, Your Grace," Tray said, as they entered the front door. "I could not eat anything more, else the buttons might pop off my waistcoat."

Everyone laughed. The others headed upstairs to the library, while Reddington led her to the kitchens. When they reached them, she could hear the sound of laugher in the distance, coming from the servants' hall.

"It seems the servants are enjoying their holiday meal. Do you truly know how to brew tea?"

"I do. There are many things I have had to learn from a young age, Verina. Making tea is simply one of them."

She noticed he addressed her by her Christan name again. She did not correct him because she liked hearing her name coming from his lips.

"The first thing we must do is put a couple of kettles of water on to boil."

He did so and then moved to where the teapot stood. Unlike the one at Traywick Manor, which was kept under lock and key by the housekeeper, this teapot was easily accessible.

The duke took the tea leaves and chopped them with a sharp knife. She watched his long, lean fingers, remembering how they had cradled her cheeks.

He turned—and she believed he was thinking of the same thing. He placed his palm alongside her cheek.

"I am going to miss you very much, Verina," he said, his voice husky.

"We shall see one another at the Season," she told him, her voice faint, as she grew dizzy from his touch. "I have thought about our kiss. Often," she admitted.

The corners of his mouth turned up. "Have you?"

She nodded. "And I believe I would like another kiss from you, Your Grace. One for me to remember you by until we meet again this coming spring."

He gazed at her a long moment. Then his hand shifted, taking her chin and tilting it up toward him. He bent, pressing his lips against hers, causing a hunger to grow within her. Without thinking, she brought a hand up, cupping his nape, holding him to her.

She felt his smile against her mouth and smiled herself. Then he broke the kiss, taking her hand from his nape and tenderly dropping a kiss into the center of her palm. He turned her hand over and brushed his lips against her knuckles, sending a rush of chills through her.

"I would like to kiss you for hours, Verina," he admitted. "You are not ready for the kind of kisses I wish to give you, however. I know how important it is for you to have the Season you have longed for your entire life. I want you to experience that, my darling. But know that I intend to be your most fervent suitor."

Suddenly, a Season did not mean very much to her. Not when this man stood before her, and a deep yearning filled her.

He turned away from her, though, as one kettle began to whistle, and then the other did. He carefully measured the tea leaves and placed them into the strainer, placing one inside each kettle, allowing the tea to steep.

Together, they silently prepared a tray. He put the silverware, tongs, pitcher of milk, and a bowl of sugar upon it, while she added cups and saucers. Then he collected the two kettles and placed them upon a different tray. They carried these two trays up to the library, where Tia and Her Grace poured out for them.

The entire time, Verina could feel the duke's fingers on her chin. His lips against hers. His mouth pressed into her palm.

And with no doubt at all, she knew they belonged together.

CHAPTER SEVENTEEN

Four months later . . .

IT WAS THE eve of the Season, and Verina sat in Val and Eden's drawing room. Con and Rowena were also there. She liked Con's new wife quite a bit. Rowena was due to give birth in late August. She and Con would spend about a month in town, visiting with family, and then they would travel home to Somerset to await the birth of their firstborn. If Con had his way, they wouldn't have come to town at all, but Rowena had been eager to meet the others in Con's large family. Verina was glad they had come. She enjoyed Rowena's company and had fun partnering with her at cards. It seemed to be well known that Rowena was now the best cardplayer in the family.

"At least I am good at card play," Rowena had said. "Especially since I am atrocious at dancing."

Con was an elegant dancer, and it surprised Verina that he had been attracted to a woman who was not graceful on the dance floor. Then again, all she had to do was look at the pair and see the love between them. Rowena was beautiful and smart, and Con told everyone who would listen what a fortunate man he was in having won his wife's heart.

Tia and Hugo would not be attending the Season. Her babe was due at the beginning of June, and Hugo would not risk them traveling the bumpy roads to London while Tia was so large and feeling uncomfortable. Lia and Rupert had come to town, bringing Celia and their five-month-old twins with them, and Verina found the pair absolutely adorable. When Con and

Rowena left town, Lia's family would, too, but they would travel on to Merrifield so that Tia might meet Edward and Mary, and Lia could be with her twin when she gave birth.

Ariadne and Julian entered the room, Julian carrying Penelope. Verina had learned that Julian had set the standard for the men in the family. Ariadne had been the first of the ten cousins to wed, and Julian, a former dock worker who had surprisingly gained a title, was most open in his affection for his daughter. Julian carried Penelope about and spent hours in the nursery with her. The other men, as they had become fathers, took their cues from Julian, being as affectionate and loving with their babes as they were with their wives.

"Greetings to all," Ariadne said, coming to take a seat next to Verina. "Are you ready for your first ball tomorrow night?"

"I believe so. I am excited. A bit nervous."

"Tell me of your gown," her cousin insisted, and Verina did so, answering questions about it from Ariadne and Rowena. While she did so, Dru and Perry arrived, bringing Beau with them, and Lucy and Judson also stopped by, Elizabeth in tow. Soon, the men were on the floor, playing with all the children.

"This was how George was with you children," Mama said to her, wiping away a tear. "Always playing with you or singing to you."

"I recall how Papa, Lucius, and I would play with tin soldiers, lining them up for battle," Tray enthused. "When I have boys, I will do the same."

"You should play soldiers with boys *and* girls," Justina said saucily. "Men are not the only one with brains. Why, I believe if the king allowed a woman to be prime minister and another minister of war, they would find a way to defeat Bonaparte and bring peace to Europe."

Verina only wished she could remember her own papa. While Tray had been ten when the carriage accident took their father, she had been five and only had shadowy memories of Papa. Poor Justina had been four and had confided that she had no memories of Papa at all.

Lucy asked her a question, and Verina turned her attention to her cousin. It was so good to be in the midst of her large family. She knew she would busy seeing family, as well as attending *ton* affairs, over the next few months.

But what most excited her was seeing the Duke of Reddington tomorrow night.

Teacarts were rolled in, and Eden and Aunt Alice poured out for everyone. Aunt Charlotte came and took a seat beside Verina.

"I hear you and Justina had a nice, long visit with Tia at Merrifield."

"Yes. We spent about two months in Norfolk while Mama was in town caring for Mrs. Walters, one of her cousins. Mama joined us, however, and spent the last few weeks at Merrifield."

Aunt Charlotte asked Verina all kinds of questions, from details regarding Hugo's estate to the number of gowns Madame Laurent had made up for her. Aunt Charlotte was the most intimidating figure in the family. Con had often said—out of his mother's earshot—that Aunt Charlotte would have preferred being born a man so that she might have been the duke, instead of her brother.

Ariadne tapped her spoon against her porcelain teacup. "May I have your attention?" She paused as the group grew quiet. "Thank you. Julian and I have happy news to share with you all. Come October, Penelope is going to be a big sister."

Aunt Alice broke out in tears, hugging her daughter. Val kissed his sister's cheek, while Julian began accepting handshakes from the men.

"Congratulations," Eden told her sister-in-law. "You were the first cousin to wed. The first to have a child. And now you will be the first to have a second one."

"Unless you count Lia," Judson said. "She had two at the same time."

Eden laughed. "You are right. I am simply delighted that Ariadne has paved the way for us all. Not only was she the first to wed, but she wed for love. Isn't it marvelous how all the cousins since then have followed in her footsteps?"

"And Verina will be next," Tray proclaimed. "That is, if I let any gentlemen within ten paces of her."

Everyone laughed, and she found herself blushing from all the attention.

"Do you wish to wed for love?" Dru asked her. "It is not always the case. Sometimes, a marriage occurs for other reasons, but the couple comes to love one another."

Her gaze met Justina's. Fortunately, her sister did not say anything. Verina had not confided in Mama or Tray, much less any of her cousins, about her budding feelings for the Duke of Reddington. And if her family found out, she could imagine the unmerciful teasing, followed by matchmaking, where her cousins tried to constantly throw her and the duke together.

"I am keeping an open mind," she said, realizing everyone had fallen silent, listening for her reply.

"Let me say this," Dru said. "I would not look for love. Let it find you. Frankly, I was not enamored with the Season—much less marriage—but once Perry came into my life? Everything changed."

"For the better, I hope," her husband said, lacing his fingers through hers.

"Well, we have a large family with many strong social connections," Val said. "Any gentleman who shows an interest in Verina will certainly face our scrutiny."

"I believe the Duchess of Reddington will take our Verina under her wing," Mama said. "She seemed most fond of you. And it never hurts to have a duchess helping launch you into Polite Society."

"Her Grace is most fond of Verina," Justina said.

"Reddington isn't wed, is he?" Judson asked. "We have met him. A fine fellow."

Verina felt her cheeks warm and took a sip of tea, hoping to hide the blush.

Aunt Charlotte asked, "Have you met this Reddington, Verina?"

She lowered the teacup and set it back onto the saucer. "Yes, several times, Aunt. He is good friends with Hugo. Tray also has a fondness for His Grace."

Her brother said, "Reddington is a wonderful sort. We spent many hours together when I went to Merrifield several months ago."

Tray began talking about things the duke did on his estate, and the men in the family jumped into the conversation, comparing notes on what each did in a similar fashion. The women began talking of fashion and babes and new recipes for their cooks to try.

Then Ariadne asked, "Would you care to take a turn around the room, Verina? I find if I sit for too long, I become uncomfortable. At least my head is not in a chamber pot every few minutes this time around."

She rose and linked arms with her cousin, and they began a slow stroll about the drawing room.

"You are interested in this duke," Ariadne observed.

"Yes," she admitted. "He is unlike anyone I have ever known."

"Are you in love with him?"

Hesitating a moment, she finally said, "I believe I might be. I tell myself that he is the first man, outside of our family, that I have really come to know. He is great friends with Hugo and spends quite a bit of time at Merrifield. Hugo and Tia look upon Reddington and his mother as family."

"Does your heart speed up when he enters a room? Do you find yourself thinking about him at odd times—or all the time? Do you dream of kissing him?"

"Yes. All those things." Then lowering her voice, she said, "We have kissed. Twice."

Ariadne beamed at her. "Oh, that is a very good sign, Verina. Kissing you once might mean he was merely curious about you.

But doing so twice definitely shows interest on his part."

By now, they were on the far side of the room. Ariadne paused and looked out the window.

"We cannot be overheard. Speak freely, Verina."

"He kissed me once, and then he told me he wouldn't again until I asked him to do so."

Her cousin chuckled. "I already like him. And since you told me you have kissed twice, I assume you finally did so."

"Yes. It was a long time between those two occasions. And he said something quite odd. I have not been able to figure out the meaning. He said that he wished he could kiss me for hours, but he did not believe I was ready for the kind of kisses he wished to give me."

"I see."

"*What* do you see?" she beseeched. "Please, tell me. I haven't any idea what he was talking about. I have fretted over it for months. There have been times when I thought I could not breathe if I did not see him again."

Ariadne smiled. "It does sound as if you are in love. Tell me the kind of man Reddington is."

"A very good one. He is a most dutiful son, looking after his mother more than most men. He lost his father when he was young, so he came into his title as a boy. He does not trust easily because he believes people like him for being a duke, not for who he really is."

"But you do not care that he is a duke, do you?"

"Not really. I admire him quite a bit."

Verina did not want to give away the duke's secrets. Not that he had pledged her to silence, but she knew even Hugo and Tia did not know of his good deeds, so she would not be the one to share them with others.

"What do you admire most about him?"

"His character. He is a man of honor. He seeks to help those in need, using his title and wealth to do so." She did not think that gave away too much, especially if Ariadne learned how the duke had helped Hugo with his stammer. "He is also very kind. And he plays the pianoforte better than anyone I have ever met. He is jovial and loves to sing. He is most pleasant to be around."

"It sounds as if you are friends with him."

"Yes, I believe we are. I feel I know him almost as well as I do myself, and yet there are times when I am not certain I know anything about him at all."

Ariadne squeezed Verina's hand. "Ah, the mystery of men. Even now, after being wed to Julian, having had his child, and carrying another one of his, there are still times when he does or says something—and I wonder if I truly know the man I married." Her cousin smiled at her. "I would not worry, Verina. It sounds as if the two of you have much in common, as well as a foundation of friendship. Will he be at the Season?"

She nodded. "He told me he would be my most fervent suitor."

"Aha! Then you have the answer for yourself. It seems Reddington plans to pursue you. And make you his duchess."

Her heart sped up at the thought. "How will I truly know if I am in love with him, Ariadne?"

Her cousin pondered the question. "I think it is different for all of us. For me, I could not imagine my life without Julian in it. Even now, when something happens and we are apart, the first thing I think of is that I must tell Julian what happened. I want to share everything with him, from little things to large."

"And what about the kissing he wants us to do?"

Ariadne chuckled. "Your duke knows you are inexperienced. He does not want to go too far or too fast with you. But I will tell you this. If he said it to you, then a need for you is growing inside him. He desires you—and that is only going to grow stronger. I look forward to meeting Reddington tomorrow night. You will stand with the family as gentlemen come for an introduction to you. They will ask to see your dance programme. I suggest having your duke take the supper dance. That way, you not only get to dance with him, you also will be able to spend the supper hour in his company."

"That is a little frightening. What if I run out of things to say to him?"

"You won't. I promise you that. Usually, the family has a table or two in the supper room. Tell Reddington that I have requested that you and your supper partner dine with Julian and me. I promise to save a seat for the two of you at our table."

"Oh, would you, Ariadne? That would be wonderful."

"Come, let us rejoin the others. We shall keep this between us, your feelings for the duke and his for you. Of course, I will tell Julian to make him aware, but he will not tell another soul."

"Thank you. For everything."

Ariadne smoothed Verina's hair. "You are going to enjoy tomorrow night more than you think possible."

Verina did—until everything went terribly wrong.

CHAPTER EIGHTEEN

MATTHEW ESCORTED MAMA and Lady Adams to the winter parlor. It was a more intimate setting and where the three of them had decided to take their meals while they were in town for the Season. They were eating a light dinner because tonight was the opening ball. They had only arrived in town yesterday, and it had taken everything he had not to rush to Lord Traywick's townhouse and dominate Verina's time. He told himself she would be preparing for the Season she had longed to participate in, and that was the only thing which kept him from her side. He could not deny her the one thing she had been so eager to enjoy.

He only hoped by Season's end that they would be betrothed.

"Will you miss attending *ton* affairs?" he asked Lady Adams.

"Not really, Your Grace. I have never been one for social events. I only came to the Season because Lord Adams loved it so." She smiled at his mother. "And by coming, I did make good friends, ones which did not desert me."

Her gaze returned to him. "I have repeatedly said this, but I can never repay you for removing me from Throckmorton. Not only that, but you have taken me into your very home. There is nothing I wouldn't do for you or your mother. Lady Verina, as well."

"Speaking of Lady Verina, when might you be offering for her?" Mama asked casually.

Her question flustered him. "Is it obvious that I carry feelings for her?"

The two women tittered, and he had his answer.

"She is aware of my interest in her," he shared. "I also know that—as most young ladies—she has longed for this come-out Season for many years. I would not rob her of that experience," he explained.

"Do not let other gentlemen squeeze you out, Matthew," Mama cautioned. "Lady Verina is quite the beauty, and she has such a pleasant demeanor. She will be much in demand, especially by those bachelors ready to find a wife."

"Did you think to ask her to reserve a dance for you this evening?" Lady Adams inquired.

He cursed under his breath. "No, I did not think to do so."

Mama patted his hand. "Something tells me she will know to do this." Their gazes met. "I think you have chosen your duchess very wisely. Lady Verina is a caring, compassionate, and intelligent woman. She also knows of your secret life. That would have been hard to explain to other young ladies you chose to woo."

"You are right. I could not have wed a woman without her knowing something of the work I do. After all, I do not believe a husband and wife should keep secrets from one another. I would have hated to disappear for days—or weeks—at a time and not be able to tell my wife exactly where I went. Or worse, lie to her and say I'd attended to business at one of my other estates."

"Lady Verina has a good head on her shoulders," Mama said. "Those times you must be absent from Redfield, she will see to its running."

"You will be there to help her do so, Mama. You and Lady Adams."

His mother shook her head. "No, my son. It is the Duchess of Redfield who should be in charge during your absence. When you do wed, Matthew, Lady Adams and I shall move to the dower house."

"That will not be the case," he protested. "I will not see you chased from your own home, simply because I have taken a bride."

The two women exchanged a knowing glance, and then Mama said, "I will be the dowager duchess upon your marriage. I have lived at Redfield many years now. I do not wish the servants' misplaced loyalty to favor me over the new duchess. Lady Adams and I have already discussed this at length, and we are perfectly happy to move to the dower house. In fact, I insist upon it."

He swallowed the lump which had formed in his throat. "You are a very decent woman, Mama."

She smiled indulgently at him. "And as a very good son, I will expect you to invite us to dine with you at least once a week."

"You will always be welcome at my table, Mama."

They left to dress after they finished their light meal. Lady Adams said she would go to the library and read for a while before retiring for the evening.

"The one thing I will enjoy most about not attending the Season is going to bed and rising at a decent hour. I have never been fond of putting my head to the pillow as the sun comes up. Goodnight to you both. Enjoy the ball, and please give my best to Lady Verina."

Matthew returned to his rooms, where Barrow awaited him.

"I have your evening wear laid out for you, Your Grace." With a hopeful look in his eye, he added, "Perhaps this will be the Season in which you find your duchess."

"I cannot keep anything from you, Barrow. Yes, I have a particular lady in mind and will be pursuing her."

The valet brightened. "We all hope it is Lady Verina, Your Grace. She has made quite an impression upon the staff at Redfield."

"Lady Verina is my choice," he confirmed. "Hopefully, she will accept an offer from me by Season's end."

Barrow frowned. "I would not wait that long to offer for her, Your Grace. I believe Lady Verina will prove to be quite popular with the bachelors of Polite Society. You do not want to miss out on the opportunity to make her your duchess."

"I will consider your advice, Barrow."

He met Mama downstairs and escorted her to the carriage. As usual, the streets of Mayfair were crowded with vehicles. The first ball of the Season always was the most heavily attended. Matthew began worrying that he would find Verina's dance card filled by the time they arrived.

"Quit scowling," Mama admonished. "You cannot control the traffic."

"It is not the traffic I am worried about. It is Lady Verina's dance programme being full."

"If she has not been vocal this first evening and spoken up about reserving a place or two on it, you will simply have to live with that, my son. I would make clear to her, however, that you would like to dance with her at tomorrow night's ball. Be bold. Ask her to reserve a dance in advance is my advice."

His mother was right. Verina was new to the Season and everything about it. She might not wish to hurt anyone's feelings and simply would allow gentlemen to sign her programme. He told himself that even if he did not secure a dance with her this evening, he would make certain that she knew he desired one tomorrow night, preferably the supper dance. That would give them more time together.

The carriage came to a halt, the driver saying they were clogged in traffic, and he escorted Mama down the block until they reached Lord and Lady Morris' residence. Inside, they joined the lengthy receiving line. Matthew skimmed it, not seeing Verina. His impatience grew, but he kept it from showing.

Finally, they reached their hosts and thanked them for tonight's invitation.

The countess looked at him and said, "I do not wish to catch you in the card room this evening, Your Grace. There is an outstanding group of young ladies who are making their debuts into Polite Society this Season. Without a doubt, you are the most eligible bachelor of this Season. Please dance with as many of the girls as you can and get to know them."

"I plan to do so, my lady."

He led Mama to the entrance of the ballroom. They stepped inside, and he stopped, his eyes scanning the room. His gaze fell upon Verina, and a calm descended over him.

She was here—and that was all that mattered.

TRAY ESCORTED VERINA and Mama out to Val's carriage. They were riding with her cousin, Eden, and Aunt Alice to the opening ball of the Season.

As the carriage's wheels began to roll, Aunt Alice said, "You look quite lovely this evening, Verina. Has your wardrobe been created by Madame Laurent?"

"Yes, Aunt Alice. I was told she is a favorite of the women in our family. Late last year, when Mama and I were briefly in town, we made an appointment with Madame Laurent. She measured me, and we discussed several styles and chose materials for my wardrobe this Season. That allowed me to have fittings as soon as we arrived in town. Madame Laurent is a wonder with her needle and thread."

Eden said, "Ariadne insisted that I go to Madame Laurent, as well. I must say that I enjoyed giving up my plain, serviceable governess' gowns for the beautiful gowns of a duchess."

Val took his wife's hand and kissed it tenderly. "You could wear rags and still be the most beautiful woman in any room, my love."

Her cousin's words caused Verina to think of the women she had seen wearing rags, those horrible, colorless gunnysacks, as gray and washed out as the women inhabiting them. She still found it hard to believe places such as asylums existed, much less that men put their wives, sisters, and daughters into them, abandoning them. It made her extremely proud of the Duke of Reddington and all he did in trying to help as many women as he could.

That led her to reflect upon Lady Hampton. They had corresponded weekly since Verina had attended her friend's wedding, and Lady Hampton would be here this evening. She could not wait to see her again. While the duke had cautioned Lady Hampton not to reveal any details of her escape from the asylum, especially if her father were present this evening, Verina worried about that very thing happening. Lady Hampton was still a bit excitable, and it was hard to predict how she might react if Viscount Ayles did confront her. She decided to pull her friend aside and warn her again not to speak of how she was extracted from the madhouse, much less name Reddington.

"I remember my own come-out," Mama said wistfully. "I danced with your father that first night and knew he was the only one for me."

Verina wondered if she should say anything now to her relatives about her feelings for the Duke of Reddington. She decided against doing so, not wanting to put him on the spot in case his interest in her had changed in the months since they had last seen one another. She would know soon enough. Simply being in his company would tell her which way the wind blew. Though they had been apart several months, her feelings for him had not lessened. They had only grown stronger over time.

And she hoped the same might be true for him.

"You were fortunate, Mama," Tray said. "As for me, I only plan to dance a handful of times. The rest of the ball, I will be watching the gentlemen my sister dances with like a hawk."

"You will have help with that task," Val said, laughing. "Every man in the family will be on alert, keeping an eye on Verina, and seeing that she is partnered with only suitable, eligible bachelors."

"Do not frighten off too many," Mama chided.

"Aunt Agnes, we only have Verina's best interests at heart,"

Val said. "If my cousin is to enjoy her come-out Season, she needs to be in the company of the right people. We will see to that."

They arrived—or she thought they had. When she was handed down from the carriage by Tray, she saw dozens of others on foot, heading down the middle of the road or along the pavement.

"What is happening?" she asked, confused.

Tray took her arm and that of their mother's, and Mama informed her, "The first night of the Season is notorious for clogging the roads. This, obviously, was as close as Millbrooke's coachman could get us. We must walk the rest of the way."

"I am afraid I will ruin my slippers," she protested.

"That is why we ordered two dozen pairs of them," Mama reminded her. "I knew what I was doing. Trust me to get you through this Season."

They entered the townhouse of Lord and Lady Morris and joined the receiving line. Verina tried not to be too obvious as she looked for the duke. Not seeing him, she turned her attention back to her companions.

Once she had met their host and hostess, they entered the ballroom. Eden waved, and Verina saw more of her family standing on the left side of the room. They joined them, and she embraced Lia and Rupert, as well as Ariadne and Julian.

"Are you excited?" asked Ariadne. "You look radiant."

"Very much so," she replied. Glancing about the ballroom, she added, "The room is beautifully decorated."

"Are you going to give a ball for Verina's come-out, Aunt Agnes? If not, Julian and I would be more than happy to host one in her honor."

"You are such a wonderful hostess, Ariadne," Mama said. "Why don't you hold it, and I will assist you in the planning of it?"

Excitement rippled through her. She had not known a ball would be given for her.

"We must do it soon then, "Ariadne said. "With Lia and Rupert heading off to see Hugo and Tia in a few weeks and Con and Rowena returning to Marleyfield, I want to make certain as many cousins as possible can attend the ball and support Verina. I will begin working on a guest list first thing tomorrow morning."

Other family members joined them, and soon, a few gentlemen approached, asking for an introduction to her. She looked to Tray and Val, and they both nodded when the pair asked to dance a set with her.

Keeping Ariadne's advice in mind, she handed over her programme, saying, "The supper dance is reserved, but you may choose any other one, my lords."

Once they returned her programme to her, Mama leaned close and whispered, "You are saving the supper dance for someone in particular?"

Not wanting to reveal too much, she said, "Ariadne advised me to do so. She said if I found someone special, I should have that dance in reserve."

"What a wise thing to do," Mama declared.

"Lady Verina!" a voice cried, and she turned, seeing Lady Hampton approaching with her new husband. They fell into one another's arms.

"You look lovely," her friend declared.

"So do you. Marriage suits you. And it is good to see you, as well, my lord," she said to Lord Hampton. "Let me introduce you to my rather large family."

After the introductions were made, Lady Hampton said, "We must catch up with one another. Perhaps we might do so during supper."

"My family always has a couple of tables. I had planned to join them. You are more than welcome to do the same," she told the Hamptons.

Then Verina leaned in and quietly said, "Remember, try not to react if you see your father. And under no circumstances are you to mention Their Graces as being the ones who freed you from the asylum."

Lady Hampton smiled. "I plan to be perfectly cordial if he

appears. And I know to keep to myself how I came to be here tonight with my husband."

Then suddenly, a new awareness filled Verina. A tingle danced along her spine. She looked over her shoulder—and there was the Duke of Reddington, standing not two feet from her.

CHAPTER NINETEEN

"GOOD EVENING, LADY Verina," Matthew said, drinking her in. "It has been far too long since we saw one another."

"Good evening, Your Grace," she said, giving him a smile which melted his heart.

He would wed her for that smile alone.

She looked to his side where his mother stood. "Good evening, Your Grace. I am sorry I did not see you."

Mama smiled. "I believe you only have eyes for my son this evening, Lady Verina. Just as he does for you."

He watched her blush and wished he could advance the calendar to the end of the Season. That this evening was their wedding night, and he could couple with her.

"Let me introduce you to my family, Your Graces," Lady Verina said. "Oh, dear. Even more of us have shown up. This is going to take a bit of time."

Quickly, she took them through the large circle of cousins, along with their spouses, as well as two aunts. Matthew had met some of them, but he was pleased to be introduced to the others. Mama knew the Dower Duchess of Millbrooke, as well as the Dowager Countess of Marley. The three of them, along with Lady Verina's mother, Lady Traywick, moved away from the group. He noticed the others returning to their conversations, giving him a few precious moments alone with Verina.

"The first thing I should do is ask for a dance from you," he declared. "I hope I am not too late and that your programme has an opening still left."

"There are several, Your Grace. I would suggest the supper dance," she boldly said.

He accepted the card from her and scrawled his name next to it. "I am surprised you had that left, my lady."

"I was saving it. For you." She paused. "I was not certain if you had changed your mind. My time at Merrifield was four months ago. Many things might have occurred which would change—"

"My feelings remain unchanged for you, Verina," he said softly. "I told you I would be your most fervent suitor, and so I shall be. I have never sent a bouquet to a young lady the day after a ball. Never called upon one. You are the exception. Traywick will grow tired of seeing my face at his door." He hesitated. "I only hope that you do not grow weary of my presence."

Her eyes sparkling, she said, "I can never see that happening, Your Grace."

"Good. Then expect me tomorrow afternoon in your brother's drawing room. Save a dance for me at the next ball. I plan to be your shadow, my lady. Sitting next to you at musicales. Partnering with you at card parties. Strolling with you, arm in arm, at garden parties."

Her brows knit together. "Are you truly certain you wish to see that much of me? I look about and see the number of stunning women in this ballroom, both those making their come-outs and others who have already done so. Even as we are speaking, I feel the eyes of a good many upon us."

"That is because people seem to be inordinately interested in dukes." He smiled. "Especially ones who are still bachelors."

She nodded in understanding. "I see. As a duke who has yet to wed, many are interested in you, both young ladies and their mamas, hoping to see an attachment form between you and their daughters."

He shrugged. "It is the story of my life—or it has been—ever since I became the Duke of Reddington. Boys who would not have included me suddenly gave me their full attention, fawning over me. It is why I became somewhat of a loner during my school days, not knowing whom I could trust."

"That changed at university."

"Yes. I met Anthony, and we got on straight away. Then Hugo turned up, and we became as Robin Hood and his merry men."

Grinning, she asked, "And were you the famous, heroic outlaw? If not, you have still become a Robin Hood of sorts. Instead of stealing from the rich to give to the poor, you steal away women who have been unjustly imprisoned and help them to start a new life."

"Ah, that reminds me. Lady Adams asked me to give you her best."

"She came to town with you?"

"Speaking of thieves, Mama and Lady Adams have grown as thick as thieves themselves. They are good for one another, though. I have not seen Mama this happy in years. It will do her good to have Lady Adams as her companion, especially after I wed." He paused. "Because I will be devoting all my time to my duchess."

Another blush stained her cheeks. Before she could reply, Lady Martindale, one of her cousins, said, "Come here, Verina. I wish you to meet one of Perry's friends."

"I will see you at the supper dance," Matthew promised, leaving her in the hands of her family.

He casually strolled about the ballroom, speaking to a few others here and there, but he had no intention of dancing with anyone else, despite Lady Morris' suggestion that he do so. No, he only had eyes for Verina, and he had made certain she understood that.

Matthew did retreat to the card room for a while, emerging to go and stand with some of Verina's relatives. Fortunately, he had met some through Hugo at White's, as well as getting to know her brother when he had visited Merrifield.

"Millbrooke and Aldridge tell me that you have intentions toward my sister," Lord Traywick said, seeming surprised. "Is that the case?"

"I fully intend to make Lady Verina my wife," he told the earl.

"My, that is rather bold," Viscount Cressley said. "Then again, Lia told me you were smitten with Verina. My wife is never wrong about things such as that."

Lord Marley said, "As the newest married man in the family, I thought I recognized that look in your eye, Your Grace."

"And what look might that be?" he asked.

"A mixture of love, devotion, and possessiveness," Lord Marley replied. "Does my cousin know of your intention?"

"She knows," he told the group of gentlemen gathered about him. "And I suppose now that all of you do, your wives will, as well."

"When do you plan to offer for her?" Lord Traywick asked. "If you are so certain, I am surprised you did not do so when we were at Merrifield together at Christmastime."

"Under any other circumstances, I would have done so. But Verina has wanted a come-out Season. I would not rob her of the opportunity to enjoy it. She needs to wear all her pretty new gowns and make friends with other young ladies."

"That is decent of you," Lord Huntsberry said. "Of course, I would give Lucy the world on a silver platter if she so desired." The marquess paused. "Do you feel that strongly about Verina?"

"I do," he said as solemnly as he would when the day came and they spoke their vows to one another. "I have yet to tell her that I love her—and should not admit it to this circle now—but I do."

Lord Aldridge clapped Matthew on the back. "You are a good man, Your Grace. You will fit well into the family. But I would not wait too long making that declaration of love."

He thought of how all these men loved their wives and

would not keep a secret from them. They would go home and tell their spouses, and one of Verina's cousins was bound to tell her.

He needed to be the one she heard those words from.

"I will do so tonight, my lords."

The time for the supper dance arrived, and Matthew excused himself, heading toward Verina and the gentleman that led her from the ballroom floor.

"I believe this is our dance, my lady," he said, allowing the other man to hand her over. Matthew tucked her hand into the crook of his arm.

"It will not start for a few minutes, Your Grace," she protested.

"Then we will stand here and enjoy being together."

She looked at him, and he met her eyes. "You really do care for me, don't you?"

"Now is absolutely the wrong time for me to say this. I wanted us to be alone, not surrounded by a ballroom full of guests. Perhaps sitting on a bench in a garden, the sweet scent of flowers swirling about us."

He paused. "But my heart will no longer allow me to remain silent. I love you, Verina Fulton, and I wish to wed you." He paused. "I hope you will understand we will not have a traditional *ton* marriage. I want to be more than your husband. I wish to be your closest confidant. Your lover. Your friend. And I hope that you can enter into a marriage with me, knowing that I must continue to do the work I do. It will mean absences from home at times, but I—"

"Yes, you silly goose," she said, laughing. "I love you, too. With all my heart. I know you must have been reluctant in the past to consider marriage because of what you, your mother, and Mr. Larkin do, but I completely understand." She paused. "More so now that I have seen the inside of one of those places."

Beaming at him, she said, "I accept your offer of marriage, Your Grace."

He lightly took her chin in hand. "I wish I could kiss you, here and now. As it is, we will already have drawn the attention of others, and the gossip will be flying, seeing as how I touch you more intimately than I should in public."

"Do you think I care about a bit of gossip? No, Reddington. I am going to be a duchess—and I will be helping my husband in his very important work."

Others started moving toward the dance floor, and Matthew's hand fell from her chin as he escorted her to the center of the room.

"It means a great deal to me that you wish to help me. I was not expecting you to offer to do so."

She gazed at him, sincerity in her clear, blue eyes. "I want to spend as much time as I can with you. I want to be a part of everything you do, Your Grace."

"Matthew. Call me Matthew," he urged. With a smile, he added, "After all, we *are* betrothed."

That dance would be forever embedded in his memory, the one where he moved about the floor, twirling his betrothed. Everything faded away but the woman in his arms, the most wonderful, compassionate, giving person he had ever met.

When the dance ended, Verina said, "Would you mind joining some of my family for supper? And Lord and Lady Hampton had asked to join us, as well."

"I am happy to be swallowed up by your cousins and their spouses."

As they moved toward the supper room, she said, "Could we wait and tell them of our betrothal tomorrow? They will make such a fuss, and I would like to keep it to ourselves and savor it a bit before it becomes public knowledge."

"Whenever you wish to reveal our engagement, I am ready."

They entered the supper room, and Rowena spotted them, waving them over. They joined her and Con, Ariadne and Julian, and Lia and Rupert.

"We saved a place for you," Ariadne said. "And one for your

friend and her husband."

Matthew saw Lord and Lady Hampton sitting there and greeted them.

"It is a pleasure to see you this evening," he told the couple as he seated Verina. "I hope you are settling into your marriage."

"Everything has been going well," Lord Hampton said. He looked at his wife. "Shall we?"

Lady Hampton nodded. "We are to be parents," she shared with those at the table. "The babe should be here sometime in mid-November."

"Congratulations," he told the couple.

"All thanks to you, Your Grace," Lady Hampton said quietly.

He left to go to the buffet and brought back a plate with things for Verina. It had been a long while since Matthew had been truly happy, but tonight he most certainly was. He was in the midst of a closeknit group, a family he would soon become a part of. He looked forward to spending the rest of his life with Verina and hoped they would be blessed with children by this time next year.

"I believe I need to go to the retiring room," Verina told him.

"I will go with you," Lady Hampton said.

The pair left, and he talked with Lord Hampton and Lord and Lady Aldridge. Lady Aldridge rose and came to take Verina's seat.

"My cousin is glowing this evening, Your Grace. I hear that you plan to offer for her. I think you will make for a splendid couple."

"Thank you, my lady." He glanced about. "She should have returned by now. I believe I will go and see what is keeping her and Lady Hampton."

Lady Aldridge chuckled. "I will see you later, Your Grace."

Matthew left the supper room, asking for directions to the ladies' retiring room. When he turned a corner, he saw why Verina had been delayed.

A man had cornered her and Lady Hampton, a threatening scowl upon his face. Immediately, Matthew rushed to her side.

"You will regret this," the man said, wheeling and hurrying down the corridor.

"Who was that?" he asked, clasping Verina's hands, feeling the tremors running through her.

"That was Viscount Ayles. Lady Hampton's father," Verina explained.

Chapter Twenty

Verina was eager to return to Matthew. She could not believe that on the first night of her come-out, she had become betrothed. All her worries about Matthew's feelings changing for her had melted away, replaced by an incredible warmth inside her.

Lady Hampton played with her hair in a hand mirror one of the maids had given to her. Impatient, Verina said, "You look fine. We should be getting back."

Her friend patted her hair and returned the mirror to the servant. "Oh, all right. I suppose all of this is new and exciting to you. I did my Season last spring. Or at least part of it."

She saw the gloomy look fall on Lady Hampton's face. Linking her arm through hers, she guided her from the retiring room, saying, "That is water under the bridge. Be happy! You have wed a lovely man. You are at the Season once again. And I hope we will get to spend all kinds of time together."

"I am sorry," her friend apologized. "You always look on the bright side of things. I have a tendency to do the opposite. That is why Hampton appeals to me so much. He is eternally optimistic about everything."

"Well, you have every reason to be enjoying your life now." Verina paused. "And the life within you. I am so happy for you."

"I have no siblings. Only a cousin who will inherit Papa's title. You will have to be a kind of aunt to our child. Maybe you can be his godmother."

"Or hers," she said. "And yes, I would be happy to hold that honor. If that is the case, you simply must call me Verina."

"And I am—"

"What the bloody blazes are you doing here, Agatha?"

They glanced up, and she saw a man before them, his face scarlet. Instantly, she knew this was the dreaded Lord Ayles.

"You locked me away," her friend accused. "You put me in that horrible place, Papa."

"And you were supposed to remain there, not flitting about a ball!" He grabbed his daughter's forearm.

"Release her, my lord," Verina commanded, fear filling her but knowing she had to do something.

"And who might you be?" the viscount asked, keeping his grip on his daughter.

"Lady Verina helped save me," Agatha said. "And you cannot send me back, Papa. I am no longer under your thumb. I wed Lord Hampton."

"It is true, my lord," she said. "I would release your daughter now before bruises spring up, and Lord Hampton chases you down and beats you for hurting his wife."

The viscount looked at them, his eyes hard. Though frightened, Verina coolly stared at him. Finally, he said, "You will regret this," and he released Agatha, briskly walking away.

Relief filled her as she saw Matthew approaching. He took her hands in his, and she felt her body quaking.

"Who was that?" he asked.

When Agatha did not respond, Verina said, "That was Viscount Ayles. Lady Hampton's father."

Matthew's eyes widened. "What happened?" He glanced at Agatha. "Are you all right, my lady?"

"No," she said, her eyes filling with tears. "He is a vile man. I am afraid he will try to take me back. Back to . . ." Her voice broke, and she began weeping.

Verina placed an arm about her. "It will be fine. Your Grace, go and find Lord Hampton. He needs to take his wife home."

She could see he was torn, and she assured him, "He will not be coming back. Go."

Reluctantly, the duke left them.

Other ladies were starting to pass, staring as Agatha continued sobbing. Verina led her to a chair in a nearby alcove and nudged her to sit, kneeling beside her and holding her hand. She removed a handkerchief from her reticule and passed it to her friend.

"Everything I said from before is still true. Under the law, you have the protection of your husband. Your father has no rights over you. Please, try to stop crying, Agatha. It is not good for the babe."

"You are right." Agatha wiped her eyes dry. "And I am not crying because I have lost my father's love. I never had it. I was a disappointment to him from birth since I was a girl. I think that is part of the reason I became a bluestocking. I thought if I could show him how intelligent I was, he might like me a little. Perhaps even respect me."

"Men like that only think of themselves," she said. "No matter what you did or how wonderfully you did it, he would not have cared." Verina took her hand. "But you have wed a man who adores you. You carry his babe. You do not need the love or approval of your father."

"What if he tries to put me back there? I cannot go back, Verina. I simply cannot!" Her voice was rising with hysteria, and Verina tried to calm her again.

Thankfully, Matthew appeared with Lord Hampton. Agatha leapt to her feet, falling into her husband's arms.

"I will take her home now," the earl told them. "I have spoken to my solicitor about all of this. He assures me the viscount has no legal standing in the matter."

"Viscount Ayles will know this," Matthew assured Lord Hampton. "He will not bother you anymore."

"Perhaps we should retreat to the country," Agatha said, sniffing.

"No," Verina said. "That would be a victory you do not wish to give him. He is the one who wronged you. Do not tuck your tail and run away. And do not worry about him besmirching your name. If he did so, his role in placing you in the asylum would come out."

"Why don't we visit Lord Ayles tomorrow morning, Hampton?" Matthew suggested. "Clarify the situation for him so he readily understands he has no power."

Relief appeared on Lord Hampton's face. "That would be wonderful, Your Grace. From what I know of Lord Ayles and his gambling debts, he is a weak man. He would never go against us if we have the support of a duke."

"Then meet me at White's at ten o'clock tomorrow morning. We will go to Lord Ayles' residence and speak to him together." Matthew paused. "And if we have to knock some sense into him, so be it."

They bade the Hamptons goodnight, and Matthew escorted her back to the ballroom.

"I am afraid you have missed a couple of dances," he said. "Your partners will wonder where you have been."

She smiled up at him. "It does not really matter. None of this does. It took me being here to realize that. I've looked forward to the Season for years, only to see it does not have the significance I have placed upon it."

Verina took a deep breath. "Ariadne has started a new tradition in our family. She has declared the Season more about family than social affairs. She has had all the cousins make a pact. We are to bring our babes to town each year when the Season arrives. While we can go to as few or as many events as we please, the bulk of our time is to be spent visiting with family and allowing the next generation of cousins to play together and become friends. I have not discussed this with you. Would you allow this? Have us bring our children to town with us? Spend time with my family?"

Matthew tossed back his head and laughed, a deep, rich laugh that drew her in. "I would be delighted to do so. And there is no allowing to it, Verina. We are equal partners within this marriage. We should always talk things through—and together, we will make our decision. I am all in favor of limiting the number of *ton* events we attend, and I already think quite highly of your family. In fact, we should go to them now and share our good news with them."

They decided to meet at Tray's townhouse. Matthew would collect his mother and stop by to bring Lady Adams. In the meantime, she would tell her family members to come to Tray's townhouse at once.

"If Justina is not awake, then I shall rouse her," Verina declared. "I do not want my sister missing out on such an important announcement."

She caught Lia and Rupert about to slip out, and they told her Lucy and Judson had just left with Dru and Perry.

"Can you catch up with them?" she pleaded. "Have them come to Tray's now? It is important."

"Of course," Rupert said.

Inside the ballroom, she found Con and Rowena talking with Ariadne and Julian and asked them to leave now and head to Tray's. Ariadne gave Verina a knowing look.

"We shall see you shortly," her cousin said.

Con promised to find his mother, and Verina knew Aunt Charlotte would be glad to be included in this family meeting.

Val and Eden were relieved when she told them she was ready to leave. Eden went to where the dowagers sat watching the dancing and found Mama and Aunt Alice, while Val went to bring Tray from the card room. Soon, they were on their way home.

"I am surprised you wanted to leave so early," Aunt Alice said. "After all, tonight was the first night of your come-out."

Mama slipped her hand about Verina's. "Oh, Alice, I do believe there is a very good reason we are abandoning the ball."

By the time they arrived at Tray's townhouse, two other

carriages already stood outside, cousins spilling from them. They went up to the drawing room, and more of her family arrived.

Finally, the butler announced they had visitors. "His Grace, the Duke of Reddington, Her Grace, the Duchess of Reddington, and Lady Adams."

"I have not seen Lady Adams since her husband passed," Mama said.

The three entered the drawing room, and Verina rose, her footsteps taking her straight to Matthew. He captured her hands in his and brought them to his lips, kissing them reverently.

"Oh!" Aunt Alice exclaimed. "Is this what I think it is?"

Matthew led her back to the large group gathered, his mother and Lady Adams following them.

"Verina has already agreed to do me the great honor of becoming my duchess, but we wished for our families to hear the good news all together."

A cheer broke out, and tears stung her eyes as she went from one cousin to the next, receiving their congratulations. Mama hugged her tightly, telling her how alike they were.

"You knew the man you were meant to spend your lifetime with, dearest Verina. I am so happy for you."

Justina, wearing her dressing gown over her night rail, said, "I am so very pleased, Verina. His Grace will make a perfect husband for you."

Tray sent for champagne, along with food and tea, and they talked until dawn. Slowly, the couples began leaving, and Verina walked out to the carriage with Matthew. He handed up Lady Adams and his mother, and then turned to her.

"Time with your family will be something I will always cherish," he told her. "I was forever envious of those with large families, but now I find myself a part of one."

"They all adore you, Matthew. Especially me."

His lowered his lips to hers for a lingering kiss.

"And you are satisfied with wedding by special license?"

They had debated tonight whether she should have the banns

called and be wed at St. George's or wed by special license in a more private ceremony.

"I like the idea of it just being us—and our family gathered. Of course, I would like for Lord and Lady Hampton to attend, as well."

"I will take care of this business with Viscount Ayles this morning and share our good news with Lord Hampton afterward. It was kind of Lord and Lady Aldridge to offer to hold the wedding and breakfast at their residence."

"I only wish Tia and Hugo could come, but I understand why they remain at Merrifield."

"If you would like, we could go see them once we have wed. You know we do not live all that far from them."

"I would like that."

"How about the Season itself?" he asked.

She thought a moment. "Might we stay for the first six weeks? We could leave when Con and Rowena and Lia and Rupert do. Others might also at that time. That way, I could still have the experience of attending a Season, but we could then go home. Home to Redfield."

"Home to Redfield," he agreed.

Matthew kissed her again. "I will purchase the special license in Doctors' Commons tomorrow. And Mama and I will stop here and take you to tomorrow night's ball. By then, perhaps you and Lady Traywick will have decided what day we are to wed."

She laughed, happiness bubbling from her. "I will let you know tonight."

"I love you, Verina. I look forward to saying that—and showing you I do—every day of our lives."

Matthew climbed into the carriage, and she waved goodbye, heading back inside the townhouse and up to her bedchamber.

Justina waited in her room. She came and hugged Verina tightly.

"You look happy," her sister said.

"I am deliriously happy," she shared. "I never thought I

would wed for love, but I am so much in love with Matthew."

She explained how they would only stay for a portion of the Season before returning to Redfield.

"And you are not upset doing so?" Justina asked, frowning.

"Not a bit. I built the Season up in my head to be something so grand. It is. But my love for Matthew and starting my life with him is so much more important. We will come to the Season, but as Ariadne has asked, we will keep family at the center of all we do."

They returned to their shared room, and Justina helped Verina from her ballgown and into her night rail. The sisters got into bed, holding hands, and Verina drifted off, thinking this had been the best day—and night—of her life.

CHAPTER TWENTY-ONE

VERINA AWOKE AND stretched lazily. She was not at Tray's London townhouse. This morning, she awoke at Julian and Ariadne's instead. Since the wedding and the breakfast following would be held here, her cousin had suggested that it might be easier to get ready for the ceremony where it would be held, and Verina had readily agreed to do so.

She reflected on the past week of her life, a whirlwind of social activities and wedding planning. Of course, news had spread quickly of her betrothal to the Duke of Reddington, since he had been considered the most eligible bachelor of the Season. The fact that she had won his heart on the night of the opening ball had become the talk of the *ton*. Verina knew—as did Matthew—that it was not a single night which had resulted in this decision, but rather the friendship they had begun to build during her visit to Merrifield and the attraction which was a result of that friendship.

The budding romance of their relationship, however, had blossomed during this past week. Now they were an engaged couple, Mama had allowed them to be left unchaperoned in the drawing room. Matthew had taken advantage of that time alone, teaching her about the kinds of kisses he had been reluctant to expose her to before now.

And how she reveled in them . . .

She had been surprised by the depth of her emotions, as well as the sensual feelings her fiancé caused within her. Her love for Matthew grew with each passing day. Verina had learned of tender kisses. Lingering ones. Kisses which heated her blood and drove her to the point of madness, desire bubbling within her. Because of those kisses, she brought a bit more to the marriage bed than most brides. It had given her confidence, knowing she would be able to please her handsome husband, because Matthew told her over and over how much he loved her and how her kisses moved him.

Mama had sat her down for a lengthy discussion, talking of the physical aspects of the marriage bed. Her mother had explained some things to her that Verina still found a bit hard to grasp, but Mama said the love she and Matthew had for one another would guide them in what occurred between them. Knowing Mama and Papa had been very much in love, Verina trusted in her mother's words, hoping she and Matthew would have the kind, loving relationship which her parents had experienced.

Not surprisingly, they had spent a great deal of their time with her family, and she loved Matthew for it. He had wholeheartedly taken to all of them, going to White's with the men and teasing with the women.

In every household they visited, he asked if they might go up to the nursery. Matthew had come to know all the babes and young children in her extended family, and tears had misted her eyes on more than one occasion as she had watched him play with those children and cradle the babes. He did not seem to favor boys over girls. In fact, he had built the strongest relationship with little Celia. She was Rupert's niece, and her mother had died when Celia was a newborn. Rupert's brother had ignored his child, and Celia had been a wild thing by the time Rupert had inherited his title—and niece.

Now, however, Celia was the sweetest creature, and Lia and Rupert treated her as their own. Celia was very solicitous toward and protective of Edward and Mary, calling them *my twins*. Lia had been pleased how Celia had taken to her cousins, and Verina had enjoyed watching Matthew be a guest at Celia's pretend tea party.

Sarie entered the bedchamber, a tray in hand, and Verina pushed herself to a sitting position.

"Here you go, my lady. Let's get some breakfast in you before you dress."

She chuckled. "I am so excited, Sarie, I am not certain I can eat anything."

"Well, we don't want you fainting on His Grace. It's a good thing that I only brought you a little bit, my lady. Tea and toast points. You need something in you to start your big day."

The maid set down the tray and smiled at Verina. "All the servants at Merrifield think the world of His Grace. He's been a frequent and favorite visitor. I know when they hear of your marriage, they'll be so happy you've become his duchess. I'm so glad you asked me to be your lady's maid. With us living at Redfield, I won't have to be far from home. I'll still be able to see Mum and Dad every now and then. Now, you eat up. I'll be back with your wedding gown soon."

Sarie started out the door and then stopped. She returned to Verina, pulling a letter from her apron.

"I almost forgot, my lady. This came for you this morning."

The maid handed over the letter and left the room, whistling cheerfully.

Breaking the seal, she opened the letter and glanced first at the bottom, seeing Tia's signature. She had written to her cousin and Hugo the morning after the opening ball, telling them that she and Matthew were engaged to be married and that they would stay in town for about six weeks of the Season before returning to Redfield. Verina had promised to come visit her cousin once they were home.

Eagerly, her eyes returned to the top, reading as she absently nibbled on a toast point.

My dearest Verina –

Hugo and I were simply thrilled to receive the news of your betrothal to Matthew. He has been as a brother to Hugo, and I also look upon him as family. I could tell something was happening between the two of you and had hoped it would blossom during the Season. I suppose those months apart were actually good since it led to this quick betrothal. The single women of Polite Society must be weeping into their pillows, knowing that a very eligible duke has succumbed to the parson's mousetrap.

I know you will be living far from your family, Verina, but I am so very happy that you will be close to Hugo and me. I look fondly upon the months we have spent with one another in recent years, and I know our two families will grow closer over time. I can see our children and yours playing together on the lawns of Merrifield and Redfield in the years to come. That thought brings tears to my eyes.

I am sorry we will miss your wedding ceremony and breakfast, but we will see one another soon.

All our love to you and Matthew,
Tia & Hugo

Though Verina was a bit sad that she would be living far away from her immediate family, she and Matthew would build a family of their own. Having Tia and Hugo nearby, along with the babes they would make, would help.

By the time she finished her light breakfast, Sarie had returned, bringing with her Verina's wedding gown. Though Madame Laurent was swamped with orders this time of year, she had dropped everything in order to create the wedding gown of a future duchess. Crawling out of bed now, Verina fingered the delicate lace, marveling that she would be wearing this heavenly creation as she pledged her eternal love to Matthew this morning in front of their loved ones.

Everything became a whirlwind after that. Mama and Justina arrived, and a constant stream of her female cousins and her male cousins' wives, as well as her aunts, flowed into and out of the bedchamber. All her cousins had made love matches, and these young women glowed—as she now did.

Sarie had her sit at the dressing table so she might arrange Verina's hair. Various cousins gave their opinions as to how her hair should be styled. The servant waved away all their suggestions.

"I know exactly what I wish to do for my lady," the maid said. Their gazes met in the mirror, and Sarie winked at her. "Trust me, my lady."

"I always shall," she told the maid.

When Sarie finished, everyone complimented the maid's work, and Dru threatened to steal Sarie away from Verina.

She chuckled. "I have already done that by taking Sarie from Tia. I know a thief when I see one, Dru, and I simply will not let you take the best lady's maid in all of London from me."

Everyone laughed, and Ariadne told them it was time for all except the bride to go downstairs to the drawing room. Her cousin came and kissed Verina's cheek.

"You are making a commitment today, Verina," Ariadne said. "Not only to Matthew, but to yourself. I cannot imagine the two of you with anyone but each other. Enjoy your special day."

Only Mama and Justina remained behind as even Sarie left them.

Mama took Verina's hand and brought it to her cheek. "My first child to wed," she said dreamily. "I can see in your eyes how much you adore Matthew. It is the same for him, as well. I am so pleased you are making a love match, Verina. Enjoy every moment of this day—and the ones to come, my sweet girl."

Mama kissed her hand and then said, "I will leave you two sisters together. I know there are things Justina must wish to say to you."

After Mama left, Justina wrapped her arms tightly about Verina.

"What am I going to do without you?" her sister asked. "Oh, I know you are going to a good life. I saw the sparks between you and Matthew long before anyone else ever did." She smiled. "Perhaps even the two of you. I am glad that you got your Season, Verina, as well as the man who now holds your heart."

"I never thought I would wed for love, Justina, but now that I am doing so? I want the same for you. I hope that next Season you will find your soulmate."

Her sister stepped away, frowning, wrapping her arms tightly about her. She went and stood in front of the window. Gazing out, she said, "I have never been certain that I wanted a Season, Verina. Certainly, next year is too soon for me to make my come-out. I hope you might be able to help manage Mama and her expectations when the time comes. She will have such high hopes for me—and Tray—after seeing how happy you are."

She joined her sister at the window, wrapping an arm about Justina's waist.

"I am not certain I wish to wed at all," Justina confessed. "I might prefer focusing on my art. Or something else."

Verina faced Justina, taking her hand and squeezing it reassuringly. "You have always been wiser than the sum of your years. Whatever life you choose will the right one for you. I only hope that life will include the love of a good man. And no matter what comes to pass, you will always have my love and support. Matthew's, too."

She kissed her sister's cheek as a knock sounded at the door. Justina went to answer it, and Tray stepped into the room.

"It is time to make our way downstairs, Verina."

Justina smiled. "I will leave things to the two of you." She left the room.

Her brother grinned at her. "A duke? I suppose you could not have done any better, my lovely sister."

"It matters not that Matthew is a duke, Tray. What is important to me is that he is a man of his word. A man of honor and good character. I love him fiercely."

"You are exactly the woman he has needed. I have seen how others respond to a duke. How they nod and agree with everything he says. Sycophants who fight for his attention and fawn over him. The fact that you care not for Matthew's title—but love him for himself—means a great deal to him. I must agree with you. After spending time with your groom, I find he is a perfect fit for you. And our extended family."

Tray offered his arm to her. "Shall we go and make things official?"

Verina slipped her hand through the crook of his arm, and her brother led them to the drawing room. She passed a sea of faces, not truly distinguishing one from another because her gaze was focused upon her handsome groom.

Matthew stood before the fireplace, facing her, a clergyman behind him. Tray brought her to her groom's side and handed her off to him. She slipped her hand into the crook of Matthew's arm and gazed up at him, seeing the love she had for him reflected in his eyes.

The vicar cleared his throat. "If I may have the attention of the bride and groom, I will begin."

All those gathered chuckled, and Verina turned her gaze up to the man who would perform the ceremony.

"We are ready," Matthew said, stealing another look at her.

They spoke their vows to one another, and she was filled with so many emotions. Eagerness to begin their lives together. Happiness because they had found one another.

And, most of all, love.

As Matthew slipped her wedding band upon her finger, love welled inside her, making her feel as if she might burst from so much joy. The clergyman offered a final prayer, and Matthew turned her toward him for a sweet kiss.

When he broke the kiss, he quietly said to her, "I feel as if I were a half my entire life. You are my other half, Verina. Together, now, we make a complete whole."

He kissed her again, and she heard the laughter and applause coming from their guests.

Her new husband broke the kiss. Beaming at her, he said, "Let us go into the fine wedding breakfast prepared for us."

Matthew led her from the drawing room, and Verina had to agree with him.

Together, they became a happy whole. They would weather every storm which came their way, and they would sail through both good times and bad, but Verina knew they would meet every challenge as one.

CHAPTER TWENTY-TWO

Six weeks later . . .

MATTHEW CHASED VERINA around the bedchamber, leaping onto the bed and jumping to the other side, catching her. He pulled her into his arms for a long, delicious kiss.

How had he ever lived without this woman in his life?

They had been wed for six weeks now, and his appetite for his wife was still insatiable. As he framed her face and kissed her, his cock stirred. Desire rushed through him, his tongue teasing her mouth open, plunging inside to drink from her sweet nectar.

His hands slid to her shoulders, drawing her against his naked body. She was tall, her frame willowy, her breasts just the perfect size for his hands and mouth. His hands moved down her back now, cupping her buttocks, and he heard the pleased noises coming from her.

She broke the kiss. "We should be getting ready for our ball."

He seized her mouth again, their tongues mating as he kneaded her buttocks. Her hand slid down his chest, seizing his cock, her fingers encircling it as she stroked its head with her thumb.

Now, he was the one moaning.

She kept her hand firm about it, dragging its tip across her belly. His blood quickened, and he deepened the kiss, fighting her for control of it. But his young wife had learned her lessons well, and she continued to dominate him. Bloody hell, he could barely think with her stroking him, teasing him as she brushed the head of his cock against her belly.

"Enough!" he cried, spinning her around. They fell onto the mattress, her legs encircling him as she locked them at her ankles, pressing against his back.

He fondled her breasts as he continued to kiss her, something she liked. It had been a world of sensual exploration, discovering what pleased one another, and they continued to learn each day—and night—new things which made their marriage not only a partnership, but an adventure.

Knowing how she liked to take control, Matthew rolled, his back landing flat against the mattress, Verina now atop him. She broke the kiss, smiling down at him.

"Oh, I shall have my wicked way with you, Your Grace."

"Is that a threat—or a promise?" he asked lazily as she slowly took him inside her. She sat atop him now and started to undulate, as if she were a wave and he the shore. She eased from him and then took him in again, moving, swaying, practically purring. Then she rode him, hard and fast, both of them crying out as they reached their peak. Verina collapsed, her breasts pressing against his bare chest, and he greedily took her mouth with his, making every kiss count.

He finally broke the kiss, pressing her head to his shoulder, liking her close to him, feeling her heart beat as he knew she could feel his. Matthew pressed a kiss to her temple.

"I suppose we should dress. After all, your brother is being kind enough to host a ball in our honor. The least we can do is actually show up for it."

Verina lifted her head, smiling at him, stealing another kiss. "We shall be late. Thanks to you. I will let Tray know it was your fault and not mine."

"If you do, I will never hear the end of it from him."

"Good," she replied saucily, making him want to make love to her all over again.

She eased from him and then the bed, slipping into her dressing gown. As she left, she rang the cord for Barrow.

"You know he will be waiting outside the door," Matthew

told her as she scurried from the room, going through the door that lead to their bathing chamber. Her rooms were on the other side of it, and he knew Sarie would be tapping her foot and would chastise her mistress for waiting until the last minute to be dressed.

"Ah, to be in love," he said, springing from the bed, walking across the room and opening the door.

Barrow raced in. "You are cutting it close, Your Grace." The valet paused. "Then again, you look most happy. Like a cat who has lapped up all the cream accidentally left out. I fear you will set the tongues of the *ton* wagging."

"Let them talk all they wish about us," Matthew said cheerfully. "It is about time they gossiped about two people who are madly in love instead of which wife is cuckolding her husband, or what couple has to wed because they were caught kissing."

"You ought to be glad I have learned to quickly shave and dress you, Your Grace. Else you would be late to everything now that you are wed."

He sighed, contentment filling him. "I wonder if I will always be this happy, Barrow."

The servant paused a moment, studying him. "I'd say you are one of those couples who are happy—and will stay happy, Your Grace."

Matthew smiled. "I think so, too."

Twenty minutes later, he sailed through the door to his wife's bedchamber, which now served as her dressing room. She was dressed in a gown of dark blue silk, which made the blue of her eyes seem even bluer. The gown was cut low, showing a good amount of her delectable breasts, and he couldn't help but stare at them. They seemed to be slightly larger than usual, and it struck him.

She might be with child.

So far, she had not experienced any of the nausea. Then again, they had only been wed a short while. He thought back and realized that she had not had her monthly courses since they had become man and wife. That caused him to smile. Verina would be an excellent mother, and he was already learning from the unusual men in her extended family just how a father could behave. Most men of Polite Society had little to do with their children, but these cousins seemed to be enthralled with their little ones.

And Matthew knew he would be exactly the same.

Taking Verina's hands in his, he told Sarie, "Her Grace looks her usual self. Beautiful. Radiant. Fashionable. Thank you, Sarie. You may go."

The maid bit back a smile. "Yes, Your Grace," and she left the room.

"You look wonderful in this gown," he said. "And I cannot wait to strip it off you in a few hours."

"A few hours? Why, the midnight buffet will not even be over by then. We cannot leave a ball being held in our honor—"

She did not finish simply because he took her mouth, kissing her soundly.

When he broke the kiss, his wife said, "Well, perhaps we might leave a tad early."

Matthew kissed her again, and she said, "Or perhaps we will not go at all."

"No, your mama and Ariadne have gone to too much trouble for us not to make our appearance. Come, Duchess. Our carriage awaits."

Once inside, he slipped his hand into his coat's inner pocket. "Hmm. What have we here?" he asked, slowly pulling out a sapphire necklace.

"Oh! It is beautiful, Matthew."

"Turn so that I might fasten it about your neck."

She angled away from him, and he lifted it over her head, fastening the clasp and then brushing his lips along her nape.

Facing him again, Verina said, "Thank you so much. It is a lovely piece. I will wear it with pride."

He reached into another pocket. "How about a bracelet to go

with your necklace?"

Verina laughed in delight, holding up her wrist so that he might fasten it. Then she peered, asking, "Any more surprises? Jewels up your sleeves?"

Laughing, he pulled out the final gift of the set, earrings which matched the necklace and bracelet.

"Oh, dear. I shall be the best garbed and bejeweled duchess present this evening."

"Do not let Val hear that."

She grinned mischievously. "Perhaps I should. Then Eden might get a new surprise from her duke."

They laughed and kissed again, lightly, because he did not want to muss her before they greeted all their guests.

Tray had told them to park their carriage in the mews around back, and they actually cut through the kitchens, surprising servants as they raced through and went up the back staircase to avoid the receiving line which must be forming even now. They came down the corridor and joined Verina's family, who stood at the top of the stairs.

"I thought you were not going to make it," Tray said, laughing. "To your own ball."

"I bet him a guinea you would—but that you would be late," Justina said. She looked to her brother. "I will collect tomorrow."

Mama shook her head. "Oh, you two."

The countess took Verina's face in her hands and kissed her daughter soundly, and then she did the same to Matthew. While he had always felt loved by his own mother, Lady Traywick had embraced him as she would any son, and he loved her for it. Justina, too, was now as a sister to him. All of his wife's cousins and their spouses were such a part of his life now. He could not wait for them to add their own children to the family and watch them grow, making friends with their cousins.

"Your jewelry is lovely," Mama said. "Something new?"

"A gift from my husband," Verina said, smiling at him. "He seems to shower me with gifts."

Little did his wife know she was carrying the greatest gift of all. Since she had no symptoms of increasing, she might not have realized she was with child. She would, soon enough. Her breasts would swell. Her back would ache. Her belly would grow to an enormous size.

And he would love every bit of her, now—and always.

"Shall we begin greeting your guests?" Mama asked.

Lady Traywick knew everyone in Polite Society, having come to the Season for over twenty-five years. As the countess introduced them to so many, Matthew thought how gracious and graceful Verina's mother was. She was also the favorite aunt of all the cousins. Verina had told him she would model herself on her remarkable mother. Hopefully, twenty-odd years from now, they would be hosting a ball for their own child and their new spouse. The thought caused his eyes to mist with tears.

Verina looked up at him. "Is everything all right, my love?"

Smiling down at his duchess, he said, "Everything is absolutely perfect."

EPILOGUE

Five years later . . .

As THE CARRIAGE brought them closer to home, Matthew couldn't help but feel satisfied with the life he had built with Verina. She had proven to be the perfect partner for him. The one he always turned to when he needed advice or wished to share a confidence. The lover who was passionate both in and out of the bedroom. And a wonderful mother to their two children.

Marcus was four now, a bright, chatty lad who had a sunny nature and was the image of his father at the same age. Evelyn would be two in two weeks' time, and she was a nice blend of the both of them, with his cornflower blue eyes and Verina's blond hair and tall, willowy build. He would have been satisfied with having two children, but his lovely wife now carried their third child. She was about four months along, her belly beginning to round. While she had experienced bouts of nausea with the first two, this latest one had not caused a minute's worth of trouble from within the womb. Whether a boy or girl, he would be satisfied with either.

Marcus scrambled from his grandmother's lap and climbed into Matthew's. The children had been traveling in the second carriage with their nursery governess and nanny until the last changing station, but he had wanted the pair with him and Verina when they caught sight of Redfield again.

As Marcus chattered away, he glanced across at his mother, who smiled indulgently at her grandson. Lady Adams sat next to Mama, and she had become an integral part of their family, serving as another grandmother to their children. Verina's mother, whom Matthew had fondly called Aunt Agnes, as all the cousins did, had left them three years ago, passing from pneumonia unexpectedly. At least Lady Traywick had gotten to know her first grandchild. He only wished she had been able to know Evelyn, whom Verina said had much of her grandmother in her. It had been a difficult time for Verina in losing her mother, a loving, bright woman. Aunt Agnes was missed by the entire extended family.

"I like going to town," Marcus told them. "I like seeing all my cousins. When are we going to Merrifield to see Jane and Michael? But in town, we get to see lots more cousins like Cade and Theo and William."

"That is very true, my son," he said, ruffling the boy's hair. He glanced at Verina, who held a sleepy Evelyn in her arms. "It is fun getting to see your cousins. And you just saw Jane and Michael, but I promise we will visit with them at Merrifield soon."

Matthew stroked his daughter's cheek lightly. "Almost home, my sweet girl. Think you can stay awake a few more minutes?"

Evelyn nodded, sucking her thumb, something she did when she was tired. Verina said it was a habit they would soon need to break, else it would affect Evelyn's teeth and the shape of her mouth, as well as permanently damage her thumbnail. They had told their daughter when she turned two she could no longer suck upon it, and Matthew had asked what they would do to be able to stop it. His wife had laughed, telling him that her own mother had painted something vile-tasting on her thumb and Justina's when they were a similar age to Evelyn. It had quickly broken both of them of the habit.

He hated that his baby girl would suffer something such as that. Or suffer anything which hurt her or made her sad. Then again, he knew he could not stop her from growing up, and Evelyn must face everything from heartache to joy on her own, without his interference. Matthew was afraid he would blink and she would be on his arm as they walked down the aisle of St. George's, pledging herself to another man. Now, though, Evelyn was his sweet girl, and he would do anything for her. Or Marcus. And the coming babe.

And especially for his incredible duchess.

The carriage turned to head up the drive leading to Redfield, and he sensed the change in the air inside the carriage. While they all enjoyed their time in town each spring and being with family, there was nothing like coming home.

The Ridleys greeted them as they descended from the carriage. Their nursery governess and nanny hurried over to take the children. Both women had formerly been in institutions and had been absorbed into his staff. Matthew hoped he and Verina would be filling the Redfield nursery for many years to come and was happy these two women had a satisfying life now, away from the asylums they had been left in.

"I am so very tired," Mama announced as they entered the foyer. "The journey to and from town seems to get longer each time I make it. I think I shall have a tray in my room and then go straight to bed."

"I feel the same," Lady Adams said. "It has been a long day of travel."

He was glad after a year, Mama and Lady Adams had returned from the dower house. By then, Verina was firmly established as the Duchess of Reddington, and the servants knew she was in charge of the household. In fact, it had been his duchess who persuaded the two older women to once more live in the main house. She told them she wished for her children to spend as much time as possible with their grandmothers, and Mama and Lady Adams had agreed.

Knowing his wife enjoyed a long, hot bath after the journey from town, he told Mrs. Ridley, "See that bath water is brought to my chamber."

"Yes, Your Grace." She smiled at him. "If I may say so, it is very good to have you and the family back home."

"Thank you, Mrs. Ridley. It is the place we love."

He threaded his fingers through Verina's, and they slowly mounted the steps. She went to her rooms to undress, appearing several minutes later in his rooms wearing her dressing gown. Matthew knew she wore nothing under it, and that caused his blood to stir.

Barrow finished unpacking and excused himself as the servants began bringing buckets of water, filling the bathing tub.

When they left, he stripped off his clothes and untied her dressing gown, parting it, marveling in the wonderland of her body.

"Let me help you from it," he said, pulling the dressing gown from her shoulders and placing it neatly on a nearby chair.

Taking her hand, he led his wife to the bathing tub and assisted her into it. Matthew then climbed in as well, bracing his back against it, his long legs against the sides as Verina leaned against his chest. He caught the peach scent coming from her skin, one familiar to him after five years of wedded bliss. His placed a palm against her belly.

"I am so happy about the new babe," he said, stroking her belly.

"I am, too," she said softly. "Birthing a child is such a miracle, and all our children have been made in love."

His hand slid lower, slowly moving up and down the seam of her sex, causing her to give a small gasp. With gentleness, his fingers made love to her. Entering her. Caressing her. Finding her bud of pleasure and teasing it into a powerful orgasm.

"I want more of you," his wife told him, desire hot in her eyes.

With a smile, he said, "I can make that happen, Your Grace."

Matthew rose and helped her to do the same, taking the bath sheet and drying her. She returned the favor, and they moved to the bed, hand in hand.

Over the next hour, he explored her exquisite body and satin skin. He touched—and then kissed—every inch of it, entering her with one powerful thrust. Their gazes held one another's as their dance of love continued. They reached satisfaction at the same time, and he thrilled to hear her calling out his name.

Collapsing atop her, he nuzzled her neck. "That will never grow old. We may—but our love never will."

He eased from her and rang for Barrow. His valet would know that Their Graces were hungry now, having satisfied their hunger for one another first.

Matthew helped Verina don her dressing gown again and then found his banyan, slipping into it and belting it. Taking a seat in a large chair, he pulled Verina into his lap. They sat in contented silence until Barrow appeared with a large tray, which he set on the table next to them. It contained apples and pears, several cheeses, and sliced bread with a crock of butter. The valet poured wine for them, as well.

"Do you need anything else, Your Graces?" Barrow asked.

"That will do," he replied. "Her Grace and I will be sleeping in tomorrow morning. See that we are not disturbed. For any reason."

The valet did not bother to hide his smile. "Of course, Your Grace," leaving them alone again.

Verina remained in his lap as he fed her and himself. He enjoyed such simple pleasures as this.

"It was a good time in town this year, wasn't it?" she asked, opening her mouth to accept another bite of cheese.

"Very enjoyable," he told her. "I still think it was bloody brilliant of Ariadne to convince the family to bring their children to town each year. I cannot imagine how much our hearts would break, leaving Marcus and Evelyn behind, year after year. Why, I would be afraid that they might forget us."

"I only wish that Mama could have known Evelyn," she said wistfully, touching her belly. "And this new one. What do you want this time, Matthew? A spare to your heir—or a second daughter?"

"I will be happy with either addition to our growing family," he assured her. "It will be nice to take a third child to town next spring to meet their cousins and the rest of the family. You and Tia should give birth close together this time, I would think."

Tia's first child had been a girl, and Jane was now five years of age. After Marcus had been born, Hugo and Tia had added Michael to their family.

"Yes, Tia has had a bit of a rough go of it. Hopefully, her nausea will soon subside. I have been blessed to have none of that this time around."

She yawned, and Matthew kissed her. "I think it high time that my beautiful duchess gets some sleep."

"Only if my handsome duke intends to come to bed with me. You know I always rest better when you are beside me."

Matthew did leave Verina occasionally, going to retrieve a new damaged dove and bringing her to Dove Hall. Surprisingly, Mama and Lady Adams had stepped up, accompanying Larkin on more of those missions than Matthew himself. Perhaps now was the time to continue funding the missions, but retire from actively participating in them. It was becoming harder and harder to leave his wife and their children for any length of time.

They climbed into bed, and he snuffed out the candles. Gathering his wife into his arms, he dropped a kiss upon her brow.

"I may not have been a damaged dove, my love, but you saved me, all the same," he told her. "You have brought abundant love and laughter into my life and given me such precious children. Thank you, my darling. For everything."

Verina's fingers caressed his cheek. "I love you, Matthew. More than I ever dreamed possible. And this life of ours together—along with our children—is as close to heaven on earth can be."

A moment later, his duchess dropped into sleep, her breathing soft and even. He thanked the heavens above for bringing Verina into his life as he, too, fell asleep.

And dreamed of the babe to come.

About the Author

USA Today and Amazon Top 10 bestselling author Alexa Aston lives with her husband in a Dallas suburb, where she eats her fair share of dark chocolate and plots while she walks every morning. She enjoys travel and sports—and can't get enough of *Survivor* or *The Crown*.

Her Regency and Medieval historical romances bring to life loveable rogues and dashing knights. Her series include: *The Strongs of Shadowcrest, Suddenly a Duke, Second Sons of London, Dukes Done Wrong, Dukes of Distinction, Soldiers and Soulmates, The St. Clairs, The de Wolfes of Esterley Castle, The King's Cousins, Medieval Runaway Wives,* and *The Knights of Honor*.

www.ingramcontent.com/pod-product-compliance
Lightning Source LLC
Chambersburg PA
CBHW051535050726
47595CB00002B/495

* 9 7 8 1 9 7 2 0 8 6 6 1 2 *